KATIE O'CONNOR

HEART'S HAVEN

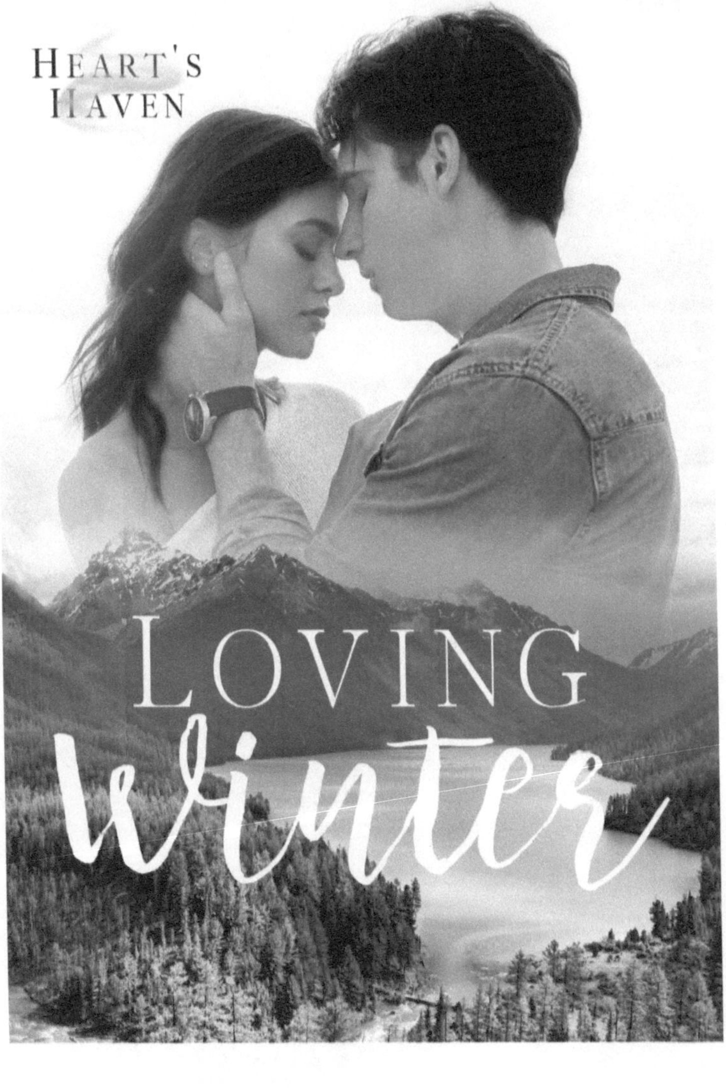

LOVING
winter

Loving Winter

Heart's Haven Book 4

Katie O'Connor

Loving Winter

-Heart's Haven Book Four-

Published March 2025 by Snarky Heart Press and Katie O'Connor. (katieohwrites.com)

ISBN: 978-1-989816-95-0 (Digital Edition)

978-1-989816-96-7 (Print Edition)

978-1-989816-97-4 (Alternate Print Edition)

Copyediting by Terri St. Clair

Cover by GetCovers

About Loving Winter

C an a man who lives for jokes and puns be happy with the most serious person he's ever met?

After an IED explosion destroys Winter Ireland's knee and her military career, she runs to Haven to regroup and figure out how to become useful again. She needs a new job and an updated life plan. She isn't looking for love, but Nick Blackstone is irresistible. Or he would be if his tendency to joke around continually wasn't so annoying.

To cope with a tragedy in his past, Nick turned to jokes and puns to survive. Winter is the most beautiful and compelling women he's ever met, and he doesn't understand why she can't be happy with him and his small town. He knows part of her problem is his fun-loving attitude, but he can't seem to stop joking. Not even for Winter.

There's so much between them, and even more pushing them apart. Can they compromise for love's sake and find happiness together?

Dedication

This one is for Andi and all my Northern Alberta girls.
Your support means the world to me.

Chapter One

Winter braced herself against the throbbing in her leg and dashed away a tear. She wished she could blame the waterworks on pain, and not a total sense of devastation over a lost career and the total hopelessness crushing her heart. She should have fully recovered from her knee replacement, but it ached and burned like it had the day after surgery. It was on days like this that she wondered if it would ever stop pounding in time to her heartbeat.

She puffed out her lips and sighed, the breath fluttering her bangs. The pain was her fault. Completely and entirely. She should have broken this trip up into more manageable blocks; two days, maybe even three. It wasn't that she couldn't afford the hotels. It was more that her inner thrifty side didn't want to spend the money for something she could get along without.

She'd served ten years in the Canadian Army. She'd gone without sleep for days and had done so more than once. Of course, that was before an IED exploded, crippling her, and changing her career trajectory in one fell swoop. Sleeping in her truck was no replacement for an actual bed and her leg was reminding her of her foolishness.

She blinked to clear the fog from her eyes. How could she be in so much pain, yet so tired all at once? She massaged her knee through her army-issue khakis.

Whisps of early morning fog drifted over the mountain road. Wind buffeted her truck, and for a moment, she could see further ahead. When the breeze died, she was back to squinting into the mist. It was like something out of a horror movie. It was a good thing she didn't scare easily.

She double-checked that her lights were on in the pre-dawn gloom. She'd been driving all night, so of course they were on. Checking was silly, really, but when your mind was exhausted, and your synapses didn't always fire properly, it didn't hurt to second guess yourself.

She rounded a curve and began the climb up another large hill. It had been years since she visited her Aunt Muriel in Haven, but some deep part of her memory told Winter she was getting close.

Driving straight through from Vancouver, British Columbia, to Haven, Alberta, took about fifteen hours if you didn't stop. Gassing up, getting snacks, and taking bathroom breaks added time. This trip was taking an eternity.

When the friend she'd been staying with had been called back to duty early, Winter had piled her duffle bag of meager belongings into her truck and set out. The plan was to leave Vancouver and stop in Abbotsford or Chilliwack overnight. Then she'd drive a bit further and stop somewhere in Alberta before she finished the trek. Instead, she'd ditched her plan and ignored her body's needs in favor of what her heart wanted.

Home.

Aunt Muriel's house was the closest thing she had to a home.

Sure, she had a mother and a father. She even had a brother, a sister-in-law, and two nephews. Living with them in their stylish mansion had never felt like home. She didn't fit into their world. She had no problems with their lifestyle, it just wasn't the one she wanted for herself.

Something moved through the fog onto the road. She braked quickly but cautiously and slowed to a stop. A female mule deer and her fawn ambled slowly across the pavement. She waited until they disappeared into the heavy trees before easing forward. Deer could be unpredictable and just when you thought they were off the road, they could dart back in front of you.

Despite her exhaustion, she smiled at the pretty picture the duo had made. Something must have chased them from their den. It was surprising to see them out in such a heavy fog. Spring often meant foggy patches at this elevation.

A road sign flashed by. Haven 30 Kilometers. Almost home. She smiled in relief and anticipation as a giddy jolt of happiness washed over her, almost erasing her exhaustion.

Aunt Muriel was her father's half-sister and the black sheep of the family. Like Winter, she'd refused to join the family business; instead, she'd gotten a teaching degree and headed out to the back of beyond, to Haven, to teach elementary school.

Muriel and Winter were kindred spirits. Despite her parents' pleas, and then orders, Winter had foregone university in favor of serving her country. She wanted to do something useful; not that her family's charity, which built houses for underserved people, wasn't meeting a need...she simply wanted to make something of herself, on her own, without the Ireland name behind her.

She massaged her aching knee. She had told her family about her surgery but had not mentioned her medical discharge. The only relative who knew was Muriel, and though Muriel wasn't home, Haven was Winter's destination. She'd spend the next year house-sitting for her aunt, who was off on a twelve-month long trip. Muriel was teaching quilting around the world, starting with a thirty-day stint on a cruise ship. Who knew that people wanted to quilt on a cruise? It wasn't an idea that would ever cross Winter's mind.

Her eyes dipped low, and she forced them open. Despite the chilly temperature outside, she flipped on the air conditioner. Maybe the cool air would perk her up. She'd drive with the window down, but she hated the thumping noise of wind battering in and out at highway speed.

"Stay awake, Ireland. You're too close to fall asleep now."

She'd taken two quick naps on roadside turnouts and had rested in Golden while she had a bite to eat. Otherwise, she was surviving on gallons of coffee and pure cussed stubbornness. Aunt Muriel would pitch a fit if she knew that Winter had made the trip in one day. Luckily, nobody would tell her because nobody knew.

A wiser person would have let someone know she was on the road. Especially since cell coverage in the mountains was crappy at best. It was sporadic enough that most houses in Haven still had landlines.

She yawned again. When she got to Aunt Muriel's, she was going to sleep for a week. Her stomach growled, reminding her it had been hours since she fed it anything but coffee. Again, poor planning on her part. She should have packed snacks. Act in haste, repent at leisure, and suffer in the interim. In her sudden, desperate need to be home, she'd ignored her military preparedness training and left without provisions.

She slowed for the last turn and in under three minutes, entered Haven. The fog wasn't as thick here, probably due to the gusting wind. The first structure she passed was the gas station/garage/café combination. She slowed down and crept down Main Street, passing businesses she recognized and a few she didn't.

A once empty turn-of-the-century log building now boasted a sign for Sid's Steakhouse. The hardware store had a fresh coat of paint. Things had changed since her last visit. Of course, it had been more years than she wanted to count since she'd come home. Funny how a place where she'd only spent a few scattered weeks over the years could feel like home.

Her truck chugged roughly. It was long overdue for a tune-up. It was her only real possession, and she'd neglected it badly while she was on duty. Vehicles needed to be used regularly, or seals and hoses dried out. She was probably facing a major repair bill, but she hadn't spent much money since she signed up, and a costly repair bill wouldn't be an issue. Especially since she was living rent-free for a year.

She'd fought with Aunt Muriel over that. Muriel wanted to pay her a monthly house-sitting fee and Winter had wanted to pay rent. After two weeks of arguing, they'd met in the middle and settled on nobody paid anybody anything. Both were doing the other a favor.

The truck sputtered and died.

"What the heck?" She pulled over to the side of the deserted road. There was no traffic this early, and she let the truck drift to a stop as close to the curb as she could. "Crap in a basket. This is a SNAFU." She loved the acronym for situation normal all fouled up. Only most military personnel replaced fouled with something earthier. She tried repeatedly to restart the truck. Whatever had quit had gone and done a great job of it.

She peered up and down the dark block. Aside from a few streetlights, it was dead. Except, was that a light farther down? Coming from inside a shop? She couldn't sit in a truck until things opened up; her bladder wouldn't let her. A quick check revealed that her phone was dead too, so she couldn't phone Nick, who had the keys to Muriel's house.

"Crap."

Rummaging through a bag she'd thrown in the backseat; she extracted a camo ball cap and thick hoodie as protection from the wind. Throwing them on, she grabbed her wallet and slid out of the truck. Favoring her knee, she jogged the short distance to the light spilling from the bakery.

She rattled the locked door.

Chapter Two

There was something he'd always loved about mornings. Nick leaned against the display case in his bakery and stared out the window at the pre-dawn darkness. Fog rolled by, stirred, and shifted by gusts of wind. The decorative spring flags on the store across the street flapped and fluttered. Depending on the day, the weather could either be great or bad for business.

Some days, it meant people showed up and drank coffee all day. On other days, it meant they stayed home, and business was dead. Knowing how much to bake could be a crap shoot.

Luckily, the weather was supposed to warm up.

There wouldn't be daylight for another couple of hours. Mid-April meant late mornings and early nights in Haven. Man, he loved it here. He'd left New York City to attend a wedding in this mountain town over a decade ago, and he couldn't imagine living anywhere else. Not even Edmonton, where he'd been raised.

A buzzer broke the quiet morning air. He set his double-double coffee on the display and strode into the kitchen. Bread was finicky, it went from baked to burned in no time flat. It was his last batch of the morning and if he ruined it, he'd run out before the day was half through and the next batch finished rising and baked. Haven might be small, but his customers loved fresh bread, which he was happy to provide. Feeding his friends nurtured his soul.

Before opening this morning, he had cakes to decorate and cookies to bake. He hurried to the kitchen, snatched up some silicone oven mitts, and pulled the loaves out. Yeasty steam washed over his face. The smell of freshly baked bread had to be his favorite thing in the whole world.

Except maybe the love of a good woman, though he'd consistently struck out on that score. He was pushing forty and had been either the best man or a groomsman at over a dozen weddings. The phrase 'always a groomsman, never a groom' was an accurate description of his love life. Still, part of his heart refused to give up hope. There was a woman out there for him. Somewhere. Maybe he'd get lucky and find love before he was too old to start a family like all his friends were doing. Occasionally, the loneliness near drove him crazy.

For a while, he'd thought Grace Winston was the woman for him. She was smart, beautiful, talented, and kind. Rather perfect wife material. They'd dated, but with no sparks between them, she'd become one of his closest friends. Two years ago, she'd married her long-lost college crush. Grace, her husband Sterling, his daughter Sasha, and their newborn son Travis, lived a few blocks away.

He pulled out all the loaves and slid in the trays of muffins he'd prepped earlier. Today's treat of the day was cinnamon roll muffins. He'd taken the best parts of cinnamon buns and spice cake and created a new muffin. He couldn't wait for Grace to show up on her way to her bookstore across the street. She'd tell him, in no uncertain terms, whether the confection met her high standards. He'd had a few failures over the years, but not many.

Failed relationships didn't count in those numbers.

"Not going there," he mumbled to himself. Life was better when you focused on the positive, and he was not going to dwell on his many failures. "Look ahead, Nick. Look ahead."

He returned to his coffee. It was early, barely after six, and he didn't open until eight. With a population of just over a thousand, Haven didn't have much early foot traffic. Anyone wanting breakfast before he opened would hit the café attached to Haven's only garage. He settled into a chair by the window, his daily to-do list in hand, and coffee at his elbow.

He checked off all the items he had finished and added extras. Most importantly, he had to double-check his stock of candy eyeballs. The bookstore had ordered eight dozen monster cookies for their spring bash.

Someone rattled the front door, startling him.

"Must be a tourist," he muttered, despite knowing that tourist season hadn't started for the year. "We're closed until eight," he shouted.

Ten seconds later, someone rapped on the window right next to him. He looked up. A woman stood there. At least it looked like a woman. Whoever it was wore an army-green sweatshirt with its hood tossed up over a ball cap pulled so low it hid her face, except for her kissable lips. His brows pinched together. What was she doing out in this wind? Any sane person was holed up at home.

"Some people." Mildly annoyed at the interruption, he went to the door.

He flipped the latch, and the tall woman pushed her way inside ringing the little bells attached to the door. She peeked out from under the cap, revealing expressive hazel eyes. His breath hissed out like he'd been sucker-punched. *Holy biscuits*!

"Hey," he greeted his unwelcome visitor. "I know that the early bird gets the worm, but this is ridiculous." He softened his words with a smile. A stranger was just a friend he hadn't met yet.

She mumbled something as she scraped her hood back.

"Come in out of the wind and warm up. What's the food emergency that couldn't wait a couple hours?" He kept his tone light and playful. He didn't want to scare her and nobody needed to be out in this gusty wind.

She slowly pushed off the cap revealing glistening, raven-black hair.

His heart jumped. What was it about black hair that was so danged sexy? Even her scowl didn't lessen its impact on his libido. She was pale with dark circles under her pretty eyes. She looked exhausted.

"That sweater is huge." He laughed. "You look like a little girl in her mommy's jacket."

"Funny. Not." She frowned.

"My apologies, princess. What can this humble baker do for your majesty?" He bowed low, and popped back up grinning at his off-kilter humor. He loved a good joke. Judging by the deepening of her frown, his guest did not.

"Are you Nick?"

"This is Nick's Bakery," he quipped. *How did she know his name? Better question, who was she and why was she disturbing his morning peace and quiet?*

"The fact that you're a man, in Nick's bakery doesn't necessarily translate to you being Nick. For all I know, Nick could be short for Nicole."

"Nick is short for Nicholas. Like St. Nicholas. Ho-ho-ho." He laughed.

She lifted one eyebrow and managed to frown at the same time. "Somehow, Nicky, I doubt that you are anything close to a saint. Are you, or are you not, Nick Blackstone?"

He bowed again. "Yes, princess, I am the saint you seek." Her brow dropped into a scowl. He was pushing his limits.

He thrust out his hand. "Hi. Nick Blackstone at your service. Please to meet you..." He trailed off, waiting for her to provide her name.

"Winter. Winter Ireland."

He bit back a joke about her being winter cold. "Ah. Muriel's niece. She said you'd be by next week. You're early." He backed out of the doorway. "Come in. I'll get you a hot drink."

"Just the key, and your washroom, please. Maybe call a cab so I can get to Aunt Muriel's house."

"Don't be silly. You're shivering. Take a minute and warm up." He glanced out the window but didn't see any cars. "How did you get here?" Haven's bus service ran once a week, on Sundays.

"My truck broke down a block and a half back. I just want to get home." She spread her legs slightly apart as if bracing for an argument.

"Come in," he repeated. "I'll call Clint and he'll check out your vehicle. You can have a hot drink, on the house, while you wait."

She rolled her eyes so hard he thought they might get stuck. "Fine. Coffee. Please." Her acceptance was less than gracious. Perhaps from exhaustion. Dark bags drooped below her eyes.

He waved her to follow him further inside. "Washroom's there." He pointed. "Help yourself, then take a seat. I'll grab that coffee for you."

"Thanks."

The response was totally without sincerity. He could almost hear her teeth grinding together as she turned toward the ladies' room after shucking her zip up hoodie. Winter Ireland was one tense woman. But man, those eyes, and that hair…dreams were made of less. And when she walked away…what a heavenly departure!

He'd seen pictures of her in uniform at Muriel's. She looked even better in person.

He swiped his half-empty cup off the table and went behind the display. After checking on the muffins in the oven, he refilled his mug, poured a fresh coffee for Winter, and threw a couple cookies onto a plate. With the plate stacked on the mug, he turned toward her.

Holy hamburgers, Batman. She sat with her back to him, facing the window. Her hair hung over her shoulders in a glorious wave of silk. He sucked in a breath. Hanging nearly to her waist, her hair was a man's fantasy.

He stumbled a bit, nearly dropping his unsteady load as he walked toward her. "Here you go. Coffee and cookies. Do you need cream? I usually keep it on the table, but it's early yet."

"Thank you. I'd love some cream."

He slid a mug toward her. "I'll be back before you can say *Beat the Clock.*" He hurried to the kitchen and pressed his head against the stainless-steel fridge door. *Holy macaroni!* What was wrong with him? His heart was beating like he'd run a marathon, not that he'd ever been crazy enough to try to run that far. He sucked in a few deep breaths and opened the walk-in fridge. The rush of cold air chilled him back to a degree of normal function. He found a dish of creamers and, with a nervous sigh, headed back to Winter's side.

Winter, that was one heck of a name for a woman who made him feverishly hot and bothered with a simple glance. Maybe it would be good to get to know her. Especially if she was going to be in town for a while. He'd promised Muriel he'd keep an eye on her niece. *Yeah, that was it, he'd befriend her...for Muriel, not because she was totally hot.*

Feigning self-control, he strolled back with the cream and sat across from her with a smile. She was thin like she'd been unwell. Muriel had mentioned an injury, but to Nick, Winter looked heartsick, though he couldn't explain why he thought that.

"Thanks. I'm exhausted. Maybe coffee will help. The drive was terrible and then my truck died. I just want to get home."

"Let's have a coffee, then if Clint's not here by the time we're done, I'll drive you home. Speaking of which..." He pulled out his phone and called the garage. Clint wasn't in yet, but the attendant promised to let him know about her truck.

"Welcome to Haven, Winter." He chuckled. "That sounded wrong because it's nearly spring." He couldn't stop the quip. He loved a good play on words.

"It feels like winter. It's frigid here. Colder than my tour of the Arctic."

"You toured the Arctic?" He suspected she meant with the army but couldn't resist the joke.

"Tour of duty," she corrected. "I'm a soldier. Was a soldier. I spent eight months in Alaska in winter. Not actually the Arctic, but close enough." Her frown indicated that she didn't want to discuss it.

"Thank you for your service." With luck, she'd hear his sincerity. He joked about a lot of stuff, but active duty was no joke. "You're no longer serving?"

"Honorably discharged after an injury." She straightened her spine, but still managed to look defeated. Her eyes glistened with tears until she blinked them away.

He took a moment to consider her words and her body language. Something bad had gone down. Probably bad enough to leave lasting emotional scars. "I'm sorry for your loss." He patted her hand where it rested on the table. Concerned for her, he barely noticed the sparks racing up his arm from the brief contact.

"What?" She jerked her hand back and her gaze flew to his face. Her eyes brimmed with more tears.

"You seem...wounded, I guess. I think something devastating must have happened to you. I'm sorry if you lost friends."

"I didn't." She swallowed audibly. "I just—can we not talk about this? I don't even know you."

He leaned back in his seat and added sugar to his coffee. "Sorry for intruding."

Chapter Three

Winter inhaled the rich scent of freshly baked bread and something deliciously cinnamon. She picked up a cookie and nibbled the edge. She wasn't hungry, but it was something to do with her hands while she gathered her thoughts.

Nick Blackstone was a strange man. Throwing out quips and jokes one second, and compassionate the next. They'd only just met, and he was an enigma, a puzzle. She didn't like puzzles. At least not the human kind, and yet she wanted to learn more about him. How long had it been since a man caught her interest? Months? Years? After just five minutes, this kooky man had her curious.

Her aunt hadn't mentioned anything about him except that he was trustworthy. She completely failed to mention that he was stunning. He was tall, definitely over six feet. He was narrow-hipped and broad-shouldered. His arms strained the sleeves of his chef's jacket. His dark hair was short but needed a trim. And his eyes, be still her beating heart, they were the exact color of the Pacific Ocean. Sea green with flecks of gray and gold. They were almost as mesmerizing as the ocean she'd grown up beside.

She stole a glance at his hands. No rings and no tan lines. Was he single? She almost laughed aloud. Did it matter? She was only here for a year. Then she was gone. Perhaps she didn't know where she was going, but she wasn't staying here. Maybe she'd take some time to travel, see the world in a way that didn't endanger her life or the life of her friends. Eventually, she'd find a job.

The people she'd served with were more than her friends, they were family. She loved them as much, if not more, than her blood relatives. Abruptly, she pushed the thoughts of her parents away. She was enjoying sitting with Nick, she didn't need their frowning faces popping into her mind.

"How did you end up in Haven? Did you grow up here?" She didn't mean to ask, but she was exhausted. Sometimes her filter slipped when she was overtired.

"I came here from Edmonton, by way of New York City."

"That's some detour." She picked up another cookie, they were delicious. The first had been shortbread; this one looked like a gingersnap and smelled of sugar and spice as she bit off a chunk. Ginger, cinnamon, and a hint of clove exploded on her tongue. If Nick made these, he was a magician. This was singularly the most delicious treat she'd had in years, maybe in a decade. She gobbled it down as fast as seemed polite. *Would it be rude to ask for actual food?*

"The Big Apple was a detour, of sorts. But that's a story for another day."

"Do you like it here? I'm not certain I can adapt to life in a small town."

"I love it here. I know everyone. The scenery is spectacular. It's everything I didn't know I wanted until I came here to visit a friend. I think you'll learn to enjoy the peace and quiet. It's soothing to a battered soul."

He had a battered soul? He didn't sound like it. He sounded like a joker. Like someone who didn't take life too seriously. She abandoned the thought; she was too tired to riddle out his puzzle.

She stirred more cream into her coffee, though the delicious brew didn't need it. It wasn't the harsh brew she'd become accustomed to in the military. It was a perfect top-end coffee. She added the cream and sugar because she needed a moment to calm herself. The spring roads had been okay for most of the trip. A few snowy spots, but no real bad weather. For the first time in her life, she felt like she needed to be home. Not where she'd been raised, but the place she'd call home for the next year.

It was all irrelevant, she was here now and ready to settle in. But something about Nick had her stomach fluttering.

She pivoted to look around the bakery. There were ten square wooden tables, each with four wrought iron chairs. It had a cute, barroom meets Parisian café vibe. Several wood and iron display shelving units held packaged coffee and teas, as well as adorable coffee mugs and other merchandise. The air was heavy with the scent of baking bread. The scent simultaneously invigorated and comforted her. While her mother had never baked bread in her life, it still smelled like home. *Ugh. She was over-fixated on home.* Her stomach growled.

Despite the early hour, the display case was filled with cookies, tarts, and other delectable treats, including her favorite. "Oh, are those Nanaimo bars?" She could almost taste them from across the room.

"Regular, mint, and maple bacon." His grin was infectious.

"What?" Not certain she heard him right, she blinked. "You messed with perfection?"

His laugh was deep and throaty. Goose bumps erupted over her skin. "It's my job to mess with perfection and create something divine. In *Life,* you have to take chances if you want a *Payday.*"

She wrinkled her brow. *Board games?*

"I don't see how you could improve on perfect," she challenged him, hoping for a taste. She should probably just ask him if she could buy something for breakfast, but she was overstepping already by being here a week early and disrupting his morning routine.

He leaped to his feet and walked to the display. Glory be, he was as delicious from behind as from the front. She fanned heat from her face.

Two minutes later, he was back with a plate and a fork. "Go ahead, try them. On the house," he dared. He stood there, hands on his hips, until she picked up the fork. A half smile played on his lips. Definitely cocky and sure of himself. Reminded her of a blowhard general.

The original flavor melted on her tongue in a wave of sweet vanilla, coconut, and chocolate. She groaned in bliss. "It's been way too long. You don't get stuff like this in the mess hall."

He made an impatient motion with his hand. She cut off a corner of the square with green filling. It just looked wrong. She eyed it warily, and after bracing herself, put it in her mouth.

The mint was subtle, barely noticeable. Like the first bar, the texture was perfect, creamy, and smooth with a hint of crisp in the chocolate crumb base. She closed her eyes to savor the unfamiliar taste. "Not bad." She banked the temptation to take a larger taste. She didn't want to give in just yet.

"Try the next one." He nudged the plate with his finger as he slipped into his chair with the grace of a dancer.

"Do I have to?" She wanted to dive into the first two choices.

"Do you like bacon?"

She nodded.

"How about maple syrup?"

She nodded again and frowned. Maple bacon seemed the rage everywhere, she wasn't sure she saw the appeal.

"Coward." He laughed. "You have to take a *Risk*."

Did he just put a slight emphasis on risk? She squinted at him.

"I dare you to take a *Chance*."

"Ha. Ha."

"I double dog dare you."

"That's so juvenile." She cut off a minuscule corner of the offensive dessert with the crispy bacon crumble on the top.

"Seriously? I thought soldiers were brave. I can't believe you're afraid of sweets."

"Am not."

"Are too."

"Am not."

They laughed together, and he nodded toward the plate.

"Fine. But just to shut you up." She hadn't laughed over something so silly in months. Maybe years.

She put the morsel in her mouth. Chocolate and bacon exploded over her tongue. A sweet hint of maple followed. The flavors were subtle but there. She was shocked to discover it was delicious.

"Okay, that's not bad. I've questioned the whole maple-bacon everything trend, but you made a decent dessert there."

"Decent?" He lifted an eyebrow.

"Okay, neither one is as good as the original, but they're both delicious. I admit it." She ate a few more bites before saying, "Can I get the rest to go?" She could devour all three, but that much sugar on top of an empty stomach was a recipe for disaster.

He bowed. "Of course." He didn't gloat or act superior, just accepted the praise as well deserved, without arrogance. He'd proved her wrong, and he wasn't acting all cocky afterward. She liked that. Add another piece to the enigma puzzle.

The door opened and a rush of frigid air blew in.

"Cold enough to freeze a witch's...." the newcomer trailed off.

"Clint, come in. This is Winter. It's her truck that's dead. Winter Ireland, meet Clint Dawson, owner of our local garage."

They made a moment of small talk, and she explained the way her truck sputtered and died.

"I'll tow it over to the garage and have a look at it. You're Muriel's niece, right? I'll call the house when I know what the issue is. Is there anything you need out of it before I tow her away?"

It took a second for her exhausted brain to assimilate everything he said. "No, I don't need anything out of it, unless it takes more than a day to repair. And yes, I'm Muriel's niece. How did you know?"

Clint chuckled. "Are you kidding? She brags about you all the time. Your picture is everywhere in her house. Her fridge is practically a collage. I'd have recognized you anywhere. Plus, you resemble her." He made a circle around his eyes. "Same eyes."

"Oh." How did she even respond to that? It was astonishing that her aunt had her picture on display. "Let me get you the keys." She grabbed them from her coat and passed them over. "Do you need a credit card or anything?"

"Nope. All good. The tow's on the house. Consider it a welcome to Haven present. My wife, Natalie, says to warn you to expect a visit from the Welcome Club, whatever that is."

"I'll keep that in mind." She kept her face from revealing her dismay. Socializing wasn't in her plans; she was here to do her aunt a favor and for some peace and quiet. All she wanted was twelve hours of solid sleep and then a hot meal. She yawned wide enough that her jaw cracked.

"Later." Clint waved and was gone before she knew it.

She yawned again and covered her mouth. "Sorry, I'm bushed."

"I'll run you home."

"I can walk. If I remember right, it isn't far." She didn't relish the idea, but she wasn't one to give in to the simple route. She'd been in worse weather in Cambodia.

"It's ridiculously windy. The gusts will blow you off your feet. You're already exhausted. Let me grab you some food for your lunch and then I'll drive you home. Give me ten minutes. I have muffins in the oven."

"Sure." What else could she say? Something said he wasn't going to take no for an answer. His long, denim-clad legs draw her attention, again, as he walked away. The man was intriguing. Or maybe she was just exhausted.

Chapter Four

Nick took the muffins from the oven. He should have been rolling and flattening peanut butter cookies, but he'd enjoyed talking to Winter too much. Her melancholy beauty spoke to his heart in a way no other woman had. He wanted to draw her into his arms and hold her there until her hurts went away.

He shook his head to dislodge the thought. Hugging a woman he barely knew would get his face slapped, at the very least.

After shutting off the oven, he grabbed a blue and white striped bakery box and started loading it. An upside-down T-shaped divider went in first to keep the savory from the sweet. On the left, he put in two mini bacon cheddar quiches and a breakfast wrap. On the right, a jumbo cinnamon bun, and two cherry tarts. Half a dozen cookies, two apple tarts, and two muffins went into a second box. He slipped both boxes and another containing the Nanaimo bars, into a bakery bag. He was never stingy with his product, but this was a lot to give away, yet he didn't think twice. Muriel had been gone for a week, her fridge was probably empty, and it was obvious that Winter lacked the energy to shop for groceries.

Besides, karma rewards good deeds.

"I'm parked out back," he said when she looked his way. "We can go whenever you're ready."

Her smile lit up the room like a sun bursting from behind clouds. It did little to hide the dark circles under her eyes. She was already pretty, and he knew she'd be breathtaking once she was rested. Wariness showed in her eyes, though, like someone who was trying hard to protect themselves, to keep the world at bay.

She really must have gone through something when she was injured. Muriel mentioned Winter being hurt, but hadn't shared any details. He'd like to know more about her injury, and her invisible wounds as well. He wasn't going to push it; she'd open up if and when she was ready. He had at least a year to worry the information out of her.

She stood and wobbled on her feet a bit. She grabbed the table for support.

"Are you okay?" He rushed to her side in case she fell. "You look like you could fall over."

"Tired," she mumbled so low he could hardly hear her. She was fading fast.

"Let's get your sweater on." He picked it up and helped her into it. After checking that she had everything she came in with, he led her through the kitchen and out the back door to his SUV. He helped her inside and strode through the swirling fog to get in on his side.

"This weather is crazy." He started the engine. When she didn't respond, he glanced over at her. Her head was tipped back, her mouth open. She had dozed off in the time it took him to get in.

A soft snore tickled his ear, and he grinned. Yup. Out like a light. She was more tired than he'd thought. It was lucky she'd made it to town before falling asleep. His heart stuttered, thinking about what could have happened to her. Clint's wife Natalie had gone off the road on her way into town. She'd been lucky that someone had called for a tow. Traffic was light this time of day, if Winter had crashed, she might have gone unfound for a long time. There were a lot of deep, tree and boulder filled gullies along the mountain highway.

Pushing away the distressing thoughts, he backed out of his stall. He turned on the defroster even though the engine was stone cold. He rarely drove. The bakery was only a couple blocks from home and nothing in Haven was far away. Peeking at her from the corner of his eye, he was half tempted to nap himself.

Three minutes later, he pulled up in front of Muriel's house. Before getting out, he pulled the house key from his pocket. He jogged up to the front door and unlocked it. Inside, he kicked off his shoes and went in, turned up the heat, and pulled the covers down on the guest bed.

Shoes back on, he opened Winter's door. "Hey, wake up. Let's get you inside."

She mumbled something unintelligible, but let him help her into the house. He hung her jacket on the coat rack near the door and stripped off her heavy boots. *Who wore combat boots to drive?*

They stumbled down the hallway, her feet barely moving, and he helped her onto the bed. He was certain she had no idea what was going on. Helping her was like leading a sleepwalker, or a zombie. Her clothing was fairly dry, so he pulled the covers up over her, flipped off the light, and headed for the bakery. He was way behind schedule.

He popped through the back door he'd left unlocked. As soon as he stepped inside, he heard Grace's voice. "Nick. Is that you?"

Shoot. He'd forgotten to lock the front door. It's a good thing Haven was a small and very safe town. "Back here, Grace," he called out.

Friends for years, she had no qualms about joining him in the kitchen. "Where were you? I was calling out for five minutes. I was about to call Mac and report you missing." Mac, also known as McKenzie Stewart, was one of two local RCMP officers.

"I had to pop out for a minute."

She raised an eyebrow at him and snatched a muffin off the counter. "I gathered that. I'm going to need details. It isn't like you to run off and leave the place unlocked. Does it have anything to do with Clint loading up that truck down the block? This muffin is good, maybe even great," she said around the bite she'd taken.

"Thanks. Don't you have a bookstore to run? Or kids to watch?" Like all small towns, Haven could be a hotbed of gossip and he didn't want to add to it. "Muriel's niece arrived. That's her truck. She needed a ride."

He cleaned his hands and started rolling balls of peanut butter cookie batter. He ignored the penetrating look she gave him. She finished her muffin and washed her hands. She flattened the balls with a fork. There were a lot of ways to make peanut butter cookies, but he still preferred the old-school method of flattening them. He'd tried a few cookie press versions but still liked his grandmother's recipe best.

"Is she nice?"

"Who?" He feigned ignorance.

"Muriel's niece. Don't play dumb with me. I've known you a long time. I thought we were friends."

"She seems nice. She was too tired to make much conversation. I drove her to Muriel's and dropped her off." *End of discussion.*

"Is she pretty?"

Pretty barely covered it. She was stunning. Hazel eyes, raven hair. Fit, firm body, from what he could tell. Something in her spoke to him in a way he hadn't felt for a long time. Her wounded warrior vibes worried him as much as they called to him. So intriguing.

"I'm going to take that as a yes." Grace laughed. "You're struck speechless." She paused. "Don't rush into anything. You've been looking for a life partner for a long time, too long for someone as wonderful as you. Take it slow. Don't let loneliness push you into something, someone, who isn't right for you. Okay?"

"I'm single, not desperate." He slammed a ball of dough onto the sheet, the force nearly flattening it.

"Oh, honey, I know that. You know that. But does your heart know that?" Her words rang with compassion.

"I sure hope so." He wouldn't take those words from anyone else, but Grace was his best friend. He was long since over his infatuation with Grace. They were close enough that she'd come to him when she learned she was pregnant and was unsure of how her new husband would feel about adding a baby to their small family. Just as Nick suggested, Sterling was thrilled with the news.

"Where's baby Travis?"

"Sterling has kid duty this morning. He'll drop Travis off at the bookstore when he takes Sasha to school. I want to get caught up on paperwork this morning. I can't do that while toting around a colicky baby."

They worked in silence for a few minutes. "Tell me about her." One thing about Grace, when she got on a topic, she didn't let it die until she heard what she wanted to hear.

"She's honorably discharged from the military due to an injury. I don't know how or how badly. I gave her coffee and treats while we waited for Clint. Then, I took her home. I'm guessing she went to bed. She seems nice. Quiet."

Grace put her fork down. "Be careful, okay?"

He nodded and removed the disposable gloves he wore to roll cookies. "I will. Let me put on a fresh pot of coffee."

"Are you kicking me out?" She laughed again.

"Yup. There's no time like the present to get to work and I'll present you with a coffee and won't charge you for that muffin, but only if you leave right away. If you hang around, you pay twice retail. Begone, foul witch."

"Evil. You're evil." She laughed. "Come for supper tonight. Bring your girlfriend if she's up to it." She waggled her fingers and sprinted from the kitchen.

He chased her as far as the coffee pot. "Not my girlfriend." *Yet.* "If I see her, I'll tell her you invited her to dinner."

Once she left, with an extra muffin and coffee, he locked the front door. He'd had enough distractions this morning. If he didn't focus, he'd never catch up. It was a good thing Uma was coming in today. Not much of a baker yet, though she was learning. She was great with customers. She'd also finally mastered getting icing smooth and writing messages on cakes. For a woman who'd shown up with a tree-planting crew, she did all right as a baker's assistant and took an enormous burden off his shoulders. Enough that he had time for a social life.

His mind flashed to Winter. He knew just who he wanted to socialize with.

· ♥ · ♥ · ♥ · ♥ · ♥ ·

Winter woke with a start. Instinct kicked in, and she bolted out of bed and crouched into a fighting stance. Her eyes searched the room for threats. She ignored the thundering of her heart. Recognition dawned. She was in her aunt's house. Still, she held motionless, unsure what woke her. Was there someone in the house with her?

She listened hard. If she were a cat, her ears would have perked forward.

Except for kids shouting outside, silence reigned. She relaxed and stretched her stiff back. Her knee hurt like a son of a gun. Slowly, she did a few cautious squats to limber her back and knee. Then, creeping on silent feet, she toured the house looking for the cause of whatever woke her.

All the bedrooms and closets were empty of life. There was nobody in the nearly empty basement. She was alone. Blessedly alone. She raised her arms and stretched again. It was good to be alive. She caught of whiff of something foul and realized it was her.

"Oh, good gravy. Did I smell like this in the bakery?" Heat flooded her face. How had she gotten home and into bed? Had Nick brought her here? Or was it the other guy? What was his name? Dang, if she could remember. She'd figure it out later. Her memory was spotty after seeing those deer on the highway. There was no sense fretting over something she couldn't fix. The information was out there, and she knew that Nick could fill her in. She'd talk to him the next time she went to the bakery. But for now, she needed to shower and de-stink.

"Shoot. My bags are in my truck. Why didn't I think of that? Probably because you were exhausted. And now, I'm talking to myself and answering. I'm losing my mind."

She rummaged through the drawers in the spare room's antique cherry wood dresser and discovered a neat pile of clothing with a note on top. She opened the note.

Winter

I know you'll be exhausted and not up for much. I grabbed these for you on my last trip to the city. I hope they fit.

Love, Auntie Muriel.

"Thank you, Auntie Muriel, you're amazing." Giggling like crazy, she headed into the shower.

Cleaned and refreshed, she peeked into the fridge. Nothing much there, except for a bag that said Nick's bakery. She vaguely remembered something about food. She'd been way overtired and shouldn't have been on the road all night. Lucky for her, she made it to town safely. She shivered, thinking about the things that could have happened when driving overtired. Sometimes, for a smart woman, she was foolish.

She pulled out the bakery bag and opened the boxes.

"Nick, you are a god among men." She ate a breakfast wrap filled with sausage, eggs, and a delicious cheese sauce. She followed it with a mini quiche, and then coffee and cookies. It had been way too long since she ate decent food. She wasn't much of a cook. She did okay, but didn't enjoy cooking. Consequently, she ate out entirely too often. Her army buddies weren't any better.

As soon as she had her truck back, she was going to have to get groceries. Her savings wouldn't last forever if she ate takeout all the time. She found a pen and paper and started a list. The cupboards held staples, but she needed fresh meat, veggies, and fruit. Oh, and milk, cheese, eggs, and yogurt. There was no way she'd be able to walk home with all that. Did Haven have a taxi? Maybe a ride share?

She sighed. Probably not.

Muriel took her car, so that was out.

She poured more coffee and carried it to the living room. She opened the drapes and warm sunshine poured in. The early morning wind had calmed. It was beautiful outside.

She picked up the small coffee table, flipped it over, and set it on top of the dining room table that had a linen tablecloth to protect it. She set her coffee on a magazine on the plush cream carpet and inched down to the floor in front of the floral sofa. Time for physio.

Slowly, carefully, she grunted her way through her prescribed workout. Her knee ached and throbbed with every motion. She hadn't done herself any favors by driving for so long without walking breaks. She was stiff and sore, but as she worked, things loosened up. With luck, she hadn't damaged anything badly enough to set her recovery back. Stretches complete, the only thing left was a walk. She had worked up to walking about three miles a day. Eventually, she'd get back into jogging. For today, she'd stroll around town and check out what had changed. If her knee held up, she'd go as far as the gas station and check on her truck.

She fired up the desktop computer in her aunt's sewing room and spent ten minutes studying a map of Haven so she wouldn't get lost. It was always best to know the terrain when you were on a mission.

She sighed in frustration. There'd never be another mission. Her entire reason for living was gone.

She needed a purpose. She'd planned on being in the military for her entire working life. She'd accepted that eventually, with age, a desk jockey position would be the way she would finish her career. But until her injury, she'd planned to be on active duty for as long as possible. What else could a lifetime soldier do? She had no other training.

The ability to play guitar and piano wasn't going to take her very far, and the recorder lessons she'd taken in elementary school were of even less value. Maybe she'd investigate some online classes and work toward a degree in something.

But what?

That was a question for another day.

She was still tired, but if she wanted a good night's sleep, she needed to stay up until bedtime. Time to finish her physio with a slow walk around the town that would be her home for the next several months. Just a few short blocks and then home. With her knee overtired, it was probably better to break her distance into shorter walks.

She found the key on the small cherry table in the front entry and locked up. She left her uncharged phone behind and started down the street.

Chapter Five

T he weather was glorious. The early afternoon sun was out. It was turning into a lovely day after a very inauspicious start. Winter smiled as a butterfly danced by on the light breeze. A cat strolled up and down behind a white picket fence, its tail twitching like mad, pretending to ignore the magpie on the grass behind it. The still-snowy mountains towered beautifully overtop the houses.

Everything smelled fresh and clean.

It was the perfect morning to start her new life. Her smile widened. Spring was her favorite time of year. The whole world seemed bursting with possibilities.

"Good afternoon," someone called out from their porch. She waved back, though she had no idea who the woman was. The greeting warmed her almost as much as the early afternoon sunshine.

She zigzagged up and down different streets, taking random turns and twists until somehow, she ended up outside the bakery. Thirsty and needing a drink, she realized she hadn't brought her wallet. She debated turning around and going home, but thirst won out.

She opened the door, and a bell tinkled happily. Had that been there earlier? She couldn't recall.

What was it about this town that seemed so upbeat and cheerful? It was nibbling away at the darkness surrounding her, and she'd only been here for a few hours. And she'd spent most of those asleep. A look at her watch said she'd probably slept five hours. Not long enough.

"Be right out," a male voice called. Nick. Funny, she hadn't forgotten his voice.

Perfect, she'd thank him for breakfast and ask for a glass of water. Two birds with one stone. Maximum efficiency.

Nick wandered out a few seconds later, drying his hands on a towel. His white chef's jacket was splattered with blue icing. "Winter, you're awake. Did you have a nice rest?" His smile turned her knees, even the titanium one, to melted butter.

"I did," her voice croaked on the last word. She cleared her throat. "I came to say thank you for the delicious breakfast. How much do I owe you?" *Ugh. Why had she brought that up when she didn't have any money with her?*

He made a waving motion. "Nothing. Consider it a welcome to Haven gift. Besides, Muriel would kick my backside if I charged you." He winked.

Sweet heaven. The man was lethal. She mentally boarded up her hormones. Not going there. When people got close, they got hurt. Or she did. Those that didn't get hurt tried to run her life.

"Well, thank you." She paused and shuffled her feet. "Can I borrow a glass of water? I went for a walk and forgot a water bottle. I guess I'm still tired."

"Sure thing." He pulled a bottle from the cooler.

"Oh, a glass will be fine." Heat rose in her face. "I forgot my wallet too."

His laughter sent shivers of heat down her spine, and his smile stole her breath. *Yup, lethal.* "It's okay, Winter. I can afford a bottle of water. Take it." He shoved it toward her. "Want a cookie or anything while you're here?"

"You can't keep feeding me."

"I can do whatever I want. Fresh peanut butter cookies, right out of the oven," he teased in a singsong voice. "You know you want one."

"Fine. You forced me into it. But if you keep thrusting food on me, I'm going to have to stop coming in. You've already fed me twice today."

"I rescind my offer. No cookie for you. You only get it if you promise to stop by regularly."

He was teasing, wasn't he?

"I make no promises, but hand over the cookie, and no one gets hurt." She waggled her finger like a mom scolding her child.

"Tsk, tsk. Manners."

"I'll have a cookie and water, please, and thank you." She couldn't stop herself from grinning at their silly exchange. He brought something out in her she hadn't felt for a long time. She felt—lighter.

"I'm ready for coffee. Why don't you join me?"

She really should refuse. She wasn't planning on getting close to anyone. Her time in Haven was a pit stop. She envisioned it as a personal tour of duty. Get in, do the job, get out. No attachments. "Sure, I'd like that."

Where had that come from? She was going to say no. Keep her distance. Do not engage with the locals.

"Take a seat anywhere. I'll just grab a coffee and join you. Did you want a cup?" His tone said that he knew she'd refuse.

"With cream, please, and thank you." Where had her refusal gone? The ability to say no? She turned and noticed for the first time that the entire bakery was empty. She pivoted toward the decimated display. There was almost nothing left in it. He must have had a busy morning.

He came out of the kitchen carrying a tray laden with two cups of coffee and two cinnamon rolls. The dark heaven of coffee tickled her senses.

"I brought snacks," He slid the tray in front of her. "I hope you're hungry."

"Not in the least. I just ate an enormous breakfast provided by the generous local baker." She picked up a plate and set it in front of herself. Who was she to turn down a free cinnamon bun? She inhaled deeply. Sweet cinnamon goodness washed over her like a soothing balm. This place, this man, was good for her soul. "Thank you." She stuffed an enormous bite into her mouth. She groaned aloud with the first sweet explosion of flavor.

She held a hand in front of her still full mouth and mumbled, "Oh, my God, you are one talented baker. This is like an orgasm on my tongue."

Heat rose in her face as she realized how her comment sounded. She choked on the bite and had to glug down hot coffee to swallow it. "That's...that's not what I meant."

Nick burst out laughing. "It's not the first orgasm I've given a woman, but it might be the first foodgasm." He laughed some more. "Thanks, you made my day."

His eyes sparkled with mirth and his grin was perfect joy. Nick Blackstone was one of the happiest people she'd ever met. It had to be a ruse. Didn't it?

"You're just complimenting me because military food sucks," he teased.

"Not always. Sometimes, we ended up with an actual chef instead of some grunt forced into the role. Those gigs were the best. There's something restorative about a delicious hot meal after a long hard patrol." She paused. "Does that make sense?" *Why in the world was she talking about this?* It wasn't like her to share deep thoughts. Okay, not deep, but not for public consumption. Semi-classified.

"I totally get it. While I was a chef in The Big Apple, I fueled up after a long shift by prepping something delicious for myself and my staff. It chilled us all out. Even after the worst day, there's something soothing about creating what *I* want." He put a subtle emphasis on the pronoun.

It struck a chord within her. Was he the type to give too much of himself? He'd certainly been more than generous with her.

Talk drifted to less personal topics. He was easy to talk to, and he listened to what she said, even the unimportant things. He had work to do, so she didn't linger too long, though she was enjoying herself. "I better be going. I need to check in at the gas station and maybe get some groceries. Is there a taxi here?"

"No taxi. But I can let you borrow my truck."

She stood and looked down at his handsome face. "I can't ask that," she demurred.

"Ah, but you didn't, I offered. I'll take a *Chance* on you. You're worth the *Risk*." He winked and stood to dig into his pocket. "Just bring her back when you're finished." He held out his keys.

She shook her head. "I couldn't."

He reached out and grasped her hand and rolled it over to set the keys in her palm. His hands were deliciously warm and gentle. "Take them. Get what you need and bring it back later. If you get delayed, no worries. My house is only blocks away. In fact, it's two doors down from yours. I'm the 1950s beauty with the new roof. The dark green with white trim."

"I noticed that one. Your lawn looks great, but your flower gardens are a mess."

"I'm terrible at gardening. I don't enjoy it. Don't get me wrong, I love the look of a well-maintained garden. But I work long hours, sometimes sixteen-hour days. By the end of the day, gardening is the last thing on my mind."

"I never minded gardening. Auntie Muriel and I used to garden together when I was young. I spent a few summers here with her. It was…I don't know…soothing, maybe? I can't wait to dive in and pull some weeds." She laughed. None of her platoon mates would understand the solace of working in the garden, though one friend loved to bake. The guys mostly unwound by playing or watching sports. A few were video game addicts.

She looked down at the keys in her hand. "Thank you, Nick. I appreciate your trust in me. I'll bring it back as soon as I can."

"No rush, Winter. And any friend of Muriel's is a friend of mine." She paused. "I guess I'll walk home, get my wallet, and come back. I can't drive without a license."

"No worries. Mac will let it slide if he pulls you over. At least he will if you can produce a license in twenty-four hours."

"Mac?"

"McKenzie Stewart, one of two local RCMP officers. Head of the department. He's a good guy. He'd cut you a break, though this time of day, he's probably patrolling the highway down by the lake."

"Good to know. I do appreciate it. Why don't I show my appreciation by cooking supper for you?" The words were out of her mouth without her even thinking them.

"You sure?"

She could hardly back down now, especially if she wanted to borrow his truck. "Absolutely. Is there anything that you don't eat?"

"Nothing. Except cauliflower."

"I'm guessing cauliflower crust pizza is out."

He fake gagged. "You feed me that and you'll be in *Trouble*." He laughed.

Again, with the board games. She squinted at him. She thought she'd imagined all the game references earlier, but apparently not. "Should I pick up a bottle of *Gin*?" she asked seriously.

His roar of laughter echoed off the ceiling right into her heart. "Beer's fine, thanks."

His smile was payment enough for making a cringe-worthy game reference. How had she fallen into that trap?

Chapter Six

S ix took an eternity to arrive. Finally, Nick closed the door on his last customer and began his nightly shutdown procedure. He'd done as much in advance as he could, such as setting the refrigerated bread dough out to rise overnight. There were still baked goods to cover, cash to count, and the floor to scrub.

Twitching with nerves and eager to get home, he was half tempted to skip his remaining chores until morning. When Winter returned his keys, they'd confirmed dinner at seven, so he had plenty of time to get ready, even if he was itching to see her again. He'd called Grace and let her know they wouldn't be coming over for dinner.

He forced himself to count the money in the register, put the deposit, and float in the safe. Their small bank didn't have a night deposit so that chore was always relegated to the next day.

Finally, he was set, and with time to spare. The sun was still shining and the evening warm. He locked up both doors and started home on foot. He needed to work off some energy. He hadn't been this nervous and excited since he opened the bakery. It felt like there was something in the air. Hope? Love? Friendship? Definitely optimism for the future.

After showering and changing, he paced his living room until it was time to leave. He grabbed the box of Long Johns he'd set aside earlier and struck out. It wasn't easy not to race toward Winter and dinner. Anticipation at seeing her rare smile prickled along his nerve endings like sparks. If he was a kid, he'd be bouncing off the walls.

Winter answered the door wearing snug jeans and a long-sleeved khaki T-shirt with a Canadian army logo on the left shoulder. Her hair was loose and brushed over her shoulders like a caress.

"Hi. I brought dessert." He thrust the package at her, totally giving away his nerves.

"Oh." She jumped back slightly. "Thank you. Come in."

He stepped inside and slipped off his shoes.

"Come into the kitchen."

He followed her past the living room with its brand-new plush carpeting and delicate, old lady furniture. There were a few knick-knacks, mostly photographs of Winter as well as Muriel's travels. A colorful quilt hung over each of the solid burgundy chairs. He'd always found this room happy...if a bit girly for his tastes.

The kitchen was equally bright and made more so by Winter's presence. She must have cleared away some pictures because the fridge was bare except for a grocery list.

"Where did all Muriel's pictures go?"

"Away. Far, far away. Do you know how creepy it is to see your face plastered over every inch of the fridge every time you walk into the kitchen? It's weird. I'll put them back before she comes home." She shuddered.

"You could have left one up," he teased.

"No way. Some things are best left hidden."

"It's a shame, really. I always enjoyed looking at them." He scratched his nose. "Of course, now I have the real thing and she's even prettier in person." He hadn't meant to mention it, it just slipped out. But her pink-cheeked smile made the unintended compliment worth a bit of embarrassment on his part.

"What's for dinner? It smells delicious." The fresh scent of basil, tomato sauce, and melting cheese made him salivate.

"Don't get your hopes up. It's just spaghetti and meat sauce, salad, and garlic toast. Nothing fancy."

"Sounds delicious." He was a sucker for a savory meal of comfort food after a day of baking.

"Take a seat and I'll put everything on the table. Did you want beer or red wine? There's a Merlot in the fridge."

"Wine sounds good. Shall I open it?"

"Yes, thank you."

"Could we be any more nervous?" He chuckled and opened the fridge. "We sound like two people on a blind date."

"This isn't a date. It's two new friends sharing a meal."

He wished he could see her face, but she kept her back toward him. They'd gotten along well earlier, but now she seemed to be throwing up a wall between them. *Interesting*. Well, he'd done some rock climbing in his youth, and he could scale any wall she built, and he was up for a challenge. Love wasn't supposed to be easy.

He paused inside the open fridge door. Love? What in the world was he thinking? He only met her before dawn today. Sure, he'd heard lots of stories about her from Muriel. But for the L-word to pop into his head? Insanity.

He shook the weird thoughts off and grabbed the wine. It was a decent brand with a twist top. He'd been served this by a few friends. "How was your day?"

"Surprisingly busy. I mean, I slept until after lunch. But I took two walks and toured town. I can't wait to hit some of the hiking trails I saw signs for. I bought groceries and checked on my truck, which Clint can't look at until tomorrow, but that's okay. I did some laundry and started turning over the potato patch. I can't believe how much snow there still is here. Some of the shadier parts still had little piles of snow. I shoveled them into the sunshine." *Good grief. I'm babbling.*

"Wow. I thought I was busy. I'm impressed. I can't wait for the snow to be gone. Being in the mountains means more snow than other places and longer for it to vanish completely. Summer's my favorite, but there's snow sense in complaining."

She ignored the wordplay as they sat down at the table. She folded her hands in her lap and bowed her head with her eyes closed. He wasn't religious, but he respected her beliefs with silence. Greedily, he took a moment to study her. Her face was nearly symmetrical, and her dark lashes rested on her cheeks. She looked like a raven-haired angel. She straightened her shoulders, and he dragged his gaze away lest she catch him staring.

"Go ahead, serve yourself." She offered. "Today felt busy because I'm still dragging from the drive. It's amazing how quickly you fall out of the habit of going non-stop from sunup to sundown. I was accustomed to hard days, but today took a lot out of me."

"That's too bad."

"It was good, though." She piled spaghetti on her plate and passed him the serving bowl.

"What changed?" He took some noodles and accepted the sauce ladle she pivoted towards him.

She sighed and stared at her plate for a moment. He doubted she was seeing the pretty rose-print placemats or the brimming serving dishes.

"Rehab." Another heavy sigh. "Rehab changed everything." Her shoulders went stiff, and she fiddled with her fork, looking everywhere except at him.

"Want to talk about it?" He twirled some heavenly-scented noodles onto his fork.

"No." Her voice was low and quivered with unspoken emotion.

"The bakery was crazy today. Not so much with customers, but with sugar cookies. It's Earth Day tomorrow. The school ordered Earth Day cookies. I've been baking and freezing them for weeks. Yesterday and today, my staff and I were decorating. Do you have any idea how long it takes to decorate six hundred and fifty cookies?"

"Six hundred and fifty?" She stared at him like he was crazy.

"Yup. My assistant, Uma, iced them in blue. I traced the continents onto them, and Betsy Cook filled in the outlines. My hands cramped from squeezing the icing bag. If I ever see blue icing again, it will be too soon."

"Why so many cookies? And is her name really Betsy Cook?"

"It really is. Five hundred cookies for the school, and the rest for the bakery. I try and celebrate the seasons with something special every year. Valentine's Day is easy. Pink heart-shaped cookies, a bit of icing, and sprinkles. Of course, I also make some fancier treats, but the cookies sell well."

He told her stories of baking disasters and after a while, her rigid posture relaxed slightly. Though she kept her erect military bearing, the hard edge to her shoulders softened. Before long, she was laughing at his stories.

He'd heard people say someone's laughter sounded like bells. Not Winter, her laugh was deep and loud and incredibly infectious. The more she laughed, the more he laughed. Her chuckles filled him with joy because he sensed she wasn't a person who laughed much. Muriel had often commented on her niece's serious demeanor. She attributed it to overcritical parents and the unbending severity of her career choice.

His first impression was that Muriel was right. Winter was a serious woman. But the more time he spent with her, the more certain he was that she had lightness buried in her heart. How he could know that after only hours was beyond him, but he was certain. And he knew just the man to bring that lightness out.

Chapter Seven

Winter noticed that Nick didn't pray with her, but he did respect her choice. She admired that. He hadn't made comments or jokes, he just sat quietly while she gave her silent thanks. There had been more than one fistfight in the mess hall over praying before meals. You'd think people would be more tolerant.

Nick was an engaging and entertaining dinner companion. He had a way with stories, puns, and plays on words. She didn't doubt that his stories were true, though she suspected he exaggerated a bit for comic effect. They lingered over dinner and, by unspoken agreement, rose to clear the table.

She had a dishwasher, but when Nick filled the sink to start washing dishes, she didn't complain. She let him wash while she dried and put things away. It was soothing in its ordinariness. She couldn't even remember the last time she'd done dishes by hand rather than dumping them into the dishwasher. Of course, on deployment, someone else handled KP duty.

"Want to watch a movie or something?" She hung her towel on the oven door handle to dry.

He glanced at his watch. "Wow, is it really nine? We spent two hours talking. That's incredible. I really should go, but maybe one quick show rather than a full movie."

She wondered if he sensed her reluctance to be alone. In the military, you rarely had time to yourself, let alone complete privacy. As much as she craved the solitude, she didn't want the evening to end. Night brought darkness. Darkness dragged out thoughts, regrets, and memories of mistakes. And sometimes, nightmares.

"More wine? I could open another bottle."

"I'm good, but thanks. Go ahead if you want more."

She declined, and they settled on the delicate sofa, side by side but not touching. His broad shoulders made everything in the room seem even smaller. She turned on Muriel's big screen television and flicked through the channels until she found a baking reality show. "How about this?"

"Seriously? I spend my entire life in the kitchen...baking, and you want me to watch more?" He laughed and his smile stole her breath.

"Yup. I didn't get much tube time. I love these shows when I get a chance to see them." She waited for him to refuse.

He waved toward the remote. "Go ahead, fire it up. I'll tell you what they're doing wrong." He made bad baking puns, poked gentle fun at the hosts, and commented insightfully on the bakers' attempts. There were some amazing creations in the first round. His companionship made the show even more entertaining. For a short while, her problems faded away.

Nick shifted slightly sideways and slung his arm along the back of the couch behind her head. He didn't touch her. It didn't feel like a play, but part of her almost wished it was. She wasn't a stranger to physical intimacy, and it had been way too long. Part of her was tempted to lean into him and see what happened. The rest of her was half relieved when it became clear that he wasn't trying to seduce her.

She relaxed and ignored the heat of his arm so close to her neck.

The next thing she knew, insistent beeping woke her. She jerked upright with a groan. Everything ached, but her neck was the worst. It took several seconds to realize she'd fallen asleep on the couch.

"Morning," Nick's voice rumbled along her spine. "I guess we fell asleep. It seems I'm not very stimulating company. My alarm woke you. I'm sorry."

She winced and tried to unlock her stiff shoulders. The room was dark except for the TV and the single lamp they'd left on. It was still night. She groaned. "What time is it?"

"Four-thirty."

"What? In the morning? Why?" She yawned.

He laughed and pointed at his chest. "Baker. Remember."

"Right." She groaned and leaned forward to stretch out her back.

"Here, let me." His hand smoothed down her spine. "You're very tight. You need to relax more." He massaged gently up and down her torso. His fingers were magic on her tight muscles. "I recommend a good long soak in the hot tub."

"I wish. Oh, that feels good. Right there." His fingers hit a particularly tense spot. Suddenly, she realized that she was letting a virtual stranger touch her intimately. A massage therapist was one thing, a neighbor another. She jerked to her feet, rolling her shoulders to release tension. "Coffee?"

"Thanks, but no. I should get going. And if you want to soak in my hot tub, feel free. I'm in the dark green house two doors left. The front gate's unlocked and there's a mechanical lifter to get the cover off. Go ahead. I don't mind. I'll be at work until six, so I won't even disturb you."

"I'll think about it." Okay, she'd more than think about it. Her aching knee was screaming for a good soak. Her surgical wounds were long since healed, and her doctor said hot tubs were okay if they weren't too hot. She'd double-check the temp before she got in...if she gave in to the temptation of a soak and went over.

After he left, she took a short nap and started her morning routine as she had the day before. Coffee, then physio. Firing up a fitness app on her tablet, she did her best to work along with a beginner yoga program. She had never been very flexible, but the long rehab from surgery had tightened her right up. She had all the flexibility of a steel bar. After much sweating, grunting, and cussing, she was done and ready for a soak in the tub...the hot tub.

Yeah, she was going to take Nick up on his offer. She rinsed the sweat off in the shower, slipped into her swimsuit, and headed over. The hot water and jets felt divine. It was a way different experience than a regular tub, even better than her friend's whirlpool tub. She could get used to this. Combat deployment never had hot tubs. Ever.

Exhaustion washed over her. She'd gotten so run down on her last tour. Then there was the IED and the damage to her body, and to her friends' bodies. Rehab had been brutal. Throw in a long drive to Haven, and she was completely and totally burned out. Weirdly, she'd slept deeply on the couch last night. Being with Nick was soothing. Almost as soothing as this tub.

She closed her eyes and leaned back against the headrest. The sun was up now, and she listened to the sounds of the town coming to life. Kids laughed and screamed in delight. Somewhere, far off, a lawn mower droned back and forth. Cars whooshed past on the street. A baby cried in the house next door. A bright female voice urged someone named Amy to hurry up, or she'd be late for school. Birds sang in the trees and a woodpecker drilled holes in a fence post.

Dappled sunlight covered her face, and she found herself focusing on the relative quiet of the day. Girlish giggles came from next door, presumably the tardy Amy. Small-town life had an entirely different morning vibe than the rush of city mornings or the harried pace of base life. She could get used to this.

A quiet click sound jerked her awake. She bolted upright, splashing water over the edge of the tub. She crouched in a ready position on the bottom of the tub and studied her surroundings. What had she heard? She quieted her thundering heart and waited with her ears tuned for the slightest sound.

Footsteps.

Soft footfalls, each followed by a flapping sound. Not Nick. Flip flops. Someone was in the yard.

"Hello?" a female voice called out. "I'm coming in."

She moved to a comfortable sitting position just as a spiky-haired blonde rounded the corner. The tips of her hair were pinkish. "Hi. I'm Lisa. I live next door." The woman smiled warmly.

"Um. Hi. Can I help you?"

"You must be Winter. I recognize you from Muriel's pictures." Her smile was warm and welcoming. "I told your aunt I'd look out for you. But to be honest, I didn't expect to find you in Nick's hot tub."

"Yeah. He said I could use it." Why did she feel defensive?

Lisa laughed. "He also told me I could use it. Mind if I join you?" She had a towel around her shoulders, and oversized shorts overtop a one-piece swimsuit.

Winter twisted her head and puckered her lips in indecision. "No?" she said, not knowing how to refuse.

Lisa laughed. "You can say no. I won't be offended," she said just as her phone rang. She whipped it out and answered it. "Yo, Nick.

What's up?" She listened for a minute. "I don't think your guest is comfortable with the company of strangers. I'll take a dip later."

"Can I talk to him?" Winter held out her hand for the phone.

Lisa passed it over without a word. "Hi, Nick."

"I tried calling Muriel's house to let you know that Lisa was going to use the tub today. Apparently, she overdid it at spin class yesterday. Don't feel you have to let her join you, since I gather you are in the tub right now."

"Yes, I am. It's okay, I'll share. Thanks for letting me use the tub."

"Just so you know," he blurted, "I don't let just anyone use my tub, and I cleaned it last weekend. Nobody's been in it since, not even me. Apologies for the double booking."

She laughed. "No problem. I need to meet my neighbors, anyway. Later." She handed the phone back to Lisa who listened again before signing off.

"Are you sure it's okay?" Lisa asked. "Today's been a year long already."

She waved Lisa in and offered her hand once Lisa stripped and climbed in. After shaking hands in greeting, Lisa slid into the water with a sigh.

"Winter Ireland. Nice to meet you."

"Lisa Zeus. My husband and I live next door. We moved in just before Christmas with our daughter Amy." She patted her slightly rounded belly. "Our second child is due in September." Her laugh was light and airy. "Cam is my second husband. Amy's father passed when she was an infant, but Cam's a great father. I did have my doubts when I met him. He was something of a playboy. I'm surprised at how much a man can change. He says he did it for love." She sighed. "Dang, I love that man."

"Aw. That's sweet. Are hot tubs okay when you're pregnant?"

"I've got about a month left before I should stop using it. I have to be super careful not to overheat. Luckily, Nick keeps this one on the lower side of hot."

Winter nodded. "Did Amy get to school on time?" She couldn't resist asking.

Lisa blushed beet red. "You heard me? Oh gosh. That's awful. I didn't mean to disturb you. I am so, so sorry. So sorry." She ducked her head. "We weren't even close to late, but today is my day off and I wanted her gone. Some days, I'm a terrible mother. I work at the café at the garage, and we've been swamped. I need a day of rest and she'd been pushing my limits since she woke up."

"At least you didn't lose your temper. You sounded very cheerful and patient."

"Whew." Lisa mock wiped her brow. "I'm usually good, but some days.... Anyway, I'm sorry you heard that."

Winter shrugged. "It didn't bother me. It's a whole lot more pleasant than city traffic or artillery fire."

Lisa gasped. "Oh, I forgot you were on active duty. That's how you were injured." She examined Winter like she was searching for scars.

Winter raised her knee long enough for Lisa to see her scars. "Total replacement." She dropped her knee below the water again. She had no problem with her physical scars, it was the mental ones that worried her.

"Wow. That looks painful," Lisa winced.

"Some days it keeps me sitting, but most of the time it's okay. Tolerable. I'm not long out of surgery and still struggling through physio, and I'm trying yoga. I lost a lot of muscle and flexibility during rehab. The surgery and the first few weeks after recovery were the worst. It gets better every day." She snapped her mouth shut. She wasn't prone to giving out secrets. Okay, not secrets, but personal information. There was just something about Lisa that invited sharing. Maybe it was her kind smile or air of empathy.

"Tell me about Amy," she changed the subject.

"She's seven. She loves all things *Barbie* and *How to Train Your Dragon*. The only thing she loves more than reading is being outdoors. She's a nature's child. That's part of why Cameron and I decided to move. Bigger yard and much closer to the park. Haven's a small town, but it's still hard to give her free rein to go wherever she wants."

"I can see that."

"Saturday mornings nearly kill me. That's when we let her walk to the bakery alone. It's good for her, but it is so hard on me." Her voice rang with love and exasperation. "She was my baby, just mine, for years before Cam showed up. I don't want her to grow up." She laughed. "Unless she's making me crazy, then I can't wait for her to turn eighteen and get out."

"Funny, that's exactly what my brother says about his twin boys."

"Twins are adorable. Do you see them much?"

She sighed. "No. My brother and I don't see eye-to-eye on some big issues. It's easier to stay away than get together and fight." She didn't want to be estranged from him. Or her parents. But they hated her decision to join the service. They wanted her at home, helping build low-income housing with their Vancouver based charity. She loved the work they did, but it wasn't how she wanted to serve humanity.

When she'd been injured, her family had told her to leave the service and had offered her a desk job. A desk job! As if she were useless. It didn't matter that she felt useless, they were her parents, they should be encouraging her. The least they could have done was offer her a construction job. She wouldn't have taken it, but they could have offered. She wondered what they'd say when they learned she'd gotten a medical discharge. No doubt the pressure to join the family business would triple.

She didn't miss them much, but she did miss her brother and his wife. Maybe she should visit. Just to see the boys. She did adore them. *Nope. Not visiting. There's no way I could see Carl and not my parents. I don't need that pressure. I'll find my way to be useful.*

"That was a big sigh. Want to talk about it?" Lisa urged.

"No, but thanks for the offer. Can I interest you in lunch? I have to get in a walk, and I'm starved. You could come, and I'll buy. Two targets, one bullet, and all that."

Lisa looked surprised, either at the invite or the figure of speech, then she smiled. "Sure. I'd love some lunch, but you're not buying. When do you want to go?"

"You just got here. Let's enjoy the water for a while first. I'm in no rush. I have no commitments." It took all she had not to frown at the thought. She'd like to have more commitments, something to give her a purpose. A nagging voice said she could get that in her parent's company, but she wanted to make a difference her way.

She was injured, not useless. There was a path for her, she just hadn't found it yet. She wiggled until she found the perfect spot on the seat, a jet aimed directly at her back, closed her eyes, and prayed for a purpose.

Chapter Eight

After yesterday's cookie decorating rush, today seemed idyllic and relaxed. Nick leaned against the counter, sipping coffee, and talking to Grace and Sterling. Baby Travis slept in his car carrier at their feet as they planned a Victoria Day barbeque at the bookstore. Their daughter, Sasha was at school. The third weekend in May was the long weekend, and it heralded the official start of tourist season. People camped year-round at the local lakes, but on the May long weekend, it got busy.

"I want cookies, but I'm not sure what," Grace said. "Sid's is doing the barbeque and the grocery store is providing drinks. I'm hoping to turn it into a celebration for the whole town, including convincing the mayor to put up pavilion tents in the town square. There will be tables and chairs for eating at."

"I thought this was your celebration. Your annual celebration," he teased. "You're acting like a commander in a *Battleship*." He winked, so she'd know he was teasing.

"She's got this plan to bring the whole town together," Sterling said. "It's making me tired."

The men laughed together while Grace tried to give them her best glare. "Funny. Very funny. You guys are a laugh-a-minute. Are you going to help or not?"

"Is this just for fun?" Nick asked. "Maybe there's an opportunity for something more. Doc's trying to raise money for a clinic, to move it out of his house. The government will give some funds, but not enough to do a new clinic outright. Could we turn this into a fundraiser?"

"That's a great idea," Grace declared. "There will be tons of tourists. I need a committee."

Nick glanced out the window just as Winter and Lisa walked by. "There's your committee right there." He pointed toward the window.

Grace sprinted to the door and hollered out at the ladies. "Come back. I need to talk to you both."

Nick introduced Winter to everyone, and they made small talk for a few minutes. "Grace has an idea to raise funds for the new clinic," he said.

"It was Nick's idea." She turned the credit back on him. "I wanted a town event to get us all outside after a long winter. Especially the kids." She explained how the town office was providing simple awnings, tables, and chairs.

"We should have food vendors," Lisa put in.

"What about crafts for the kids?" Winter suggested. "Something spring-like. Making paper flowers or something."

"I need paper, or I'm going to forget something," Grace said. "What have you got, Nick?"

"I'll grab a notepad." He hurried to his small office and came back with a clipboard and pen. He passed it to Grace. "Why don't we sit and discuss this over coffee? We need a battle plan."

"Winter and I were just going for a late lunch. Why don't you join us?" Lisa looked back and forth between everyone, clearly expecting agreement.

"I need to get back to work," Sterling said. "But I could grab a quick bite. Let me call Cam and get him to check on the new build for me." There was a small subdivision going up on the west end of town, and Cam's crew was building the first three houses. They'd broke ground earlier in the month. They'd waited until it was warm enough for their crews to live in RVs on-site, rather than having to rent rooms at Haven's one and only B&B.

Double-checking that Uma had everything under control, Nick led the group down the street.

"That's a lovely building." Winter pointed toward an old log structure whose sign declared it Sid's Steakhouse. "It's got such amazing historic vibes."

"That's our destination," Nick said, resisting the urge to take her hand in his. "It's one of the original buildings in town. Gypsy is a long-time resident. Her family erected this building as a barn. Years later, they added the windows and over time, it was repurposed for other uses. It's been a mercantile, a gym, a hardware store, and now Sid's. Sid took over about eight years ago when the hardware store went under. The plate-glass windows were replaced with custom glass to replicate the original, handcrafted glass windows from Gypsy's grandmother's era. The place was shut down for months, then one day, a sign went up for Sid's Steakhouse. It's an institution now. Fine dining at night, and breakfast café in the morning. Though typically, Sid only works evenings," Nick said as he opened the heavy wooden door.

The interior was brightly lit and buzzing with conversation. "Half the town must be here," he muttered. So much for a quiet lunch with friends. They followed Sterling to a table in the back, away from most of the patrons. The thirty-something server wandered over with menus in her hands.

"Hi, Molly," he greeted their server.

"Afternoon." Molly greeted them. She flashed a bright smile and flipped her long black hair over her shoulder with one hand before passing out the laminated sheet of lunch specials. "Can I get anyone a drink?"

"I would love a coffee with cream," Winter spoke first.

Nick's gaze flashed to her. "Wow. That only took half a second. You sure know how to *Beat the Clock*." He laughed.

"What? I can't need coffee?" Her voice was level and completely civil, but he got the sense that she was annoyed at him.

He held up his hands and shrugged. "My bad. I thought I was the only one who mainlined coffee." Then he added, "Sorry, I am," in his best Yoda voice.

"Don't even start," Grace warned him. She smiled at Winter. "He has the most annoying habit of making a joke out of everything. Watch out for the board game references," she warned.

"I had hoped I was imagining those." Winter gave him a pinched look.

"What can I say?" He raised his hands in mock helplessness. "I have a cluttered mind. It holds two things exceptionally well, recipes and jokes."

"You should focus on the recipe side," Lisa suggested.

Winter smirked but didn't smile or laugh outright. The woman was too serious by far. He wished he was sitting across from her so he could see her better, but somehow, he'd been trapped between her and Lisa when Grace, Sterling, and Travis's car seat took up the entire other bench.

He didn't need to read the menu, so he leaned back to rest and study his companions while they studied the menu. Grace and Sterling were a cute couple. Lisa was smiling and humming to herself, no doubt happy to have time away from her family. She'd spent years raising Amy without help until she bumped into Cam at the garage diner where she worked for Clint. Clint was married to Natalie, a socialite who had been wrongfully accused of killing her first husband. They were blissfully happy and had a new baby at home to adore, along with Natalie's first son.

Haven was growing. Not too fast, but fast enough that even in winter there were new faces appearing in the bakery. It both pleased and annoyed him. He loved people, but the more people, the busier he got, and it wasn't easy to find competent bakery help. What he needed was an actual trained baker and more ovens. Maybe he should think of expanding.

The thought shocked him, and he sucked in a breath. Minty shampoo and light, flowery perfume whirled around him. *Dang.* Winter smelled wonderfully like summer. He shifted closer and pretended to be reading over her shoulder, just so he could get another whiff of her deliciousness. "What are you having?" he asked.

"I'm not sure. The steak sandwich looks good, but so does the salmon, or the crab cakes."

"Grilled cheese and salad for me," Lisa said.

"I'll have calamari," Grace said.

"I'll have a cheeseburger platter and bruschetta," Sterling said. "I'll share with you." He smiled down at Grace who cast him an adoring look in return. Everyone needed someone to look at them like that...like they hung the moon and stars.

Molly took their orders and they chatted for a minute until Grace said, "Okay, let's plan this thing." Conversation flowed back and forth with ideas.

"Maybe we could get local businesses to donate prizes for a silent auction. Some of the major hotel chains in the city might give prizes too, or we could find a way to sponsor a vacation trip as the biggest prize. Maybe we could plan a vacation and raffle tickets to it. I mean, who doesn't love a vacation? Right?"

Nick managed to keep his mouth shut for most of the conversation. He was already in for providing snacks for the volunteers and baked goods for sale. "Where are we going to sell the food? This is in May. It always rains or snows on May long weekend."

"What about party tents?" Lisa said. "You can rent them for a week pretty cheaply."

"How many vendors are there in town?" Winter asked. "What if we gave them first shot at tents, then opened up to vendors from out of town?"

They worked on the idea for a while before she spoke again. "This will be like a farmer's market to raise money for the clinic. This will be spring, and hopefully nice weather. We could charge table rental and get a donation to the silent auction from every vendor."

"You're a wizard at this," Nick exclaimed. "Have you done this before?"

Her blush was beautiful. "No. It just came to me. I just thought about the markets I've been to. I went to some of the best markets in Cairo and again in Mexico City. Even Alaska has winter events with crafters. Cairo's tourist market sells virtually everything, and then there is a deeper, more hidden market that serves locals. You get two entirely different vibes and different quality of products, as well as price differences." She shrugged. "It made me think of different rates for outsiders." She frowned at the term.

"You're not an outsider," Grace said, taking the words right out of Nick's mouth. "You're one of us now. After all, your aunt is one of us. That makes you family too."

Winter's eyes widened, and a shy smile crept across her face.

They bandied ideas back and forth as they ate, until finally, Grace's phone rang. She took the call and her smile morphed to a frown as she hung up. "I have to run. Problem at work. Sterl, can you get the bill?"

"Got it, babe." He slid out of the booth and helped her out, then reached in to pull the car seat and its sleeping occupant closer. "Do you want me to go with you?"

"No, finish your coffee and go back to work. I'll take Travis." She hoisted the diaper bag like a cross-body bag and dropped a kiss on Sterling's mouth. "Love you."

"Love you most," he said with a grin and handed her the heavy car seat. "Are you sure you don't want me to carry this for you?"

"*This* is our son," she teased. "And yes, I'm sure. It isn't far and the weather's nice. It was lovely to meet you, Winter. Catch you guys later." She strode out of the restaurant like the baby weighed nothing.

"That's one strong woman," Nick said.

"She slings boxes of books around all day. Travis weighs nothing in comparison."

"Oh, she left her clipboard," Winter said. "She runs the bookstore, right? I can run it over there when we're done. I need something to read, anyway." As if that settled it, she picked up her fork and finished her meal.

Nick tried not to stare. She kept pulling his attention without even trying. He barely tasted his lunch. It might have been sand for all he cared. Where had all his chef's tastebuds gone? He thought he was doing a good job of keeping himself distracted when Sterling kicked him under the table and gave him a slightly bug-eyed questioning look.

"I guess I should get back," he said, not wanting to leave Winter's side.

"Me too," Sterling agreed.

"You ladies finish your lunch. I've got the bill," Nick said as he waited for Winter to move so he could slide out.

"I've got it," Sterling countered.

"Ugh. Men and their stupid testosterone," Lisa mocked them.

"Mind your Ps and Qs little lady," Nick said, "or you'll be paying for your own lunch."

He was one hundred percent joking, and she knew it. Even Winter chuckled.

"You're a good egg, Nick," Lisa said. "Probably rotten, but a good egg."

"I'll have you know I'm an eggcellent person and all-around good egg. I eggcell at baking too."

"Lisa, did you have to get him started?" Sterling groaned and strode away without waiting for an answer.

"Ladies." Nick tipped an imaginary hat and followed his friend to the register.

Chapter Nine

Winter grunted and groaned as she attempted her second physio round of the day. After the long truck journey, eight busy days of walking, and two long walks today, she was paying the price for not pacing herself. A go-getter, she wanted this physio over with. She wanted to get on with her life. She was pushing too hard. Everything was stiff and sore. She ached like crazy, and sleep was nearly impossible.

She flopped onto her back and sighed.

The whole reason for the excess walking was boredom.

She'd never gone weeks without being told what to do and now that she had all the time in the world, she didn't know how to fill it. The gardens were weeded and ready for bedding plants. She'd dropped in the early vegetable seeds and, as instructed by Aunt Muriel's notes, was waiting until June first to plant the rest of the seeds. She didn't want new seedlings to suffer from an unexpected frost. Flower beds she could cover, but the entire one-hundred-foot by one-hundred-foot garden was virtually impossible to cover. She had no idea why her aunt needed so much produce, or why she wanted it planted while she was away, but working the soil made Winter happy, so she planted as directed. She could always give away what she couldn't use.

Maybe she could get some flowers for the areas of the front garden where there were no perennials. It would be something to fill her time with aside from walking. She grinned and rose to her feet. Despite the stiffness in her legs, her knee was gaining some flexibility, but could do with a good soak.

"You just want to see Nick," she taunted herself.

"Merow." Her aunt's cat meowed in agreement. She'd picked up Henrietta from the vet where she'd been boarding before Winter arrived. She wasn't much of an animal lover, she'd never owned a pet, but having someone around, even an animal, was nice. It felt like she had company.

Henrietta always responded when Winter spoke aloud. "I think I'll call Nick and see if I can use the hot tub."

"Merow?" She almost swore the cat was doubting her decision.

"Yup. Really."

Nobody answered at the bakery or at Nick's house. Almost everyone had a house phone because, during winter, cell service was notoriously unreliable. She didn't have his cell number. "Well, Henrietta, I'm going over anyway. Maybe he's not home and I can sneak in and out unnoticed." She'd used the tub quite a few times, each with permission. Though he'd told her to use it anytime, she always called first. Today would be an exception.

She walked through the cool night to Nick's. Nobody answered her knock on the front door, so she headed around the house and let herself into the backyard. Nick was in the tub.

"Oh, sorry to interrupt." She turned to leave.

"Hey, Winter. Don't run off. Join me." She turned back toward him. "The water's fine." He winked. "Plenty of room for two."

The wink went straight to her heart. She could fall for this generous and attractive man if she let herself. Which she had no intention of doing. Nope. Haven was a pit stop. She wasn't staying here, no matter how nice the people were. No matter how many hours she'd put into the May long weekend celebration.

"I won't disturb you. I'll come back another time." Heat flooded her face. Why did the idea of getting in the tub with him titillate her so much?

"Don't be silly. It's a big tub. There are no sharks." His grin was pure seduction. "Except me." He patted the edge of the tub. "I don't mind at all. Company would be nice."

She waffled for a moment. "Sure, why not?" Trying her best not to think about him watching her, she stripped out of her clothing. As a soldier, she'd been in tough situations, but in that moment, nothing seemed as hard as getting undressed in front of her neighbor.

She climbed into the tub as quickly as she could and slipped into the water with a blissful sigh. "Thanks," she murmured.

"I already told you, you're welcome anytime." He leaned back and looked up at the sky. "Oh, look. A shooting star."

She gazed up but couldn't find it. Had it been there, or was he trying to put her at ease? "I missed it." The sky wasn't fully dark yet. It was more of an inky gray, with a few specks of light shining here and there. The air was warm and still, a sign of summer's approach. "It's beautiful. I missed the stars when I served in cities."

"They're part of the reason why I fell in love with Haven. New York stars are more the human kind." He pointed to the sky. "Look, there's a satellite. You can tell because it moves much slower than a shooting star."

She followed the satellite as it moved. A few moments later, she spotted another. "There's one. I had no idea there were so many."

"It seems like there's one every few minutes."

"You'd be amazed to know just how many surveillance satellites there are up there, orbiting around, watching everything. Recording everything."

"Another reason why I'm here. No cameras on every corner."

"You have something to hide?" She couldn't stop herself from asking. Since she turned eighteen, her job had been protecting her country. Was he a threat of some kind?

"Nope. I just like my privacy."

She stared at him in the yard's dim light. He wasn't flinching or looking away. He didn't seem nervous. All her training said he was telling the truth. "Good to know. I'd hate to have to kick your ass."

His laugh made her smile. "You could try, *Winter Soldier*, you could try."

"Did you just equate me to a superhero movie?" She pinned him with a stare.

"If the movie fits."

"I've never seen it. Not much movie watching during combat duty."

"But you've been stationed outside of combat zones."

"I'm more a reader. Mostly history. And I dislike movie theaters. The seats are uncomfortable." She shrugged. Pop culture wasn't important to her. She rarely gave it more than passing consideration.

"You've never tried my movie theater."

"You mean Haven's theater. Where is it? I haven't noticed it and I've put in a hundred miles on my feet since I arrived." She couldn't possibly have missed something as large as a theater, though she hadn't been down every street.

"No. Haven doesn't have one. But I do." He grinned at her. "I work hard, but I play hard too. Well, relax hard. Is relaxing hard a thing?" He shrugged. "I decided that if I was going to spend time watching television, I might as well do it in comfort. I splurged and built a media room." He pointed to an extension off the back of the house. It blended perfectly with the old house's design.

"I built a room and furnished it."

It seemed a ridiculous expense to her, but then she'd never settled in one place for long, and who was she to judge him for such a harmless vice? "Interesting."

"Interesting as in that's cool, or as in this guy is nuts?"

"Maybe a little of both?"

·♥·♥·♥·♥·♥·

Nick laughed. Winter was so serious, and in her seriousness, she was compelling. Everything in him wanted to help her relax and lighten up. He wasn't dissing her former profession, but not everything in life was serious. Play was important too, and he was going to teach her how.

"Have you eaten?"

"That's an abrupt subject change." She lifted her head just enough to squint at him.

"Not really. I haven't eaten yet. I was thinking of ordering takeout and vegging. I thought you might like to join me." He really wanted her to join him. She'd been in town for over a week and except for a few chance meetings, he'd barely seen her. He didn't know her at all, yet he missed her when she wasn't around.

"Didn't you used to be a chef? Before you became a baker?"

Her head rested against the back of the hot tub, exposing the long lines of her neck. His fingers itched to travel that length, to explore the heated softness of her skin. His mouth begged to taste her. He swallowed down a wave of desire.

"I was a chef. Classically trained in New York. I've worked under a few big names. I can cook with the best of them, but baking makes me happiest. It's a different world entirely. Why do you ask?"

"We ate lunch together, you've delivered me baked goods, now you want takeout. I thought I must be mistaken, since you never seem to cook for yourself." Her voice was serious, not in the least joking.

"Cooking for one sucks," he admitted. "I love cooking for friends. I'll tell you what. Why don't we order in, and watch a movie? Friday night, I'll cook you dinner. Something nice." If she said yes, he'd have finagled two dates. Well, in his mind they were dates, perhaps to her, they weren't.

"Would that be you cooking for a friend, or are you looking for something more? You should know I'm not open to a relationship."

It was like she'd picked the idea of dating right out of his mind. "Friend*ship* is a relation*ship*," he quipped, to hide his disappointment. "I'm not looking for anything beyond the pleasure of your company, Winter. I like talking with you." He did like talking to her, though he'd only had a couple of opportunities. Something about being around her filled him with peace and excitement. He was simultaneously soothed and aroused.

He shifted to get a better view of her face. "Winter, will you have dinner with me as a friend and neighbor?" He offered the friend card, hoping it would lead to the lover or life partner card.

"Yes, Nick, I will let you cook a friend's dinner for me on Friday. Did you want to invite anyone else?"

Not a single person. "I'll see who is around, if that's what you want."

"Sure. Thanks."

Great, now he had the dilemma of asking friends like she wanted, or doing what he wanted and spending the evening alone with a strong, compelling woman. He hated moral dilemmas.

"Friday night then. Say about seven?" He'd take the afternoon off and prep something impressive. "Is there anything you don't eat or anything you'd like to have?"

"I eat almost anything. I have no food allergies." She fell silent. "I'd love an authentic Mexican taco."

"Tacos?" he mocked. "I'm a chef, not a fast-food line cook."

"And can't a skilled chef elevate simple foods to something more?"

For the life of him, he couldn't tell if she was teasing. "I'm going to take that as a challenge and cook you the best danged taco you've ever had. Now, what do you want to eat tonight?"

"How about you?" she countered. "What do you want?"

"I'm flexible. I'm not craving anything, I'm just hungry." The truth was, he'd kill for a burger and onion rings, but he was more than happy to bow to whatever she wanted. Pleasing Winter by letting her choose dinner seemed like the right course of action.

Her look said she didn't believe him. "Fish and chips," she blurted. "And deep-fried shrimp."

"Done!" He dried his hands, grabbed his phone off the tub's ledge, and made a call.

"I didn't think we'd have to get right out. I'm enjoying the jets on my knee."

"It'll take at least half an hour, maybe forty-five minutes. It's Friday. Sid's is busy, but the food is worth waiting for."

She nodded. "Lunch was delicious last week. I'm glad I still have time to soak before I run home to get dressed."

He nodded and slid down in his seat and pretended to close his eyes. She did the same but didn't sit still. Shifting one way, then the other, she appeared restless. *Was she in pain? Was she nervous? Excited?* He could only see part of her face because her face was tipped up toward the stars again, making it impossible to read her mood.

She intrigued him. He wanted to know everything about her. It was crazy. He'd been attracted to women before, more than one had been extreme-like extreme like at first sight. But this — this mixed-up feeling he had for Winter was different. He snickered to himself. It was exactly what he felt for actual winter...the season. He loved the beauty of the season, and wished the cold would go away, all at the same time.

He studied the woman across from him. He adored her beauty and wanted to get closer to her, in every way, but he was wary. She wasn't here forever, and she was so serious. Sure, she cracked a smile now and then. He'd even heard her laugh a time or two. But she was solemn. Was it her nature, or the result of the trauma she'd experienced when she was injured? Heaven knew trauma had changed him.

He lived for jokes and puns, could he be happy with the most serious woman he'd ever met? Probably not. "*But maybe,*" his heart whispered.

"*Or maybe not,*" his logical brain countered.

His parents had been quite different from each other. Dad had been an accountant, his mother an artist. Somehow, they had balanced each other. When his father and grandfather died in a car accident, his mother lost her drive to create. As a teen, it had been heartbreaking to watch. How did a person survive that kind of loss?

He closed his eyes at the pain the memories wrought. His mother hadn't managed well. She'd gone into her room and stayed there. He missed three weeks of school, bringing her meals and keeping an eye on her. She probably hadn't been suicidal, but earlier in the year, a friend had taken his own life and that thought played over and over in Nick's teenage head.

He refused to leave his mother alone until she returned to normal. The only thing that made her smile in those first few days were bad puns. His father, rest his soul, had been a bit of a joker. Nick figured if he copied his dad, it might cheer her up.

One joke had become many. Puns and wordplay got to be a habit. When his mother finally emerged from her room, she stopped smiling at his attempts at humor, but the pattern was set, and he couldn't seem to break it. In fact, he loved being a joker and making people laugh.

"You look like you're thinking hard," Winter's voice broke him from the past. "Are you okay?"

"Yup." She frowned, and he knew she wanted more. "Bad memories. You know how it is, sometimes your mind just goes where you don't want it to." *Crap. Why did I say that? I know she's got scars from her past. Way to ruin an evening.*

"I do."

She agreed with his statement, but his mind jumped to wedding vows.

Holy crap.

He'd been alone way too long. He had plenty of friends who didn't marry until they were in their forties. But at thirty-eight, he was starting to lose hope. Until Winter arrived. But leaping to vows was ridiculous.

His heart thundered. Man, he was getting way ahead of himself. He barely knew her. So why did it feel like she was part of his soul?

"I was thinking about my mom," he said. "She passed two years ago. My dad died when I was seventeen — mom was never the same." He banked a sigh. "Memories hurt."

"You know what? They do. I try not to let terrible memories in, but sometimes there's no stopping them. I cope by letting myself feel the pain for a while, then getting up and doing something to distract myself. It's probably not the best technique, but it helps."

"Thanks. I'll try that." It seemed unlikely that something so simple could be helpful, but he was willing to try her suggestion. He rarely got caught up in the past, but he knew it had shaped who he was. He didn't need a shrink to tell him that.

Chapter Ten

Winter stared bug-eyed at Nick's media room. This was a man who took his television seriously. The south wall had no windows and held an enormous television and sound system. Opposite was the doorway into the rest of the house, featuring a gas fireplace. The east and west walls were primarily windows, all of which opened. Right now, the shades were down most of the way, blocking the neighbors' view into the room which jutted out into the backyard.

The room held two love seats, which looked like recliners, and were angled toward the television. One was slightly closer and would probably provide the best view. Two rocker recliners faced the fireplace but could be easily moved wherever someone wanted. It was like a theater, and it was pure decadence.

"Wow, you weren't kidding about this being a theater," she said. "How much television do you watch?"

He laughed. "Not as much as you'd think. What do you think of the space? The main house is old. I had it wrapped in insulation and new siding and added new windows, but the rooms are small. When

I watch a movie, I like the full theater effect. Since there isn't a theater in Haven, I built my own."

"I can see that." She examined the room again. The chairs even had trays for snacks. It was either awesome or ridiculous, she couldn't decide which.

"It's a great room for company. I might be a bachelor, but I do have friends." His tone was joking. "My house is paid off, and I make good money. I give to charity. I've got enough money to retire on. Why shouldn't I indulge myself?" He sounded defensive. She wondered who had been pestering him about how he spent his own money. An old girlfriend? Family?

"Do you have family?" She blurted the question as soon as she thought it.

He answered without pause. "A younger sister who I don't see much. She lives in Montreal with her fiancé. Both my folks are dead, but I do have a few aunts, uncles, and cousins scattered around the country. A lot are in Newfoundland and Nova Scotia. How about you?"

"Just my parents, and my brother. Well, he has a wife and kids."

"Are you close?"

The man had a way of asking hard questions and making them sound simple. "Not really. Though, I think I mentioned missing the boys." If she could just get her life plan together, she'd be able to go see the kids again. "What are we watching?" She threw the question out to change the subject. Enough about her family.

"*Captain America: The Winter Soldier*, of course. You said you've never seen it." His brow wrinkled. "Are you okay with violence in movies? I should have asked that first. We can always try something else."

"I'll live. I'm not immune to it, but televised violence isn't a trigger or anything like that. But inaccurate portrayal of combat, now that'll get me going for sure." Poor portrayal of the horrors of war irritated her because they did a disservice to those who served.

"I can see that. Luckily for us, this is pure fantasy. Prepare to suspend your disbelief. Let's do this. You sit here," he waved at a loveseat. "Do you mind me sitting beside you? These are the best seats in the house."

"I don't mind." She'd never admit having him beside her stirred up things she wasn't ready for. Okay, things she didn't want at all. But she was a soldier. She was tough enough to resist the temptation of a man. Even one who smelled and looked as delicious as Nick.

He rotated the table beside her chair, it became a tray over her lap. "Wow," she exclaimed as he set the food on her tray. He loaded up his own table, sat, and pivoted his own table into place.

"Dig in before it gets cold."

"Copy that."

He gave her a puzzled look.

"Military for I can do that. Or yes, sir. Or for general agreement." She shrugged. "Old habits die hard."

"*Die Hard*, now there's a series worth binge-watching."

She rolled her eyes. "Yippie kiyay."

He laughed until he was clutching his stomach.

"What?" she glared.

"I had no idea you had it in you. Bad movie jokes, gratuitous movie quotes? Who knew the solemn Winter Ireland had a sense of humor?"

He was joking, and when wasn't he? But the jab hit home hard. Just because she wasn't frivolous all the time, it didn't mean she lacked a sense of humor. *Jerk.* "Play the movie."

He sobered at her grumpy tone. "Yes, sir, captain, sir." He saluted and, surprisingly, he got it right. Maybe he wasn't all buffoon.

She sighed to herself. That was unfair. She didn't know him well enough to make that call and she had no intention of getting to know him better. *Yeah, right. If you don't plan on getting to know him better, why are you in his home theater eating dinner he paid for?* She shushed her mind and settled in to eat.

Bits and pieces of the movie confused her, and Nick had to stop it to answer her questions.

"The *Marvel* universe is complicated, and all twisted together," he explained. "Maybe we should have started at the beginning chronologically. Next time. Unless you want to watch something else."

Cocky of him to assume there would be a next time. She wrinkled her nose, and he hit play to restart the movie. She had no intention of seeing him again after their Friday dinner. Avoiding him around town might be difficult, because who could resist the delights in his bakery? But she could run a reconnoiter and figure out where he went and when. Then, she'd be able to plan her life according to the best way to avoid him.

Avoid him? For the next year? Not likely. Darn it. Accepting his first dinner invitation had been a mistake. Why had her truck broken down so close to his bakery, the only open business? Why couldn't it have died near the garage?

Because fate is fickle, that's why. She didn't believe in fate, not exactly. No predestination for her. She was a living, thinking human being. She made her own choices and decided where to go and when. So why was she feeling like she was being thrust into Nick's path? She would have been anyway because her aunt had left the house key with him.

Stop using his hot tub. That would help. And give up all that blissful warmth and those jets? Not likely. Just use it when he's at work.

Problem. Solution. Done.

Luckily, Nick was laughing at something in the movie, because she chuckled at her oversimplification of her problems. Eventually, s She focused her mind on the screen and ended up enjoying the movie. She still had questions, but asking them might show how little attention she'd been paying. Maybe she could find the movie on cable and catch up.

The credits rolled, and he turned to her. "Want to watch something else?"

"Thanks, but no. I need my beauty sleep. I'm still drained when I do my physio. It's been eight months since my accident, and I'm still not back in combat condition. Thanks for dinner, and the movie. Extra thanks for the use of your tub." The soothing water was helping with her physio. She was still weaker than she'd like, but she was recovering.

"You are welcome on all counts. Use the tub anytime." He shut down the entertainment center and followed her to the front door.

"Thanks again, Nick. It was nice."

A frown flitted across his face. "Yes, it was. Your company was *Marvel*-ous." He grinned.

The abrupt change of expressions and the silly joke had her wondering what he was covering. "Ha. Ha." She looked at him. His eyes were dim, almost sad looking. Maybe she wasn't the only one with scars and secrets.

It didn't matter. She was moving on, and had no business or intention of getting to know him better. She had a life to plan. "Thanks again, Nick. It was nice. See you around town."

All traces of levity vanished from his face at her words. He slammed his hands into the pockets of his sweats. "I'll see you tomorrow."

"What?" She had no idea what he was talking about.

"May long weekend planning at Grace and Sterling's tomorrow night at six-thirty? Remember?"

"Right. I'll be there."

"I can pick you up."

The hope in his voice was devastating. "I'm walking but thanks. I'll meet you there."

Another frown. Where had the jolly joker gone? Odd.

"Sure. Want me to walk you home now?"

"Nick, it's half a block. I'll be fine. Didn't you tell me Haven was the safest place in the province?"

"True. Tomorrow then. Good night, Winter."

Hurrying through the darkness, she regretted her refusal. She missed him already.

Chapter Eleven

Winter began her reconnoiter, okay stalking, of Nick, the next morning. She noted the bakery hours and made the reasonable assumption that Nick would be there during those hours. Now, if she could figure out where he spent his off hours, she could avoid him entirely. Maybe she could get some ideas at the planning meeting tonight. Plan solidly in mind, she headed for the grocery store.

She saw a face she recognized in the checkout line. "Hi," the woman said. "You must be Winter."

"Um. Yeah. I am." It was disconcerting that total strangers knew her. She avoided the woman's gaze.

The woman thrust out her hand. "I'm Uma. I work at the bakery." The short, round forty-something woman virtually bounced with energy. "I love the job, and Nick lets me work around my kids' school hours. Nick's teaching me how to do the basics. Frankly, I wonder why he hasn't fired me yet. I've messed up a lot of stuff."

"Nice to meet you, Uma. You can't be that bad."

"Ask Nick about the salt instead of sugar incident." She laughed. "It's funny now, but I nearly ruined a fiftieth-anniversary party. Thank heaven Nick decided to double-check the cupcakes before we iced them."

"He sounds like a good boss." What else could she say? Uma seemed amused by the event, and it seemed like Nick took it well. Winter's smile was awkward.

"He's an amazing boss, and a great person. If I wasn't totally in love with my husband, Reuben, I'd be after Nick like a pit bull on a porkchop." She put a few items onto the cashier's conveyor. "I mean, he's cute, he's funny, he's got money, he's kind. He's the best. Except my Reuben, of course."

She already knew about all of Nick's good qualities. They were why she was trying to keep her distance. She didn't want to fall for him. Besides, his constant joking would get old fast.

"You should come to quilt night. We make quilts for charity. You'd love it."

She couldn't imagine a more boring evening, but didn't want to dampen Uma's enthusiasm. "I'll keep that in mind. Thanks. What does Nick do for fun?"

"I honestly don't know. Haven's small, but we don't socialize outside of the bakery. I know he does a lot of community work. He hangs out at the bookstore. Grace was his best friend, or vice versa until she married Sterling. I mean, they're still remarkably close. Anyway, the quilters meet in the craft store, Thursdays at seven. Every week. We'd love to have you. Maybe I'll see you there."

"I'll try." *More like try to avoid it. Grannies quilted, soldiers did not.* Maybe she should take up something more suitable to a soldier. Gunsmithing? Welding? Woodworking? All noble hobbies — and not any more appealing than sewing. Ugh.

They parted ways on her vague promise, and she took her small bags of produce home. Then she walked to the garage to check on her truck.

Clint greeted her. "Hey, I was just going to call you. Your truck is ready. Sorry, it took so long. Getting parts for these old beasts can be brutal."

"What was the issue again?" He had told her, but she couldn't remember.

"A combination of old gas in the tank and a plugged fuel filter. Plus, the gas gauge wasn't working right. It was stuck."

"But I filled up six times on the way. How could it be old gas?"

"Gas has a shelf life. Every time you filled up, you diluted the old gas. Eventually, it can cause issues with the way a vehicle runs. I'm surprised you didn't have issues before it died."

"It chugged a few times." She was no mechanic. She could check her oil and change a tire, that was about it. Though she knew that new noises meant a trip to the garage for investigation. Until just before it died, her truck had been running perfectly. "Thanks for looking after it for me."

He handed her a computer printout. "I'd recommend these maintenance items. Nothing is urgent, but if you want them done, let me know in advance so I can order parts. No sense keeping your truck longer than I need to."

"Thanks. I'll do that." She took her keys.

She was halfway out the door when he called out, "Have fun at the meeting tonight. My wife Natalie will be there. I'd come too, but I'm babysitting. Sorry, I'm parenting. She hates when I call it babysitting." He rolled his eyes.

"No doubt." She waved at the genial mechanic and headed for her truck. This was the friendliest town she'd ever been in. Everyone knew everyone, and they all talked to her like she belonged. She didn't want to feel welcome, after all, she was leaving eventually, but in so many ways, Haven reminded her of her old unit. Everyone took care of everyone else.

She had expected to feel like a bug under a microscope, and it wasn't that way at all. It was friendlier and caring, but still disconcerting, to say the very least.

She drove through town and down the highway toward the lake. Lisa had drawn a map to her destination. Two miles outside of town, she turned left onto a well-maintained gravel road. Flora Flora was just ahead. Two short rows of greenhouses stood beside a small farmhouse. According to Grace, this was the place to buy bedding plants. It was early yet, but if she covered them at night, they'd survive the cool nights of late spring. She could use something pretty to brighten up her aunt's yard. The phlox was already budding, and there were a few tulips showing their faces, but she wanted more, and the earlier she put them in, the earlier they'd bloom.

Haven needed a flower shop where you could buy blooms year-round. She'd grabbed a small potted cyclamen for the kitchen table when she was at the grocery store. Until she saw it, she hadn't realized how much she missed flowers while on tour. Denmark had been her favorite deployment. The fields of tulips brought a smile to her face every time she saw them.

She had billeted at a hotel in Anchorage for a while and the lobby had flowers, but the rooms were utilitarian and colorless. That bright spot had cheered her every day.

After nearly a decade in the service, she needed more beauty in her world. She hopped out of the truck and rubbed her hands together. She was excited to see what was available. A tiny voice whispered that tough, ready-to-kill soldiers didn't plant flowers. She considered the thought and discarded it.

Tough soldiers did whatever the hell they wanted.

She stepped out of the cool morning air into the blissfully moist heat of the greenhouse. She paused to inhale, and peace washed over her.

"Good afternoon," a perky voice called out. "Or is it still morning? I've lost track."

Winter turned to her left, where an elderly lady stood behind the counter repotting a cactus. "Still morning. Almost lunch, I think," Winter said.

"Welcome to Flora Flora. I'm Ginny. How can I help you?"

"Hi. I'm looking for flowers, or rather bedding plants. Something hardy for full sun, and something that will take deep shade."

"What do you usually buy?" Ginny came out from behind the counter.

"It's my first time. I'm staying at my aunt's place. She usually has flowers. She's away, and I thought I'd put some in. I just need some guidance."

"Oh, you must be Muriel's niece."

"That I am." She wasn't going to escape that connection anywhere. As much as it annoyed her to be recognized via someone else, it also gave her a sense of belonging. "What do you suggest? Let's start with full sun."

"Dozens of choices. Follow me. I've got them segregated by shade tolerance." They walked deeper into the greenhouse. The greenhouse was about a hundred feet long, with four rows of plants. Two wide ones in the middle, and two narrower rows down the sides. Bees buzzed between the plants, stopping here and there for a rest or some nectar.

"The bees don't bother you?" she asked.

"Not a bit. I've got hives out back. Twenty, actually. My husband and I sell honey. You'll find it near the register. The world needs more bees." She stopped before a table laid out with rows of colorful plants. "These are petunias. They love the sun. So do marigolds. Your first choice will be whether to plant in rows or clumps. Rows give a more structured look."

"Clumps, I think." The answer came without thought. She'd had enough regimented structure in the army.

"Do you want a color theme? Or a mix? Some people stick to one or two colors; others mix them up. It's entirely personal."

"How do I decide?" She didn't realize there was this much involved in buying plants. She just figured she'd get in and get out. A phone started ringing somewhere in the building.

"I must get that. Just look around. These tables are full sun. Just make note of what you like. There are tags in each about height and climate conditions." Ginny hurried off.

In the end, she settled on bachelor's buttons, petunias, marigolds, and a few pre-made planters. For the shade, she grabbed begonias in six colors, and one more in a pretty pot for the kitchen window. It was a good thing she had a truck to haul them all home. She'd probably bought too much, but she was sure she'd find a good spot for them. Maybe Lisa would take the extras. Ginny had advised her to buy a few and come back for more. Winter declined, but she had accepted care sheets and had taken Ginny's advice and bought a book on annuals.

She was still putting plants in when Nick walked up several hours later.

"Are you coming?" he asked.

She squinted at him. He looked amazing in jeans and a navy button-down shirt. "What time is it?"

"Six-twenty-five. Did you forget?"

She jumped to her feet. "Holy crap." She brushed frantically at her dirt encrusted jeans. "I had no idea. I was totally lost in my plants. I'm a mess. Oh no!"

"Chillax. Go wash up. I'll let them know we'll be late. You might want to shower." He stepped toward her. "You've got dirt right here." He brushed a knuckle across her cheek.

Sparks seemed to arc between them. She sucked in a breath. His eyes went wide as if he felt it too. He cleared his throat. "Go on. I'll wait for you. Did you eat?"

"No!" she wailed. "I didn't get lunch either." Her stomach growled and Nick laughed.

"I'll grab a snack from my place and meet you back here in ten minutes." He made a shooing motion like he was hurrying her along. "Go, go, go."

She looked at the shambles she had on the lawn and sidewalk. "Food'll wait until I get back," she declared and sprinted toward the house. It wasn't until she was in the shower that she realized she'd taken the stairs two at a time without pain in her knee. Nor had it bothered her as she kneeled in the yard planting flowers. If she wasn't already in the shower, she'd have done a victory dance.

She was in and out as fast as she could. She slapped a ponytail in her hair, leaving it to hang damply over her right shoulder and stared at her reflection, wishing she had some mascara, or maybe some lip gloss. "You are not going on a date. This is a business meeting among friends." When had she gotten so vain? Probably about the time she bumped into Nick.

He stood staring at something in the garden bordering the house.

"What's wrong?" she asked.

"Just looking at plants. What are those?" He pointed to some spikey green stalks just poking out of the ground.

"Tulips, I think. Why?"

He grinned. "Tulips in the garden, tulips in the park. The tulips I like best are two lips in the dark."

She frowned when the words sank in.

"What? It's cute. My grandfather used to say it to my grandmother when he wanted a kiss. It's totally adorable."

"Let's go. We're already late." She strode down the walkway, carefully stepping over packages of fertilizer and empty pots.

"Wait. Don't you want your snack?" He hurried to walk beside her. "Here." He thrust a paper lunch bag at her. "A muffin, cookies, and some cheese."

"Thanks." She felt bad for ignoring his joke. She hadn't realized it was important. She didn't know how to apologize. *Why was he always so damned jokey?*

Chapter Twelve

The woman was exasperating. One hundred percent. She had no sense of humor. Who didn't like jokes? Weirdos, that's who. He hoped the meeting was short because he'd suddenly lost all enthusiasm for the meeting and the event. He was ready to head home and lose himself in an action flick or a hard workout.

She pulled a muffin from the bag and managed to peel the paper off and break it in half without missing a step. She took a bite off the bottom and exclaimed, "What is this? It's amazing."

"Chocolate peanut butter chip. I made it high in fiber to reduce the heart-stopping effects. Muffins are essentially cake without icing." He chuckled at her frown.

"Did you have to ruin it for me?" She glared as she took another big bite. "Isn't your thing making stuff funny, not stealing the fun?"

"Obviously it isn't stopping you from eating it," he teased. "Wait until you hit the middle."

"Oh my!"

"Yup, chocolate whipped cream center."

"Nick Blackstone, you are an evil, evil man."

She didn't meet his eyes, but he was almost certain he saw a smile curve the corner of her mouth up. Baker-victory. He watched her devour the muffin as they walked the short distance to the meeting. "Wait until you try the cookie," he warned.

She pulled out the thick treat and stared at it. "What is it?"

"No hints, taste it." She gave the chocolate-covered cookie a wary look.

"Okay…" She bit it and immediately groaned, and stopped walking. She closed her eyes and sighed. She savored the bite and turned to him. "Like I said evil."

"What? It's just a chocolate chip cookie layered with an oatmeal raisin cookie with icing between and dipped in chocolate. I thought they'd be good together."

"They are. They absolutely are. I can see I'm going to have to avoid the bakery, or I'll end up weighing a million pounds."

He knew better than to comment that he thought she could gain a pound or two.

Her body was her own, and he had no right to an opinion. She was looking less exhausted than the day she arrived and was obviously fit and strong, but a few more curves wouldn't hurt. Not rude or foolish enough to mention it, he changed the subject. "Eat up, that's their place. The big yellow one."

"That's where Sterling and Grace live?" She stared at the house. "I noticed it while I was walking around."

"Sterling does okay in the construction business," Nick jested. "He's doing okay in the game of *Life.*"

"Clearly. They seem so down to earth."

Nick laughed. "They are the most down-to-earth people you'll ever meet, and Sterling's daughter is adorable. Grace adopted her after they married. You'll love her."

"I didn't realize she wasn't Grace's child. I saw them together at the bookstore. Interesting."

She seemed to pick up on everything going on around her. No doubt a trait of a good soldier. It was fascinating because she didn't seem to catch on that he was interested in her as more than a friend. Or maybe she did, and she was just ignoring the idea. He gestured for her to walk up the sidewalk ahead of him. It was wide, but not quite wide enough for two adults. He took a moment to enjoy the view of her denim-clad legs and shining hair. By the time they reached the porch, she had finished her snack.

"I can give you something more substantial to eat after the meeting, or we could go for a late dinner if you'd like."

She paused on the bottom step. "Let's see how late this runs. I know you have to get up early and bake bread. I wouldn't want you to be overtired and burn it."

He sighed. A brush-off. Definitely avoiding him. What he couldn't figure out was why. He was a good guy. He'd dated several women over the years, but none had touched his heart this way, not even Grace. None of them seemed to have complaints either, at least not beyond the lack of sparks. It was weird how Winter affected him. After just a few minutes of knowing her, he wanted to protect her and keep her safe.

He was a protective guy, looking out for those weaker than he was, but what he felt for Winter was different and intriguing. They hadn't spent much time together, but he liked her. A lot. She was serious, but kind. She'd only been in town days when she volunteered to help with a town event which spoke to her giving, caring personality. Plus, Muriel had told him a hundred stories about her. Enough that it felt like he knew Winter before she arrived. Maybe it wasn't attraction at first sight, maybe he was smitten before he even met her.

He reached past her to open the door.

"Aren't you going to knock?" Her brow wrinkled.

"Nope. They're expecting us." He opened both doors and a wave of laughter assaulted them. "Sounds like everyone else is here." He nodded for her to go ahead while he held the doors. She hesitated and walked in.

He stepped inside, right behind her, and sucked in a deep breath. He'd never tire of her light, flowery scent. It reminded him of a spring meadow or a flower shop.

"Hey, guys. We made it."

"Nick," Sterling called out. "Come in." He came to the door and patted Nick on the shoulder. "You're late, man. That's not like you."

"Yeah, I got caught up in something. It won't happen again."

Sterling chuckled. "No worries. Winter, come in. We're in the living room. What can I get you to drink?"

"Water's fine, thanks."

Nick took her coat and hung it alongside his in the front closet. Hand on her back, he guided her forward into the room. Her back was strong and solid under his fingertips. Its warmth chased the early evening chill from his entire body, and his fingers itched to delve deeper under her soft sweater to test the softness of her skin.

He tore his gaze away from where it rested on his hand, low on her back, just above her backside. He looked around the room. "Hey, guys. You all know Winter, right?" Aside from their hosts, Lisa was there, a couple of teachers from the school, the mayor, and Natalie Dawson.

"We haven't met yet," said Natalie. "Nice to meet you, Winter, I'm Natalie, you know my husband, Clint, from the garage."

Winter stepped toward her, and Nick's hand fell from her back, leaving him cold and bereft. After the introductions, everyone took a seat. Winter sat beside Nat on the burgundy leather loveseat, leaving

Nick the only empty chair in the room, a straight-backed kitchen chair.

A deliberate slight? Or just the mechanics of the seating?

Or just your overactive imagination, his mind suggested.

Grace wasted no time getting the meeting started. Before he knew it, plans were made, committees organized, and the meeting was breaking up. He hadn't heard a word that was said. He'd been watching Winter interact as if she belonged.

"Nick!" Sterling's voice broke through his thoughts.

"Yo."

"I need a hand in the kitchen." He turned away without waiting for agreement. When Nick got into the kitchen, Sterling hissed, "Dude. Stop staring. You'll freak her out. What's wrong with you? You're being disrespectful. You stared until I thought Winter would melt into the floor in embarrassment."

"I wasn't staring."

"You were. Did you hear anything that went on in the meeting? I mean, actually hear?"

"I heard every word."

Sterling smirked. "You know you agreed to bake a thousand maple leaf cookies for the event? Each has to say Welcome to Haven. You caught that, right?"

"What?" The single syllable flew out of his mouth, and he clamped it shut.

"Yup. You agreed."

"Crap. I should have been paying attention."

"Listen." Sterling stepped closer. "I get it, you like her. But you're acting like a creep. Back off. Give her time to get to know you."

"Thanks, Sterl." He clapped him on the back. "I appreciate it." He had been staring. He couldn't help himself. She drew him like a thirsty man to water. She was sustenance to his heart and soul. It didn't make sense, but that's how it was, and Sterling was right, he needed to back off before she freaked out.

The meeting broke up and he waited for Winter to be ready to leave. He had to back off and stop pressing her for dates. No matter how strongly he was attracted, she wasn't interested, and he had to respect that.

Why did the idea make his stomach hurt?

·♥·♥·♥·♥·♥·

The air had cooled by the time they stepped outside an hour and a half later. She was starving. There had been cookies to go with the tea and coffee, but after a large cookie and muffin, she wanted proper food, not sweets. Even the chunk of cheddar Nick had put in the bag hadn't helped.

They left the house and Nick turned toward home rather than toward downtown. He'd asked her out for something to eat earlier. It seemed he'd change his mind. It was difficult to bring it up because he'd been staring at her all night and now wouldn't even look at her. *What the hell had shifted?*

"Lovely night," she commented, trying to get him to engage.

"Mm hm."

"Look at those stars. They're beautiful. Don't you think?" She paused to stare up at the sky. It wasn't late, but darkness was coming, and more and more stars popped out as she watched. Nick didn't stop to look. She had to race to catch up.

She grabbed him by the arm and yanked him to a stop.

"Can I buy you dinner?" she asked.

"I ate before the meeting. But thanks." He shook her hand off his arm and resumed walking.

What the heck? "How about a snack? I'll buy you a snack."

"I'm good. I'll just walk you home and call it a night if it's all the same to you."

"You invited me out before the meeting. Why the sudden change of heart, Nick?" She pushed past him and turned toward him, hands on her hips. He stared at the ground before looking up at her, then looking away again.

"I asked you out, you didn't seem interested, so I didn't push it. Now you want to go? You *Boggle* me. I could ask you why the sudden change of *Hearts*." He waited for her to answer. The questions in his eyes were hard to bear.

It was her turn to look away. "I don't know. I feel like we could be friends, but I get the idea that you want more. I'm not looking for more, Nick. I told you that." It wasn't easy to voice her thoughts, especially when she didn't understand her own mixed feelings. "I'm here for a year, not a day longer. I have a life to build. A future. Which can't happen here. I'm only here for Aunt Muriel, and because I need time to plan my life."

She inhaled a steadying breath. "I wasn't hungry when you asked, I just finished that delicious muffin. I am hungry and right now, I'm asking you, as a friend, if you would like to join me at the pub for something to eat. Maybe even a beer?"

"Are you saying you have no interest in me as a man?"

She nodded, though she couldn't meet his eye because the simple action was a lie. She was entirely too interested in him, that's why she was dead set on staying away from him. Only right now, her stomach was taking priority, and she hated dining out alone and loathed the idea of cooking this late in the evening.

"Yes, Nick. That's what I'm saying. I like you as a friend and neighbor, but I'm not looking to date you or anyone else. My entire life is in flux, and until I muster things into formation, I'm not dating."

He crossed his arms over his chest and frowned until his brows met in the middle. Something flashed in his eyes, and he gave her a sad smile. "I can live with that." He slung his arm around her waist and turned them back toward the pub. "Come on, friend, let's eat."

His arm was warm around her waist, and her body came to life. She wanted to lean into him and suck up that warmth. A sweet glow of contentment washed over her, only to be dashed immediately.

She had just made a colossal mistake. What happened to her plan to avoid him? She needed a new action plan. She had to remember her time in Haven was just another deployment, even if she was a civilian and not a soldier.

After tonight it would be friends, only friends, and her lonely heart could just shut up. Someday, maybe next year, when she had her life together, she'd think about a relationship with another human being. Until then, it was just her and Aunt Muriel's cat.

Chapter Thirteen

After staying way too late at the pub talking with Winter, Nick was exhausted. He didn't need much sleep, but three hours wasn't enough. They hadn't left until the bartender kicked them out. Smiling through his yawn, he loaded loaves of yeasty-smelling bread dough into the oven before pulling out his binder of special recipes.

He knew dozens of recipes by heart, but always worked with the recipe close at hand. Mistakes could be costly. Too costly for a small business. He had a solid local clientele year-round, and a larger group during tourist season when the local lakes were jammed. Christmas meant being extra busy. He even did a bit of mail-order business. None of that success meant that he could waste ingredients. Especially with Uma around. She was getting better, but when he first hired her, she was a definite liability in the kitchen. He hadn't been much better when he started baking when he was twelve years old.

He'd hired Uma because she was amazing with customers. Slowly but surely, he was turning her into a pastry chef. Thinking of all her failures made him smile.

Not as much as thinking about his time with Winter did. Winter was an enigma. She seemed to blow hot and cold. One minute she was all-in on friendship, the next she backed off. With no set plans to leave, and no commitments lined up, why was she so averse to putting down roots?

She didn't realize that she was already transplanting herself as surely as she was transplanting seedlings into her garden and was already making friends in town. He had a hunch she could be happy here, he just had to convince her. He whistled as he flipped through the recipes. As soon as he had today's specials and basics out of the way, he'd start on a solid freezable cookie for the May long weekend celebration.

Winter had informed him that they were being donated for sale to raise money for the new clinic. With one or two new houses going up every summer, Haven was fast outgrowing the clinic in the back of Doc Hardy's house. By city standards, the growth was minimal. But for Haven, it was a population explosion.

He wasn't sure how big he wanted his hometown to become. He liked the peace and quiet and the solid view of the mountains, no matter where he looked.

After discarding the cliché of maple-flavored maple leaves, he flipped through recipes until he found one for lemon sugar cookies. They'd be perfect. Especially if he flavored the icing with a hint of lemon. He knew he had a maple leaf cookie cutter. Chuckling to himself, he realized he probably had every shape imaginable. He'd ice the event cookies in spring green and get a Welcome to Haven stencil made for dusting the tops with colored powdered sugar or a swipe of colored icing. Of course, the first step was to bake at least two hundred more than he needed. He'd sell the basic cookie in the store as a daily featured cookie, knowing there were always a few mishaps in the creation process.

One batch at a time.

He prepped the first batch and slid it into the fridge for chilling before rolling and cutting. Now, it was time to prep today's muffins. Raisin bran and blueberry seemed like good choices. He'd have them in the oven long before the sun rose.

The bell for the delivery door chimed. Who would be delivering this early? He had a few friends who dropped by before he opened, but they usually texted first. Nobody came to the back door. He peered through the peephole he'd added when he hired his first female employee. No sense having women, or anyone, open the door to strangers. Even in a safe place like Haven, the risk of injury was too great.

What was she doing here?

He popped the double deadbolts on the steel door and pushed it open. "Winter, what brings you by?" He held the door open and let her enter. "It's awful early for most people."

She sighed and stepped inside. "I don't know. I was awake and couldn't fall back to sleep. I knew you'd be up, so I headed over. Can you spare a cup of coffee? Please tell me you have coffee." She clasped her hands together in a gesture somewhere between a double fist and a prayer pose.

"Out front. Help yourself. The mugs are under the counter. You can't miss them. Would you mind refilling mine while you're at it?" He passed her his oversized mug. She reached for the mug and their fingers brushed. He nearly dropped it in shock at the electricity that arced between them. *Holy Snap.*

She sucked in a little breath. Had she felt it too? He searched her face for clues, but she was focused on his mug, which read World's Greatest Baker in elegant blue script.

"That's cute."

"A gift from Grace and Sterling."

She hurried away with the mugs, and he wondered why she was here. After declaring them nothing more than friends, they had spent hours together yesterday. He half expected her to stay away for a while. When it came to Winter, he didn't have a *Clue*. He shrugged the contradiction off and started putting ingredients into his biggest stand mixer. Muffins waited for no man and getting stuck on figuring out what was going on in Winter's mind was a trap worse than a YouTube rabbit hole. Still, he thought about her as he measured everything.

"Here you go. Where do you want it, and is there cream?"

"Cream's in the walk-in cooler, just left of the door. There should be an open jug. Take your pick, one percent, five percent, and whipping cream. Don't let the door slam. I'm waiting on parts; it locks you inside sometimes. Just set mine there, beside the mixer, please. I drink it with two cream and two sugar."

After she doctored their coffee, he gestured to a high stool. "You can sit there if you like. Put it wherever you want. Just not in this area. He drew a small circle in the air, indicating his immediate workspace. She sat and sipped her coffee. After five minutes, she hadn't said a word.

"What's on your mind?" he asked as he measured batter into paper-lined trays.

"Nothing. I just couldn't sleep." She shifted on the stool and smoothed her hands against her khaki-green jeans. Had he ever seen her in anything besides army green?

"Does that happen a lot?"

The black circles which ringed her eyes had returned, and she was pale. She looked like she needed a nap and a hug. He was half tempted to give her the latter. He couldn't recall a single time where the urge to comfort someone was so strong that it was almost a compulsion...except right now.

"They wake me up now and then. Dreams...you know." She shrugged like her bad dreams didn't matter, but she was hiding something.

He did not know from personal experience, but he'd read a lot on PTSD. But reading and living were two entirely different things. Like comparing cookies to chickens. "That must be difficult. Would it help to talk about it?"

"Not really, no. But thanks. I appreciate the offer."

With the trays full, he sipped his coffee before he began cleaning the mixer for the next flavor. He leaned back against the counter and inhaled deeply. Even without the timer set, he'd know by the distinctive scent and color when the bread was close to fully baked. Yeasty and golden.

He searched for something to say. "I'm off tomorrow. I was thinking about taking a walk around the lake. The smaller lake. With a bit of bushwhacking, you can get all the way around. I think it's a seven-mile hike. There's no real difficult terrain. Want to join me?"

"Are you saying you don't think I can handle rough terrain?" Her voice had a bite.

He met her stare. He thought she was serious until her lip twitched slightly. "No, definitely not. I'm saying *I* can't handle rough terrain. I've still got my winter fat stores." He patted his belly. His weight was up a bit, he always was after winter, but he was far from flabby. The bonus pounds would be gone by the end of the month at the rate he was working.

"Don't you have cookies to bake?"

"Technically, yes, but until the long weekend, I'm closed on Sundays and have no intention of changing that. If I'm a few cookies short, so be it. It is a donation after all and one I didn't sign up for. I wish I knew who suggested it."

Her cheeks flushed.

"You?" he squawked. "I can't believe you'd do that to a man you hardly know."

"I know you make the best cookies. Speaking of which," she slipped off her stool. "Mind if I steal one from the display? They look amazing."

He'd never begrudge anyone a cookie or two and only in part because he knew most people would end up coming back to buy more. Giving away treats fed his heart. "Be my guest. But only after you tell me why."

"I'll tell you after the cookie."

He waved her away. "Whatever."

He scrubbed out the mixer and began measuring ingredients. As soon as she was back with her cookie, he asked. "Why?"

"Because you were totally oblivious to the meeting, and everyone was staring at you staring at me. It was awkward. I turned the heat fully on you and you never even noticed. You just said, 'Sure' when Grace asked you to do it." She nibbled a second cookie. His girl had a sweet tooth.

"What's with you and Grace, anyway?"

"We're friends. No. She's my family. I have a sister, but we aren't close. My folks passed years ago. We tried dating and didn't click, and we ended up friends. I'm sure you know what that's like."

"I've dated a few guys that became friends. People say you can't be friends with someone of the opposite sex, but that's not true. Look at all my platoon mates. We're both friends and family. Look at you and I — we're friends and not dating."

True enough, at least on the surface. She had no idea what was going on in his mind and his heart. Frankly, most of his body didn't believe what she said. He could be friends with women, just not with her. He wanted more. But if all he could have was her friendship, he'd take it and try to be grateful.

"We are friends." He measured in some baking powder. "Now, my friend, can you grab me the bucket of blueberries from inside the fridge?"

"I can do that."

"Watch the door."

·♥·♥·♥·♥·♥·

Winter wasn't sure why she was here. Her dreams had been no worse than usual. With her therapist's help, the dreams were becoming less frequent, but last night, they'd been back with a vengeance. She couldn't stop the visions of her friends lying on the ground bleeding and screaming after she hit the IED with their jeep.

Something must have triggered the dreams. Something someone said, or something she'd seen. She knew better than to try to figure it out. Focusing on the dreams made them worse. But it was hard to forget the accident that still felt like yesterday, even though it was nearly eight months ago.

Following her report and the investigation, it was determined that she was not at fault. Logically, there was no way to prevent the accident, but she was at the wheel, and they could have all died. Ergo, in her mind, it was her fault. Logic and emotion often failed to go hand in hand in tragic incidents.

The fact that nobody died was irrelevant. Jeb had lost an arm, and Tink would never walk without a cane. Tiny and Reaper had only minor injuries. Her shattered knee would be a constant reminder that she failed to keep them safe. She had a lot to atone for, and finding a job that helped people would be a good start. There was nothing like that here in Haven. She checked the ad board every day. She'd even done some volunteering at the church.

"I can't help much with the bad dreams, but you're welcome to come keep me company any time you want to. You can use the hot tub too. Even at night. More than once, I've found myself sitting in it, staring at the stars, trying to work out *Life, the Universe and Everything*."

She frowned. "First, it's board games, now it's book titles? What's with that?"

"If the pop culture reference fits...I'm pretty good with gratuitous movie quotes as well."

"No doubt."

"Well, are you going to hike with me tomorrow? I leave at eight. I'll throw together a picnic lunch for us. I'll bring cookies."

Chapter Fourteen

Aside from a few quick stretches, Winter skipped her morning physio and walk because she'd get a good workout with Nick. Nick. His name alone was enough to confuse her. He was brilliant company and very generous. In other circumstances, she could easily see herself in a relationship with him. At this point in her life, two major barricades were preventing them from being together.

First was her messy life. With her lack of career, bad dreams, and somewhat unstable future, she wasn't a good potential partner for anyone. Second was Nick's continued joking. He didn't seem to take anything seriously. Even when he was being empathetic, he joked and quipped, and it grated on her nerves. What was he hiding, or what was he running from? It had to be something. Sometimes he reminded her of an old platoon mate who took to joking when he was scared.

She was watering her newly planted flowers when he pulled up right on time.

He rolled down the window and called out, "Good morning. Your plants are looking great. I can see the growth from here. You must have a green thumb."

She grinned at him. "Thanks. I like looking after them. I planted some veggies and they've got little sprouts already." She sounded ridiculously proud, but didn't care. After years of death and destruction, it was nice to nurture growth. Hers and the plants. There was something soothing and healing about getting her hands dirty in a way that led to growth and beauty.

"Ready to go?"

"Sure am. Just let me grab my pack." She locked up the house and tossed her small backpack into the back of the truck. She climbed in. "Lead on, Macduff."

"I think you mean...to the lake, James."

They laughed together. Now there was an appropriate joke.

It barely took ten minutes to get to the parking lot. She hopped out and looked around. The early morning sun glinted off the water, making the minuscule waves sparkle like diamonds. In a nearby tent, a baby cried and was immediately shushed by its mother's soothing voice.

The wind rustled through the small leaves and buds on the poplar trees. She watched a squirrel make a flying leap between two enormous jack pines. Everything smelled fresh and clean. The morning felt like a new beginning.

She hoisted her pack on her shoulders and adjusted the built-in straw for easy access to her water supply.

"Wow. You come prepared, don't you?"

"Always. I've got a first aid kit, food, matches, a survival blanket, a compass." She trailed off without listing everything she carried. His mouth hung open in surprise. "I like to be prepared." Even with all that and the geographical coordinates in her pack in case they needed to get home without the compass, she felt woefully underprepared. She'd give her eyeteeth for a satellite phone, especially with the shoddy cellular service.

"Good to know. I've hiked this route a dozen times. We aren't going to get lost." He pointed west. "We'll start here and come out there." He indicated a path on the opposite side of the parking lot.

The pathway was tiny red shale chips, well packed and traveled. For a while, they walked side by side. After twenty minutes, the path narrowed until they had to walk single file. She took the lead despite not knowing where they were headed. There was only one path with no other paths in sight.

"I guess most people don't go past those benches. The path seems wilder here." She turned to glance at him as they had passed a cluster of benches in the shade of some pines. It was a lovely resting spot facing the water.

"We'll probably run across a few people, but it's early in the season. Later in the year, we'll be dodging hikers and bikers on fat-wheeled bikes. It gets incredibly busy. I, for one, am glad of the quiet."

"It's very peaceful."

"Soothing."

It was soothing. The tension of two nights of bad dreams slipped away. There was something soul-satisfying about being out in nature. Especially with someone who understood the need to be quiet and enjoy their surroundings. She always found it curious that many people didn't know how to be together and not chatter away.

"Look," Nick whispered. His arm shot over her shoulder to point to a small clearing ahead.

So wrapped up in the quiet and what was immediately around her, she hadn't even noticed the elk with enormous antlers standing there. She stopped in her tracks, her heart thundering in her ears.

"She's beautiful."

"He's handsome," Nick corrected. "Female elk don't grow antlers." He stepped up to stand beside her.

"Is he dangerous?" She hated the quiver in her voice. She'd faced armed insurrectionists, been shot at, survived explosions, and near drowning, but this magnificent animal made her knees knock together.

"Not if we don't startle him. It isn't rutting season. If we approach slowly, he'll probably take off. If he doesn't, we'll back away and leave him to his home. He'll grind his teeth or pull his ears back in warning if he's bothered."

The elk stared back at them and resumed eating. "So far, so good," Nick whispered. He scuffed his hiking boot on the path. The elk looked up and stared at them.

She clutched his arm. "Don't freak him out." Didn't Nick know not to startle a potential enemy?

"He knows we're here, even if he isn't looking. The breeze is blowing his way. He smelled us long before he saw us." He took a small step forward. "Come on, Winter. I think we're good." He stepped around her and walked forward.

They were still a hundred yards away. The elk watched them as they came closer. At fifty yards, about when Winter was ready to bolt and run, the elk snorted and wandered slowly into the trees.

"That was incredible." Her heart was still pounding but with excitement instead of fear. It was amazing to be so close to such a magnificent animal. If she saw no other wildlife today, this would be enough. She sipped her water to moisten her dry mouth. Why did your mouth dry up when you were afraid? She knew, but at this moment couldn't remember. Maybe something to do with the fight-or-flight response.

"It was incredible. In the fall, you sometimes see cow elk with their calves. Last year, I saw one with twins. The females hang together in a herd. The most I've seen together, from a distance, is about twelve. Though under the right conditions, they gather in hundreds. Males and females separate from each other."

"Do you hunt?" The idea of anyone killing one of these magnificent animals broke her heart.

"I do not. I don't mind if others hunt responsibly, and I enjoy wild meat, but I don't hunt."

Not having a solid opinion either way, she just nodded. They walked along in silence; each enjoying the sights and sounds around them. For a while, it was peaceful. Then her brain kicked in and she started thinking about her future.

"Do you know anyone looking for a grunt laborer? I'm bored. I need something to fill my time. I'm not used to doing nothing all day." So far, she'd managed to keep busy, but she needed something more mentally stimulating. Shoveling dirt would be better than nothing.

"I'd pay you to plant flowers in my yard. I've been meaning to do it. I don't mind watering, but I don't care for planting or weeding."

"I'm not joking. I'm thinking about getting a job."

He glanced over his shoulder at her. "Aren't you rehabbing that knee?"

"I am, but that's an hour a day at most, plus some walking. I need to fill my time." She needed to get past her thoughts of the accident and of this man. She hadn't slept well last night. After waking from another nightmare, she'd taken melatonin and finally fallen into a restless sleep and dreamed of Nick.

In the hot tub.

Bare-chested.

Aside from those dreams, she couldn't remember the last time she'd had a dream that even approached hot. And when he'd gotten out of the tub? Yikes. That body.

She stumbled on the path and nearly fell into Nick. Her hand brushed his shoulder, its heat branding her palm. "Sorry," she mumbled. "Must have been a root there." Her fingers twitched with the need to stroke his back.

"No worries." He glanced at her like he was ensuring she was okay, then turned forward. "There's a great place up here to rest."

"Okay." She dropped her eyes when he turned around. Her gaze traveled down his back and lingered on his backside for a moment before carrying on to his muscled thighs and calves. He had great legs. Strong. Tanned. Sexy.

She licked her dry lips and took another sip of water. Man, it was hot out today.

"So, how about it," he asked as he walked onto a rocky beach beside the lake. "Are you going to plant my flowers for me?"

"You're serious?"

When he slung off his pack and sat on a boulder, she sat on another one, two feet away. The dappled sunlight of the shore was warmer than the full shade of the forest path they'd been hiking on, but it felt nice. She shucked her pack and her army hoodie.

"Absolutely. I will pay you to spruce up my yard." He opened his pack and brought out a container of strawberries. He held it out to her, and she took a couple, placing them in the palm of her other hand. "I'll pay you and let you put in whatever you want," he added.

"Hourly or fixed rate?" *Did it even matter?* It wasn't about money. She had a decent nest egg. It was about doing something useful. She already had ideas running around in her head about what would look great in his yard.

"Fixed rate. I'll go with you to the garden center and pay for the plants. You prep the beds and put them in. I'll pay you to weed once a week."

"I suppose you want me to mow too?" she teased.

"Would you?" He grinned eagerly.

"Sure, why not?" She'd already run the mower with the thatching attachment over her aunt's yard. The labor made up for the physical challenges that came with being a soldier.

"I'll pay by cheque through my business. Legit, since my company owns my house and rents it to me."

That had logistics she didn't understand, but his business was just that. His. "Okay. I'll get you my social insurance number."

They snacked and talked wages and ideas for the yard. He was totally open to letting her have her way. It was invigorating. She wanted to rush home and get started, but she wanted to linger here with him. Just sit and enjoy the beauty of nature and the company of a good man. Especially since he wasn't cracking jokes with every other sentence.

The splash of a fish jumping in the lake surprised her. She looked toward the sound, and the fish jumped again. "Oh, look."

"Rainbow trout, I think. It's the wrong colors to be a jackfish."

"You know a lot about nature. Though not much beyond basic survival skills."

"I live in a small town surrounded by forests and mountains. It's in my best interests to be informed about my co-inhabitants." He looked thoughtful. "Technically, I'm an interloper on their terrain. I try to remember that. I spent a week at a wilderness camp shortly after I moved here. It was aimed at teaching about nature and survival. I could hold my own here for quite a while. Probably not as well as you. I'm sure you have a lot of survival training."

"More than you can guess. But survival isn't the same as understanding the surrounding wilderness. The animals, I mean." She was having trouble organizing her thoughts.

Being near Nick was damaging her mental processes. She stepped out of her combat boots and socks. After rolling up her jeans, she made her way to the water by stepping from large rock to large rock. Most of them were smooth river rocks, probably dropped when the lake was formed.

The water was perfectly clear and blue. She dipped her toes in and yanked them back out. "Yikes, that's cold."

Nick laughed as he stepped up beside her. "There's still snow in the mountains, what did you expect? The ice hasn't been gone long. It melts slowly at first, then disappears all at once. I used to think it sank to the bottom, but it doesn't. It just breaks up smaller and smaller, and with more surface area melts faster."

"It's cool that you know so much. Thanks for sharing." He always had a lot to say on a variety of subjects. He seemed well educated. She glanced at him. His cheeks were pink.

"Thanks. I read a lot." There was a wry tone in his voice indicating he meant that to have a double meaning somehow. *Was that a hint that he felt they didn't spend enough time together? Or was she just imagining things?*

They fell into talking about books and wildlife documentaries. The discussion continued through lunch and another hour of walking. Eventually, they fell silent again. He was comfortable to be around. She could easily get used to being with him more often

Don't go there. He's not for you. He's married to this town and you're leaving.

She sighed.

You could stay.

No, I can't.

She argued with herself for a while. Maybe she needed to take some aptitude tests and see what sort of work suited her. One thing she knew for sure was that a desk job with her parents' company wasn't it. They did good work, but she didn't want to be tied to a desk. There had to be a way to be useful and happy simultaneously.

As they walked, the idea of doing yard work for a living struck her. She'd have to research small business rules and see what she came up with. Just for Nick, she could be an employee, but if she were to branch out during her time in Haven, she'd need a business license.

"Do you think people would pay me to do their yardwork? Is there someone in town who does that already?"

"There's a guy who does new home landscaping, but not yard maintenance. Check with the town office they'd know. Planning to stay around?"

He sounded entirely too hopeful for her sanity. "Well, I'm here for a year. I could take contracts for that length of time. Who knows, maybe I could sell the business later. I can't spend my life doing nothing. I'm trying to find a way to fill my time." She paused on a stone outcropping that overlooked the lake, her mind whirling with possibilities.

"Well, Haven is growing. Maybe there's room for that type of service. You never know unless you give it a shot. I'm sure you could research the idea without any difficulty."

Huh. He'd missed a perfect opportunity to throw in a game reference. He could have said without *Trouble*. The miss surprised her. It had been quite a while since he'd cracked a joke or made a game reference. What was going on in his head?

Eventually, they stopped at a rudimentary picnic site, obviously made by some locals. They sat on rough wooden benches overlooking the water and watched canoes gliding across the lake. The water was so clear and blue they looked like kites flying through the sky.

"I guess we should get going," Nick said at last, not sounding like he wanted to move at all. "There's a documentary on the challenges of living in a small mountain town, like ours, tonight and I don't want to miss it."

He stood and brushed the dust off his shorts. She couldn't help but admire his physique as he did so. He was as fit as many of her platoon mates had been. Only she'd never lusted after any of them. She followed as he led the way down the winding path. The sun had risen high and was now beginning its descent. The day had passed so quickly.

She stepped over a massive log on the path, barely keeping from falling when her bootlace caught on a bit of branch. She kneeled to tighten it. No sense taking a spill if she didn't need to. Back in her army days, she'd have checked her laces every time they stopped. Today it had totally slipped her mind. She considered it just one more indication that she needed to find something to keep her physically active and mentally challenged.

"This hike is taking longer than I thought," she said.

"We're not going particularly fast. I'm enjoying your company."

"Me too." Surprisingly, it didn't pain her to admit she liked his company. She liked him entirely too much. It was more the discomfort of admitting it out loud. She vowed to keep her mouth shut for the rest of the walk. No more confessions.

Chapter Fifteen

Nick walked home from work ten days later and pondered the thought that he hadn't seen Winter since their hike. She'd ghosted him. Again. Honestly, he'd expected it after she admitted she enjoyed his company. She made the statement and then clammed up. She must be fighting her attraction to him. Lord knows he was crazy for her.

Ahead of him, a kerfuffle was going on, just down the block from his house. Parked outside of Winter's place was a delivery truck. She was on the front step, gesturing wildly at a pair of delivery men who ignored her, climbed into the truck, and drove away, leaving what appeared to be parts of a treadmill on the front sidewalk.

He kept walking past his place and stopped at the end of her sidewalk. "Hey, what's up?"

"Can you believe those guys? They flat out refused to carry this to the basement. I paid for delivery to the basement. How am I supposed to get it there alone? I can't believe their gall." She paced back and forth on the front step, gesturing wildly, her hair flying around her head in the light breeze. She was glorious.

"That doesn't seem right," he commented, not wanting to fire her up further. "How do they expect a lone woman to get that inside?"

"Right?" She brushed her hair off her face and gathered it in a rough ponytail with an elastic she pulled off her wrist. "What do I do now?" Her shoulders sagged as she let out a heavy breath. "I can't leave it outside in the weather."

"I can call a couple guys to come help us. They won't mind."

She winced. "I don't know."

He strolled up the walkway and gave the biggest piece a tentative shove. "This thing weighs a ton. There is no way you and I can get it downstairs. We couldn't even if you didn't have a wounded knee."

"My knee is fine," she snapped.

"Maybe, but two of us aren't enough to move this thing." There was a box of parts on the grass, and the base was the only part assembled. It likely weighed a couple hundred pounds and was incredibly awkward looking. "Let me make a couple calls. Everyone needs a hand now and then. You can repay them with a beer." When she didn't answer right away, he realized she didn't want to accept a favor and added, "They all owe me for helping them move, and you can pay me back by roto-raking my lawn."

"Okay." She still sounded hesitant, but he made the calls anyway.

Ten minutes later, Clint, Sterling, and Cameron pulled up in Sterling's SUV. "Let's do this thing," Sterling called out.

Nick made sure everyone knew each other.

The biggest trouble was that there were no convenient spots to grip and no good way to carry it with a dolly. Working in slightly uncoordinated unison, they wrestled the awkward device into the basement.

"Thanks so much, you guys," Winter exclaimed. "Can I buy you a beer in thanks?"

"Hell, yes." Cam laughed. "I'd never turn down a brewski. "But did you want help assembling it first?"

She paused. "No, I think I can manage. If I get stuck, I'll call Nick."

Nick was surprised that she'd even consider asking for help after how reluctant she was to get help carrying it inside. "I'm around if you need assistance. Why don't we hit the pub for that beer? I haven't eaten, and I'd love a burger."

Ten minutes later they were crowded around a small table with a couple pitchers of beer in front of them. Nick ordered a burger, and Winter ordered a round of appetizers for everyone. Huge plates of wings, nachos, calamari, and sliders. It was enough food for an army, but barely enough for four hungry men and one retired soldier.

He'd hoped to sit beside Winter, but somehow in the shuffle ended up down the table from her with Sterling between them. He banked down disappointment that he couldn't watch her or touch her. Then he had to stifle self-critical thoughts that Sterling had been right the other night, he was acting like an ass and practically stalking her. He contented himself with knowing he'd helped her out of a jam and would get to walk home beside her. Small victories won the *War*.

They had barely finished their first round of beer when Natalie, Grace, and Lisa showed up. They dragged two tables together and finally; Nick was sitting beside Winter. He kept a respectful distance from her and concentrated on talking to everyone while surreptitiously watching Winter. Tonight, he was extra careful not to stare.

He shifted to lean past Lisa to ask Cam a question and his knee brushed against Winter's. She didn't shift away, and when he straightened, he kept the contact between them. It felt intimate, secret, and filled him with hope that she was adjusting to him in her life.

When the impromptu party broke up two hours later, he held up Winter's light jacket so she could slip into it. His finger brushed her neck, and he quickly banked the desire swamping his senses.

After bidding their goodbyes to everyone in the parking lot, they headed for home in the chilly night air. The full moon was shielded behind a thick bank of clouds.

"That was nice. You seem to be fitting in with my friends."

"It was. You have great friends. I appreciate the help with the treadmill. I am a bit annoyed that Natalie paid the bill before I could. Why would she do that?"

"That's Nat for sure. She's generous in so many ways. Don't fret about her paying. Not to tell tales out of school or anything, but she can more than afford it. She's probably a billionaire or more. Her first husband was a business tycoon of some sort. She doesn't always cover the check but probably gets it more often than not. She's got a big heart, and I accept it as a gift. I used to fight her about paying, but I've learned to do nice things for her instead. You know, take the kids for a couple hours, bake her some cookies. That type of stuff."

"I don't know..." she trailed off like she didn't know how to finish.

"She hasn't put in flowers yet, maybe you could offer to plant them for her as repayment." Natalie was a unique individual. Fleeing a very abusive marriage, she'd crashed her car and ended up in Haven. She'd been secretive on arrival, but now eagerly took part in everything Haven had to offer. She was a kind and generous person and a wonderful friend.

Nick understood Winter's independence and how she probably felt gypped by not being able to pay for tonight's festivities, letting her know Nat might need flowers planted was an easy way to help them both out. "I'd pop by the bookstore. She works there, part time. You can ask her about the flowers. Maybe mention that you're thinking of starting a business and need practice."

"I'll do that. When did you want to start your garden?"

"How about Sunday?" He didn't care what she put in, but he'd take the chance to spend time with her.

·♥·♥·♥·♥·♥·

"I can't believe you only want white flowers," Winter declared. She stared at Nick like he'd lost his mind.

"What's wrong with that? I think white petunias will be amazing. My house is white and green. My lawn is green, why shouldn't my flowers be white? You know, make the whole thing matchy-matchy. Don't women like that?"

His smirk was probably the most annoying thing she'd ever seen.

"Besides, you always dress in shades of khaki and green." He threw the statement out like it was supposed to make sense.

"Don't be ridiculous. I wear what I wear because it's what I own." She'd never needed anything else. Until recently, she'd lived and breathed her job and had precious little social life. She sure as heck wasn't going to admit that she'd visited Haven's only clothing store and picked up a few things in brighter colors. Right now, she was in her jeans and an army T-shirt. Her gardening clothes.

"I think you should consider a variety of flowers. Just for interest." She paused and threw out a taunt. "Take a *Chance*, Nick. Boldly go where no one has gone before." She dropped the Star Trek reference without meaning to. She snapped her mouth shut, hoping he wouldn't notice her slip.

"Nice gratuitous television and game references. For that, I'll give you your way. Pick whatever you want. I bow to your greater judgment."

She suspected he'd probably intended to give her free rein to begin with, and was arguing just for the fun of it. Unfortunately, she was enjoying the back-and-forth between them entirely too much. Maybe even as much as he was.

"Excellent." She rubbed her hands together like an evil villain. "Finally, I can make your yard as girly as I like. Watch yourself, Blackstone. You're about to touch your feminine side." Laughing, she dropped some pink begonias onto the empty cart he was pushing.

She loved working with plants. She'd done her gardens, added a few leftovers to Lisa's, and put in both annuals and perennials in Natalie's garden. Grace's place was up for later in the week. Every minute of this work, if you could call it work, was bringing joy. She had clients lined up for the next two weeks. Her knee rarely bothered her. Gardening and running on the treadmill had strengthened it to near normal. It had been busier than she liked, but moving felt better than doing nothing.

"What are you planning to do once winter comes?" His question echoed one that had been running around in her head for days.

"I'm not sure. I don't mind winter, but I'm not sure I want to spend it shoveling other people's sidewalks and driveways." She paused and put some lemon balm on the cart. "It's not even May. I've got time to figure it out." What was she going to do? Her mind circled around a few ideas.

She'd debated going into security, like a couple of veterans she knew were doing, but there wasn't much call for it in Haven. Not that she planned to stay here. She wanted something to generate income. Something that she could sell and move on from at the end of her tour. Maybe she could link it to this gardening thing.

"How do you feel about roses?" She asked Nick. "I put in a couple for Natalie. I think they'd look nice on either side of your front step."

He shrugged. "Okay. I guess."

"It gets cold up here, you'd have to wrap them in the late fall to protect them over the winter. There are zero-hardy varieties that would be nice. Of course, they aren't cheap." When he didn't comment one way or the other, she said, "A deep pink color would work. Especially if we flanked them with your white petunias."

"Whatever you want." His voice was toneless as if he didn't give a crap. First, he wanted his way, then gave her free rein, and now he didn't have an opinion at all. What was that all about?

Something inside her snapped. "Why did you even bother to come with me?" she ground out through teeth gritted so hard her jaw ached. "First you refuse to consider anything, now you won't comment at all. I'm done, Nick. Done with your games and game references." She grabbed her jacket off the cart handle and stormed out of the greenhouse.

The man was infuriating. Outside, the chilly morning breeze cooled her temper. She didn't even know why she was so upset. He was so danged perplexing. He made her crazy. She stood in the parking lot, hands on her hips, staring down the gravel road. She was going to have to walk home. No way was she sitting in a truck with him.

She paced a small circle, trying to get a grip on why she was upset.

"I'm sorry." Nick's voice came from behind her. She hadn't even heard his footsteps on the gravel. "I don't know what I want. I honestly thought all white would be nice. My comments about your clothing were out of line. I should have admitted that I have no idea what I want. I trust you. How about if I give you a budget and you do what you want within that budget? Just give me care instructions to go along with the plants. Please."

She turned to look at him. He seemed serious enough. But his statements did nothing to explain his vacillation.

"I am sorry. I tease and joke a lot. Sometimes it isn't appropriate. Honest to God, Winter, you make me say and do things I shouldn't. I'm out of my comfort zone with you. I acted like an idiot. I apologize. I'll try not to let it happen again."

She liked that he didn't make a promise he couldn't keep, choosing to promise to try instead. The apology was nice as well. She got a giddy feeling, knowing he felt discombobulated around her. "Apology accepted."

"So, can we go get flowers?" His voice raised in hope.

"Will you give me your opinions when I ask?" His wordless nod was good enough for her. "Okay, let's do this." They returned to their cart, which was standing where they had abandoned it. They were nearly finished shopping before he voiced an unsolicited opinion, though he'd answered all her questions.

"What are those?" he asked. "I like the leaves; well they're not quite leaves. They remind me of a succulent."

She checked the tag. "It says Portulaca. Full sun. Do you want them? They'd go well on either side of your sidewalk at the end." His yard had narrow gardens running on either side of his front walk.

"I'd like that." He looked at the tag. "It's nice that they bloom in different colors. Let's get them."

She added six plants to the cart, and they headed toward the cash desk.

"Oh, what about these?" He pulled the tag. "Coleus. I like the red and green leaves." After discussing the merits of the plants, they added them to their order.

"I think that does it," she exclaimed. They had two pallets of plants and baskets. "Your gardens aren't that big, and don't forget you already picked out hanging baskets and planters for your steps. You've got a lot of watering ahead of you."

"True, but I don't have any in the backyard. What if we got a couple of those hanging planter poles and put flowers by the hot tub? Something that smells nice."

"What if we wait until these are planted? We're probably above budget, anyway. We could see if we have leftovers to use in planters." They shouldn't have, she'd gotten pretty good at knowing how much it took to fill a space. Her nights were filled with reading and researching garden design. At one point, she'd gotten lost watching videos on flower arranging. Video rabbit holes were the worst.

On the drive home, he asked when they were going to plant everything.

"*We* are not going to plant them. *I* am going to plant them. You're going to go do something else and leave me to the work you're paying me for." It wasn't that she didn't want to work with him. It was that she enjoyed being with him too much.

He was a pretty decent guy when he wasn't wisecracking.

"We could make this a two-man, sorry two-person, *Operation*."

"We could, but we won't. I don't want you to *Risk* your precious baker's hands." Ugh, now she was doing it, too. How pathetic was that, especially after she jumped on him for doing it.

Chapter Sixteen

Nick stayed inside for as long as he could. He paced back and forth and snuck peeks at what Winter was doing in the yard. She wore funny rubber pads on her knees and traded her combat boots for pink low-rise rubber boots. She wore a green plaid work shirt and the most ridiculous straw hat with a band made of silk flowers. From behind, she looked like an old granny crawling around his yard. From the front, she was the most beautiful thing he'd ever seen.

After half an hour, he gave up all pretense of not watching her and took her a glass of iced tea. "I brought you a cool drink."

"Thanks." She chugged it down and handed the glass back to him. "That was good." She waved at the flowers she had planted. "What do you think?"

He walked up and down before making an honest appraisal. "I think they're awfully far apart. Do they need to be closer?"

She pulled a tag from the earth and handed it to him. "See how big they grow? I've left room for spreading, and I planted the taller plants behind the shorter ones. See how the back row is staggered next to the front? It gives a fuller look now, but still leaves room for growth."

He read the tag and picked up another. "That makes sense. I'll let you work." He went to the step, but instead of going inside, he sat down to watch her. She worked in silence for five minutes and then turned toward him.

"Must you watch me? Don't you trust me?"

"I do trust you. Implicitly. I just like watching you." He shrugged.

"I don't like it. Either go inside or pick up a tool. I'd prefer the former."

He jogged down toward her. "Tell me what to do, boss." She dug holes and instructed him on how to fill them with water and fertilizer. Once the water soaked in, she dropped in the plants and lightly packed soil around them.

"There may be settling later, just keep your eyes open for holes and fill them in as you find them."

Working with her, though done in near silence, was relaxing. A jolt of electric awareness raced through him each time their arms or legs brushed. By the time they were done, he was as aroused as a teenage boy at the beach.

He picked up the empty pots and stacked them to return to the garden center for reuse while she swept up stray dirt and coiled up the hose. "Beer?"

"That would be perfect, thanks."

He jogged inside after brushing himself off and returned seconds later with two opened bottles and a big bag of all-dressed chips. He sat beside her on the step. "It looks great. Thank you."

She chuckled. "You did half the work, so thank you."

He brushed a bit of dirt off her sleeve, and another off her cheek. "How did you get dirt there?" he asked.

"I don't know. How did you get it in your hair?" She brushed a bit of dirt from his hair and T-shirt. "You're a disaster. Though I suppose I am too."

"No. You're lovely." He stroked her cheek and, unable to help himself, brushed a quick kiss where his fingers had been seconds before. "You're irresistible."

"Thanks?" She sounded like she didn't believe him, but she didn't complain about the kiss.

"Trust me on this," he said. "Every day I am more and more drawn to you. It's very difficult to be around you and just be your friend. I like you. A lot."

"Nick." The single word held a wealth of warning.

"I know." He clenched both hands around his bottle to keep from touching her again. "Friends. Just friends."

"Thank you."

They sat in silence, sipping their beer and watching kids playing down the street. "I'll type up some instructions on watering and drop them at the bakery."

"Sounds great. I'm going out to the lake later. Not the one we went to the other day. There's a second lake further out. I'm going to watch the stars." He wasn't, but if she was willing to go with him, he'd make it happen. "Want to come with me? There's a hill that overlooks the entire lake valley. You can see for miles in the daylight. At night, it offers the best view of the night sky you'll find anywhere."

"That would be nice. What time?"

"I'm thinking we'll leave about eight. Dress warmly. You might even want a toque. The view is better outside the vehicle and sometimes it's windy."

·♥·♥·♥·♥·♥·

Winter was silent as they drove past the lake. Eventually, Nick pulled down a long narrow lane through some trees and then whipped a U-turn. He reversed the truck until the rear bumper was inches from a cement barricade and shut off the engine.

"Sit tight for a minute and I'll get things all set up."

"Set up?"

"Trust me. We want to be comfortable for this."

He got out and rolled back the tonneau cover of the truck box. She heard him hop inside and shuffle around for a few minutes before coming around to her side of the truck and opening the door for her. He held out his hand. "My lady." His other hand held a small flashlight. Its dim light made her surroundings just clear enough to see her immediate vicinity.

Taking his hand, and accepting his unneeded help out of the truck was one of the most natural things she'd ever done. He assisted her onto the tailgate. She froze in amazement. "Wow."

He'd set up two folding canvas lawn chairs, each covered with a fuzzy blanket. Just in front of them, a plastic crate turned on its side held an enormous thermal jug and two mugs. Inside the crate, there was a bag of marshmallows and a plastic container.

He'd stuffed two tiki torches into the box corners and she got just the faintest hint of evergreen and lemon emanating off them. They gave off almost no light. "Have a seat." As soon as she sat, he bent low, lifted the corners of the blanket, and wrapped her shoulders. He spread another blanket over her lap and did the same for himself.

The chairs were close enough that their arms would brush if they placed them on the chairs' small armrests. "Ready?" he asked.

For what, she wasn't sure, but she said. "Ready and waiting."

He switched off the flashlight, plunging them into total darkness.

"Oh." The surprised exclamation slipped out unbidden.

Slowly, stars popped out in the night sky. First one, then another. It was breathtaking. "It's amazing," she whispered, strangely loath to disturb the quiet.

"This is one of my all-time favorite places. I've taken snowmobile rides up here in the depths of winter. Before Natalie came along, Clint and I used to winter camp up here. It was a lot of fun when the weather was nice. We'd snowmobile in and stay three or four days and just chill.

"Pun aside, that sounds amazing." She leaned her head back. The lightweight chair was surprisingly comfortable. She closed her eyes to savor the moment, to commit these precious seconds to memory. She opened them again, and it seemed like the number of stars had tripled. "It's so beautiful."

"Yes, it is." Something in his voice caught her attention. She turned toward him. He wasn't looking at the stars, he was staring at her. It was dark enough that he had to be having trouble seeing her properly, even so, he stared. A bit uncomfortable and entirely too pleased by the attention, she focused on the stars once more.

"Did you want a cup of cocoa?"

"Oh, yes. Please. Cocoa wasn't something I got a lot of in the service. It was especially rare in the heat of Afghanistan. In Alaska, it was a daily treat."

"Coming right up. Marshmallows?"

"Is there another way to drink it?"

He fixed the cup and handed it over. Their fingers brushed, and a wave of heat shot through her hand and into her core. She wished she could blame it on the cocoa, but she knew better.

Nick was kind and giving. They got along famously well. Perhaps too well. She was trying her best to keep her distance and failing miserably. Tonight was just another example of that. Still, for all her attempts to keep her heart safe from him, she was glad to be at his side right now.

"Have you made any plans for your future yet?" Nick asked, his voice low and deep.

"No. I've been doing a lot of research. I'd planned on staying in the army until I retired. I didn't have a Plan B."

"What about gardening? Or something similar?" he asked.

She rolled the questions around in her mind. Something sparked deep inside. It was the hint of an idea, right there, at the front of her mind, on the tip of her tongue, but just out of reach.

"I'm enjoying the gardening so much. People have approached me to design their yards. Jeb Collins asked if I'd be interested in working with him. He does rough landscaping, but there's a market for someone to do the prettying up of his work."

"Are you going to work with him?"

"I might. But that still leaves me a long, cold winter." The darkness gave her a feeling of safety that the daylight didn't, to open up to him. "I want to do more. I spent so many years in combat that I want something..." she struggled for the right words, "something happier. I want to...to bring light to people's lives. Year round. Like I do when I plant flowers. The joy on people's faces when they see my finished work is so...so uplifting, gratifying."

"Haven could use a flower shop," Nick said. "Giving a girl wilted blooms from the grocery store seems inadequate." He chuckled. "The last date I went on, the blooms totally disintegrated when she pulled them from the plastic sleeve. I was mortified."

"Aw. Poor Nicky." They chuckled together.

"It might be something to consider. There's an empty storefront four doors down from the bakery. It's been vacant as long as I've been here. I have no idea who owns it, but the town office would know."

"I suppose if I started something, I could sell it later. I don't know that I want to be that involved. My stay here is temporary." Somehow, it felt like she was trying to convince herself. Tension pinched her shoulders together and made her neck ache. Surprisingly, Nick didn't comment, he just let the subject drop and stared up at the sky.

She forced herself to breathe deeply and relax. He was just trying to help her out. He wasn't planning her life. She got enough of that from her parents. She leaned back and watched some satellites go past. Slowly, the tension ebbed away.

"It's so peaceful here," she whispered.

"Beautiful sky, good company. It's darn near *Perfection*."

Weirdly, his game reference didn't grate on her nerves. Maybe it was the peace of the night, or maybe she was getting used to him. Either way, she was thoroughly enjoying herself.

Funny how his flower shop idea mirrored a passing thought she'd had days ago. Silence reigned once again as they stared up at the stars. She sipped her cocoa and wished she didn't want to kiss him.

When was the last time she'd wanted to kiss a man? She'd had a brief relationship during basic training, but her civilian date hadn't liked her limited availability and had broken things off. Good grief, she was thirty-two years old. She hadn't had sex since a one-night stand in Alaska five years ago. *Holy crow*. She'd rarely been kissed since then. When had she turned celibate? Being in the service didn't mean you joined a monastery. "Wow." The word flew out without her meaning to speak.

"Wow, what?" Nick asked, turning to look at her.

"Sorry. Thinking aloud. Pay no attention." She shuffled lower under the blanket to hide her heated face.

"No way, Winter. You can't drop a wow bomb, and then not fill me in on the deets."

"The deets? What are you, twelve?" She hid her smirk under the blanket.

"Thirty-eight actually. Quite a bit older than you."

Clearly, he was fishing for her age. "Thirty-two for me. The age gap isn't that great."

"Good to know I won't be robbing the cradle."

"I beg your pardon." *What was he implying?*

"Tell me about this thought that made you say wow."

"It's, it's nothing."

"Nothing is not wow worthy. You can tell me. There's nobody here but you and me and the stars. I won't share it with anyone else."

Somehow, she wanted him to know that she didn't have much dating experience. "The military has been my life since my eighteenth birthday. I signed up immediately, much to my family's displeasure."

"That's very noble of you."

"Not really. It started as a way to avoid joining the family business. But I love it. Loved it. What I didn't realize until just this moment was how lonely it was. Don't misunderstand, I have great friendships with my unit, and with people I met around the world. But sitting here, under the stars, with someone who is supposed to be my friend, and nothing more, made me realize how little romance there was in my life." She swallowed a lump of sadness.

"Nick, do you realize that it's been years, too many years, since a man has shown interest in me as a woman? It's been so long since I've been kissed that I can't actually remember it." A soft sigh slipped out.

"Winter, that might be the saddest thing I've ever heard." Slowly, Nick lowered his blanket and reached out and pulled hers until it rested well under her chin. He stood and lifted the plastic crate table to the side, set it down, and crouched in front of her.

"We're going to have to do something about that."

"Oh?" The word was a sigh pushed past the sudden surge of anticipation in her throat.

"Oh, yeah." He leaned toward her. His eyes shone in the dark. His stare caught hers and held her trapped. "Speak now..."

He didn't finish the statement. It was a warning. He was going to kiss her. He paused, waiting. Two seconds. Five. Ten.

Just when she thought her pounding heart would explode with anticipation, he leaned all the way in and brushed his lips over hers. Sparks exploded, and she closed her eyes and leaned into the gentle touch. Fire raced through her veins.

He pressed forward, and she pressed back with equal force. Tilting left, seeking better contact, needing to be closer, she swept her tongue over his...testing. Tasting. Delicious. Man. Cocoa. Marshmallow. Sweet and savory, just like Nick.

He was gentle and forceful at once. She could have leaned away or could have denied him from the start. But she wanted this, more than she dared even consider. Worse than that, she needed this. The human contact, the expression of caring, the man.

As their lips moved in unison, something shifted in the vicinity of her heart. She soared and for a moment, she was free.

Then reality hit.

She could not, would not, become attached to Nick Blackstone.

Not now.

Not ever.

Chapter Seventeen

"How do you feel about dinner and dancing?" Nick did a little dance step across the front of the bakery where they were sharing a coffee before he opened. It had become a tradition for her to go for her morning walk and stop for coffee with him.

It had been over a week since their kiss. That crazy, delicious, heart-stealing moment in the back of his truck. The one that haunted her dreams and made her long for things she couldn't have. The kiss that drove her to his side every morning. And he hadn't tried again.

"Dancing? Me?" she squeaked.

"You. Me. The long weekend bash is this Friday. I'm asking you to go to the dance as my date." He executed another fancy step and pulled her from her seat to dance with him.

"I can't believe a community fundraising event turned into a dance." She let him spin her into a circle. The man could dance.

"This is Haven. We're coming out of a long winter, and one thing you need to know about this place is that we take every opportunity to celebrate. And what better thing to celebrate than the end of snow?"

"I thought it always snowed on May Long," she quipped as he pulled her back into his arms to waltz between the tables.

"It does. That's why we're having the dance at the community center. Tickets are ten bucks. There's a cash bar and a free taxi service home. Well, not taxis, but some of the local teens will act as designated drivers. I've already got two tickets."

"That was presumptuous. What if I don't want to go?"

"Then I shall go and pine away in the corner, wishing your love-liness was with me." He twirled her again. "Or perhaps I'll *Scrabble* about trying to find a date. Maybe Gypsy will go with me."

She was tempted to laugh, but he seemed so serious. "I think you mean scramble about, and isn't Gypsy in her eighties?"

Winter could use a night out. Aside from a couple of trips to the pub with Natalie, Lisa, and Grace, she'd spent most of her nights at home, or over at Nick's watching television. She could use a change. Not that she didn't love being with him. Even though he hadn't tried to kiss her again. *And why hadn't he?*

"She is. But she still dances."

"You know what?" She stepped out of his arms. His silliness convinced her to go, which made no sense since it usually annoyed the heck out of her. "Going to the dance sounds nice. But only because it appears that you can dance. It's not because I like you."

"Liar." He laughed.

The single word echoed her own thoughts. She loved spending time with him. Nick Blackstone was an all-around nice guy, and he was a good friend. He'd honored her request to remain friends and, except for that amazing kiss in the truck, he'd been a perfect gentleman. Of course, it wasn't like she was going out of her way to spend time with him beyond their daily coffee, though she dearly wanted to.

She shrugged. "You don't have to believe me. It's no skin off my nose."

"I'll pick you up at six on Friday."

"Isn't that early?"

"This is Haven. It's a family dance. I made dinner reservations at Sid's for six-fifteen. I'm going to wine and dine you, and take you to the dance."

"Family dance?" Interesting concept. The only dances she'd been to since high school grad were military affairs. Adults. No kids. This was going to be an experience. She was almost giddy.

"Every family in town will be there. It's a potluck of snacks mid-evening, so I'll be dropping off my contribution early. I could drop yours too. I'm bringing desserts."

"Obviously. What should I bring?" She baked a mean broccoli casserole.

"Anything you want as long as you have your dancing shoes on." He attempted to pull her back into his arms for another swing around the room, but she avoided him by picking up her coffee. Already off-balance with excitement, she didn't need him making it worse.

She nibbled on what was left of her morning blueberry muffin. "Is there a dress code?"

"It's not formal, but it is an opportunity to dress up a bit. I'll be wearing a shirt and jacket, no tie if that helps."

"It does. Thanks."

Okay, not thanks. She had nothing to wear. Ugh. She sounded like her brother's wife, the clothes horse. Maybe Lisa would go shopping with her.

"So, you'll go with me?" he asked, sounding uncertain.

"It's a date." She put up a hand. "And by that, I mean we'll go together. As friends. As friends, Nick. Nothing more." She didn't want him getting the wrong idea, even if her heart was.

He saluted. "Got it. You don't need to draw me a *Pictionary*."

·♥·♥·♥·♥·♥·

"I love a road trip," Lisa exclaimed. "A full day without kids. It doesn't get any better than this. Thanks for inviting me, although I'm not sure why you need to shop for something special for the May long weekend dance."

"Thanks for coming," Winter said. "I need to shop because I only have cargo pants and jeans. Almost everything I own is khaki. I haven't dressed up for years, at least not in anything besides my dress uniform. Probably my high school prom. This is my first event as a civilian and I intend to enjoy it to the max." And she was as nervous as hell.

"Are you going with Nick? You guys are so hot together." She waggled her eyebrows.

Winter checked her surroundings for cars before pulling out to pass a slow-moving VW Beetle. "We're going. As friends."

"Come on, admit it. Nick's hot stuff and you've got a thing for him. You can't keep your eyes off him and he's even worse. You nearly set the planning meeting on fire the other night."

"Did not." Okay, maybe a little. She'd ended up sitting across from him and had gotten lost in his eyes more than once. She barely managed to keep her wits about her and take part in the meeting. It was worse than the first meeting because it went both ways.

There was no denying that the man was sexier than most men. She was crazy attracted to him and, as much as she tried to avoid him, she kept finding herself spending time with Nick.

She chatted back and forth with Lisa until they got to the city. "Where should we go?"

Lisa suggested a mid-sized mall.

"Don't you think we should go to the big one? Wouldn't they have more selection?"

"Maybe. But I like the smaller malls. They're less crowded with tourists and often have the same shops. This one has the sweetest boutique shop with hand-crafted dresses. You'll love it."

"Sounds expensive, but I'll trust you. I so want to look nice tomorrow night."

"We'll find you the perfect dress or die trying." She laughed. "If need be, I have a friend here and we can crash on her couch and go home in the morning."

"Good to know. Where do we start?"

"With lunch, of course." They parked at the mall and headed for the food court.

Winter grabbed a burger and fries while Lisa found herself a heaping tray of teriyaki chicken and rice. They slid into a small table and started eating. After a moment, Lisa asked, "What's with you and Nick?"

"We're friends." Winter took a huge bite of her burger to avoid saying anything else.

"Don't try and kid me. I live on the same street as you. My kitchen overlooks his hot tub. I've seen you two out there. A lot. You pass by my house to get to his. I see you both coming and going."

"You're stalking us?" She didn't believe it, but hoped for a deflection.

Lisa's laugh rang out across the food court, and people turned to smile and stare. "Not at all. My favorite chair faces the road. Remember that life in a small town means everyone knows everyone else's business. I'd never gossip about you two, so I haven't mentioned it to anyone else, but I am curious."

"I swear, we're just friends. His hot tub is great for my knee, especially when I strain it. Some lawns I mow are on brutal hills, and my knees ache afterward."

"So, what's with the dress then?"

"Didn't we talk about this? I have nothing but jeans. Who knows, I might buy a nice pair of pants instead." She ate a few fries. She could almost see the gears turning in Lisa's head.

"I thought we were friends. Friends don't lie to each other. I'm disappointed."

Winter sighed and sipped her cola. "Okay, here it is. I like Nick. He's a great guy. He's handsome, sexy, and kind. His stupid jokes and puns are growing on me, and if you tell him, I'll use one of the fifty-two methods I know to end you and nobody will ever find your body. But I'm only in Haven temporarily. I can't and won't start something I won't be around to finish. It wouldn't be right."

Lisa ate a few mouthfuls and waited until a gang of noisy teens passed by before she answered. "I didn't realize you had a plan for after your time in Haven. Could you change that plan? You know, fall in love with a great guy, stay in Haven, and live your happily ever after? Be my BFF forever."

"I need to build my life. I need to find my path forward. Independent of my family, the military, and a man. Even if that man is Nick."

"I didn't think Nick was a guy who'd try and control another person. He's pretty easy-going and supportive."

"He's not trying to control me, or guide me, but experience tells me he will try. Dad controls Mom. My brother controls his wife. My only ex wanted me to quit the service for him. It happens to every woman."

"Bullshit. Cameron doesn't control me. He doesn't even try. Clint doesn't. Sterling doesn't. Don't let a few poor examples ruin what could be amazing for you and Nick. Don't give up a chance at love because you're afraid." She sipped her drink and added, "Love doesn't come around often. I was blessed to have it twice. First with Darren, and after he died, with Cam. Don't throw away something potentially amazing because something might go wrong. Love is worth it, even when it sucks."

Something resembling hope surged in her heart. She pushed it aside. Heartburn. That's all it was. Heartburn after eating too quickly. "Are we going to shop or what?" She stood and picked up her empty tray. Lisa joined her with a grin.

The boutique, Angel Designs, wasn't tiny, but it was small. Each article of clothing was unique. There was almost nothing available in more than one size. You either choose from your size, or custom ordered what you want. Winter winced a bit at the prices, but for custom creations, they were quite reasonable.

She wandered through a rack of slacks, then skirts and blouses, trying to determine what she liked. Eventually, she decided to just pick something and try it on. She was thin but quite muscular, so form-fitting wasn't an option.

"Have you got something with shape, but that isn't clingy? I'm going to a semi-formal dance." *Did people even call it semi-formal anymore?* "A family dance. I want to look nice, but not too done up."

The sales assistant sized her up and down. "Hang tight. Angel's working on something in the back. Let me see if she's close to finishing. It should be about your size."

"Oh, you don't have to do that. I can just look around."

"Would you please check?" Lisa interrupted. She turned to Winter. "I've got a few of Angel's pieces. You won't be disappointed."

The young woman vanished into the back room. Winter flipped through dresses in her size and selected three to try on while she waited for the sales clerk to return. A shorter, flowing, pale blue knit. An emerald, green knee-length one with floaty sleeves, and a floor-length purple gown of some light filmy fabric she couldn't identify.

A second clerk invited her to the changing rooms to model the dresses. Lisa followed them and waited in the viewing area that held two sets of three-way mirrors. She slipped into the purple one; it was too short to work with her height. Instead of brushing the tops of her feet, it came to mid-ankle. The pale blue was the perfect fit, but the color wasn't quite right for her skin.

"I don't know," she said to Lisa as they looked at the green one. "This is okay, but something isn't quite right. It is beautiful, though."

"Try this." The clerk brought in the dress she'd gone to get. "I think it will be perfect."

Two minutes later, Winter stared in the mirror, stunned. The dress was a shimmery golden-silver color with a fitted bodice and a princess neckline high enough to conceal her breasts, but low enough to hint at them. It had long, flowing gypsy sleeves and a loosely fitted skirt that would end just above her knees once hemmed. It brought out the color of her eyes and made her hair shine like black silk.

"You look incredible," Lisa exclaimed.

"It's better than I imagined," a new voice said. "It's like I created it just for you."

Winter whirled around. "Did you make this?"

"I did. I'm Angel. That is the perfect dress for you. It will only take half an hour to hem it for you."

Winter chewed on her lip. The dress was a confection and likely costlier than the others she looked at. "How much?" She hid a wince at the price.

"Do it," Lisa encouraged. "It's perfect. Nick will be struck senseless when he sees you. How are you going to do your hair? Sexy updo?"

"I'm going to cut it."

"Wait. What? No way."

"I'll take the dress."

"Let me mark the hem."

She returned to her conversation with Lisa as she changed out of the dress. "Yes, way. I only grew it to donate to an organization that makes wigs for cancer patients. They need twelve inches to make it work."

"Oh, there's a salon in the mall that does that," the clerk said. "Second floor, down by the sporting goods store. Did you want us to call and see if they have an opening?"

"Would you? That would be amazing."

Angel made a gesture and her associate hurried off.

"Your hair will be so short," Lisa lamented.

"No, it won't. It'll be just to my shoulders. Honestly, I can't wait to lose the weight. It's so thick and heavy."

"What about Nick?"

"What about him? It's my hair, not his. Why do you ask? You've got a short pixie cut, and it's changed color twice since I've met you."

"Wash out color." Lisa laughed. "I guess it doesn't matter what Nick thinks. It's your hair and you're doing a good thing."

"Darn right."

Chapter Eighteen

Nick hadn't seen Winter for three days. Not since he asked her to the dance. He'd invited her over several times. She didn't want dinner, or to watch television, or just to hang out. She hadn't been by the bakery at all. Not even once. He had the nagging feeling that she was avoiding him. Again. She was off and on like a light switch.

If she'd changed her mind, he wouldn't show up to take her out tonight. Barely surviving in the friend zone, he wasn't sure he'd live through being ghosted entirely. He shot her a text.

Nick: Are we still on for tonight?

Winter: Yes! I'm looking forward to it. :D

Nick: Still on for dinner? I can pick you up at six.

Winter: Six sounds perfect. □

He wanted to send another text or call her, but it was already four and he understood that sometimes women wanted time to get ready to go out, though he didn't think Winter was like that. She was always ready to go at the drop of a hat. Her beauty was entirely natural.

Anticipation thrummed through him as he showered. He'd gotten distracted at work by a rush of customers and barely got out in time. Uma was going to close for him, as she had no dinner plans.

He whistled his way down the street. They'd decided to walk to dinner and then the dance, just in case they had a couple of drinks. Haven was small enough that you could walk anywhere, no matter the season. So far, the weather was holding up. It was a balmy seventeen Celsius and there was no wind.

He straightened the tie he'd put on at the last minute and smoothed his jacket before he rang the bell.

He heard a muffled curse from inside, and then, "Just a minute." Footsteps raced down the hall and after a moment the sound of heels clicking on hardwood met his ears. He rubbed his hands in anticipation and wiped his sweaty palms on his thighs. He was ridiculously nervous.

Lisa's daughter, Amy, called out to him, and he turned to watch her do a small jump on her skateboard. "Well done," he praised as the door opened behind him. "See you later, munchkin." He turned and nearly fell backward off the step at the sight of Winter holding the screen door open.

Geez Louise. His heart thundered in his ears even though all his blood had pooled below his waist.

She was a beautiful woman at the best of times. Tonight, she was stunning. Shimmery gold hugged her form without being too tight. Her long legs were in some kind of silken hosiery. Glittering shoes with three-inch strappy heels took his mind to steamy places. He swallowed hard. "Wow." She reached out and stroked his tie. "You don't look so bad yourself. Come in while I find my wrap."

She turned, and he realized she'd cut her hair. It hung on her shoulders in a neat bob. She had to have taken off at least thirteen inches. There was something way too sexy about the way it brushed her shoulders. He'd been in lust with her long hair. This stunning cut was simultaneously devastating and intriguing. He wanted to run his hands through its softness and slide it aside to nibble her neck.

Yup. Definitely sexy.

Her sparkly dress accentuated her curves, and he nearly followed her forward just to put his hand on the dip in her waist just above her tempting backside. *Ho-ly Space Balls!*

She spun a quick circle. "Do I look okay?"

She bit the corner of her lip, and he nearly lost his mind. *Hells Bells.*

"You look incredible. Not that you don't always look nice. I like the haircut. It suits you." It brushed the top of her chest, drawing his eyes to the heart of cleavage there. Tonight was going to be a long, damned night. He didn't want other men looking at her. Not for one second. "Can I help with your wrap?"

"Thank you." She handed him a wispy gold shawl that was more airy than substantial. It wouldn't do much to keep her warm, but it added to the intrigue of her outfit. He held it up, and she turned so he could wrap it around her shoulders.

She picked up a glittery evening bag and smiled at him. "Shall we go?"

"Absolutely, though I think we should stay home." At her puzzled look, he quickly added, "I don't want to share you with anyone." He grinned. "Are you sure you want to walk in those heels?"

"Of course. They're amazingly comfortable. I could dance all night in these." She lifted one foot, and they both stared at her shoe.

"Good, because I intend to keep you in my arms all night." He slammed his mouth shut. *Friends, she wanted to be friends.* He had to keep that in mind and not frighten her off before he convinced her they could be more. And he would not give in to the fantasies those shoes evoked.

"Oh? I was planning on taking a few others for a spin. I noticed that Sterling's construction company has a pretty hot crew." She fanned her face, winked, and slid past him and out the door. Her light, flowery scent lingered to tease him.

He turned the lock on the door handle and pulled the door closed behind him. She waited for him on the sidewalk, a mischievous light dancing in her eyes. She was totally playing him, which brought up whether she was more interested in him than she let on. He tucked the idea close to his heart for later.

Sid's was packed, and he was grateful that he'd reserved their most romantic table weeks ago. Long before he'd invited Winter to the dance. The hostess seated them, and Sid hurried over to greet them. She believed in keeping tabs on her regular patrons.

"Winter, you look stunning. I hope you know you're much too good for this reprobate. He may be the best baker in town, but I'm sure you could do better." Her voice was full-on teasing, and her smile amused.

"Indeed, I can." Winter laughed. "I'm just using him to make potential dates jealous." She winked at Nick in a way that Sid wouldn't see. "You know how it is, Sid. A beautiful woman must keep her dates on their toes."

Sid roared with laughter. "You know it." The women shared a fist bump. "Tonight's specials are chicken souvlaki, chicken taco lettuce wraps, salmon almondine, and a Greek steak salad plate. I went light because I knew there'd be food at the dance. I'll leave you with the menus and check back in later. Enjoy your evening."

"She's so nice," Winter said after Sid walked away.

"She's a great person. She gives a lot back to the community." Nick picked up his menu.

"So, do you. From what I hear, you donate to every town function. Baking and manpower. You're a good man, Nick Blackstone, and you know it."

Heat rose in his face, and he mumbled his thanks.

They'd barely finished eating when Sid appeared at their table for the second time. "I hate to interrupt your date."

"Not a date, two friends sharing a meal and supporting the community," Winter corrected.

"What's up?" Nick asked.

"It's the mayor's wife's birthday. He ordered a cake for her. I've got a cake, but nobody to decorate it. My pastry chef is out with the flu. I can't decorate to save my life. Can you please, please, please, come do something simple? It's already iced in white, and the colored frosting is ready." She clasped her hands together like she was begging.

Nick looked at Winter. "Do you mind? It will only take a few minutes."

Her smile was breathtaking. "Can I watch?"

They both looked at Sid.

"Absolutely, and your dinner is on the house for this."

Winter paused inside the swinging doors to the kitchen. It was quietly chaotic. People rushed back and forth with plates, pots, and utensils. She'd never been in a full commercial kitchen except Nick's. This one dwarfed his tiny space. It was a buzzing hive of activity.

"This way." Sid led them through the kitchen to a counter near the back door where a small white cake sat waiting. Someone called her name. "Oh, I'll leave you to it. I have to check this. Thanks, Nick. Thank you too, Winter."

Nick started working on the cake right away. Winter watched for a moment, but found herself distracted by the activity in the kitchen.

Not counting Sid, there were six staff members. "Is it always this crazy?"

Nick didn't look up from the cake. "I think there's usually Sid, two cooks, and a dishwasher. They're heavily booked for the first night of the tourist season. There are also usually only one or two specials. More customers and specials must equal more cooks."

"You know a lot about business."

"Well, I do run one." He winked at her, and her toes curled in her shoes. "Plus, I read a lot and I used to run a kitchen before I opened the bakery."

"Right, I'd forgotten that. I should read more about business."

"Thanking about opening up a business beyond yard work?" He quickly changed the tip on the green icing bag.

His hands moved swiftly and surely, and she wondered how they'd feel on her skin. Her breath hitched.

"Maybe. I kind of have an idea perking in the back of my mind. I'm not ready to discuss it." She was more than ready, but if she told him she was considering opening a flower shop that also did yardwork, she knew he'd get his hopes up about her staying. She hid a sigh. It would get her hopes up, too. And there were far too many details to work out.

He piped on a few roses, scrolled the birthday girl's name out in script, and put down the icing bag. "What do you think?"

She leaned past him for a closer look. The flowers were lovely, the text was simple and elegant. "It's beautiful."

He inched closer and whispered to her, "It won't taste as good as mine."

Sid slapped him on the back. Winter hadn't even noticed her approach. "I heard that, Blackstone. I'd be offended if you weren't right."

He sketched a quick bow. "We each have our skills."

"Ha. I visited Tamier when you were head chef. I expect you could out cook me any day. Thanks for coming to my rescue tonight. I owe you one."

"You're welcome. Now I have to get my date to the dance before she runs off without me." He washed up and removed his apron.

Chapter Nineteen

Winter passed her shawl to the young teen running the coat check in the community hall. Hundreds of paper and cloth Canadian flags in a variety of sizes decorated the foyer. Brightly colored flowers and red maple leaves, like the ones on the flag, hung everywhere, including from the ceiling. The decorations wouldn't be out of place at a Canada Day celebration. Tonight, they looked summery and patriotic. She was once again moved by her love of her country. And maybe of this community.

The inner foyer doors were closed. Bright strains of country music vibrated through the doors, along with an occasional bark of laughter. The party was in full swing. Excitement tickled down her spine.

It reminded her of the one dance she'd attended in high school. Only tonight she was certain her date wouldn't ditch her for the 'easy' girl. She hadn't minded being ditched when she realized what an absolute pig her date was. She'd been eager to see him go after he refused to take no for an answer.

"Are you ready for this?" Nick asked, taking her hand in his and squeezing lightly. "I can't wait to dance with you." The strength and calluses of his hand sent her mind whirling to intimate places and activities they could share.

The music thrummed at her core as they got closer to the door. His hand was warm in hers and his light cologne tickled her senses. She was as giddy as a schoolgirl. Nick was a great guy, and she was itching to be in his arms. He opened the door, and the music hit in a wave of sound that was almost physical. Surprisingly, it wasn't as loud as she'd expected. It was at a decent level. If you sat close to someone, you'd be able to have a conversation.

The music morphed into a classic rock ballad, and Nick immediately pulled her into his arms and onto the dance floor. As they swirled around, she was caught up in the joy of the people surrounding them. They danced in pairs, individually, and in groups. They sat in clusters at round tables lining the edges of the hall. Everyone was smiling, chatting, and laughing.

To her shock, the music came from a five-man band on stage rather than a DJ. The drummer was a teen, the bass guitarist in his sixties, and the other three members were somewhere in between. The sign in front of them read Pete and Company. It seemed a weird name for a band, as she idly wondered which one was Pete. They wrapped up a Taylor Swift number and rolled into an excellent version of *Beth* by KISS. A well-rounded band, they covered music for all generations.

Nick pulled her close, one hand holding hers in the classic waltz pose, the other holding her tight around the waist. She shivered in excitement as the heat of his body penetrated hers. Bliss stole over her as they waltzed and swirled through the crowd. He was graceful and led amazingly well. She'd taken hours of dance classes as a teen, and he far outdanced many of her fellow students, and probably some of her instructors.

A graceful dancer, a talented chef and baker, and a community-minded man, just the type of person she'd be proud to take home to her family. Not that she had any interest in taking him home to meet her family. Her family was out of her life for now and maybe longer. She decided not to think about them. Tonight was for pure pleasure, nothing more, nothing less. She had no future with Nick or in Haven, but she was going to enjoy tonight. She'd revel in the dancing, the companionship, the snacks, the drinks. Every single minute.

The song wound to a close and, after a brief pause, morphed into one of last year's top ballads. It seemed tonight was the night for slow dancing and being close to the person who brought you. Nick didn't let go, not for a second, and Winter couldn't find it in herself to object. She felt safe and cherished in his arms. It was a feeling she could easily get used to. They pivoted and swirled. Once he even dipped her down and her breath caught with excitement. He didn't drop her, he just bent them over, stood again, and spun her in a small circle. It was exactly how she had always wanted to dance, to be romanced. It was a pity that this was with Nick, a man she couldn't have. A man she wanted, but didn't want to want.

Screw it. I'm going to take tonight and commit it to memory. I'll dig it out later, when I'm cold, when I'm lonely, when I'm wishing that I hadn't been afraid to take a chance.

As the song ended, she needed a moment to herself. She said, "Let's take a quick break, and could we please get a drink?" She needed more than a drink. She needed to regain her composure. Shaken to her core, Nick was bringing out feelings that she didn't dare have.

He led her to a table where all their friends were hanging out. It astounded her to think how many friends she'd made in the short time she'd been in town. It was only weeks, and she had dozens of friends. Friends who were as close to her as her platoon mates had once been. Something about living in a small town was warm and comforting. It was a feeling she'd never had at home with her parents and brother.

"Have a seat I'll go get us both a drink. What would you like?" Nick asked.

"I'd love a soda, something without caffeine, please. And maybe a glass of white wine." She'd danced up a serious thirst.

"You've got it." Nick took off, and she sat between Grace and Lisa.

There were pitchers of water and glasses on every table, and she poured herself a cool drink. "Wow," Lisa said. "You two are sure burning up the dance floor. You guys are hotter than a bonfire together. When are you going to make it official and start dating instead of just faking that you're only friends?"

Lisa had a knack for blunt. The words didn't bother Winter because it was a question she'd been asking herself. *Could you make a relationship work with Nick? Could she find happiness here in this small town?*

If she found a way to have a career that paid enough to live on, maybe she could. She stuffed the thought aside. In the words of Scarlett O'Hara, she'd worry about that tomorrow.

"Seriously, Lisa," Winter laughed. "Nick and I are just friends. Friends and neighbors."

"Friends don't buy red-hot sexy dresses to go to a dance with their friends," Grace threw in. "And unless I'm mistaken, Nick's wearing a new suit. You guys spend time together most nights, you're at the bakery almost every morning when I get there for my coffee, and now you're dancing together like an old married couple." She chuckled. "No, that's not right. You dance together like you can't keep your hands off each other. Like you can't wait to get him into your bed." Her tone went sly. "Don't even try to hide it. You're attracted to each other. Maybe even more. Just how deep do your feelings go?"

"I admit it," Winter said. "Nick's a great guy. In other circumstances, he could be the perfect guy. Which, as you know, we talked about over coffee the other day." The day Nick invited her to the dance, she had gotten together with Lisa, Grace, and Natalie, for lunch and to discuss the final plans for the May Long Weekend events. Her three new friends had pestered her for details on her relationship with Nick. For some reason, they didn't understand that a man and a woman could just be friends.

Oh, who was she kidding, she was falling for him and if her life was different, she could love him. But for now, she wasn't going to let herself fall anymore into 'like' with him, and love was completely out of the question. One hundred percent. That was an absolute certainty. A near certainty. She was pretty certain they weren't meant for each other. *Right?*

Nick came back with her drinks and instead of taking a chair of his own, slipped onto the edge of hers. It was a bit presumptuous but something about the proprietary action tickled her heart and made her giddy. It's not like there was room to squeeze in another chair, anyway.

"I've had enough of sitting here, listening to you old ladies gossip," Nick said three songs later. "Come on, Winter, dance with me. You do know how to two-step, don't you?"

Winter laughed. "I'll have you know that I can properly perform twenty-one dances well enough to give dance classes. There is no way on Earth that a small-town boy like you can out-dance me to any music."

"I'm not going to let you challenge my masculinity and besmirch small towns that way. Time to put up or shut up." He smirked. "Let's find out what's *Truth*, and what's just an empty *Dare*." Nick stood and grabbed her by the hand. He pulled her to her feet and urged her towards the dance floor. "I'm a bit offended," he teased, "I'll have you know that I took dance lessons in New York. There is no way you can outperform me."

"Now that's a challenge I can't refuse. This soldier is going to dance your socks off." She laughed when the music morphed into a raucous jive number. Nick's laughter rang with hers, causing several heads to turn their way.

They hopped and bopped around the floor, dancing and swinging until they were breathless.

The jive flowed into a waltz, which flowed into a two-step. Dance after dance they moved in unison as if they'd been dancing together for years. As the evening wore on, she found herself falling deeper and deeper in like with Nick. If she were being honest with herself, she would admit she was well on her way to love. She wasn't ready for that. She had to get her life together. Only after she had re-established her career, away from her family, could she consider a permanent long-term relationship with a man. Until then, it was nothing but friendship for her.

Still, she couldn't stop herself from leaning into his embrace. Each dance brought them closer and closer. Her body warmed against his, her fingers stroked his skin and threaded their way through his hair. Their breaths mingled together as they moved slowly, and their hands tangled...never fully separating, even as they danced further apart. Each separation, though only a song in duration, made her heart and her body yearn to be back in his arms.

At length, the band announced the last song of the evening. It was crazy how quickly the time in Nick's arms passed. They'd barely paused for snacks and drinks. She never wanted the evening to end. He shifted even closer and whispered in her ear.

"Winter, I want to take you home with me."

She gave him a puzzled look. "What are you talking about, Nick? You're my date. You brought me here. Who else would I go home with?" Surely, he wasn't hinting at what it seemed like he was hinting at. Was this his not-so-subtle way of asking her to sleep with him?

She didn't think that even Nick had balls that big. *Could she do that? Could she sleep with Nick?* Or would the aftermath destroy their friendship and her heart?

"Come on, Winter. You know what I'm talking about." He stroked a finger down her arm. Goose flesh rose at his touch. Her entire body was hyper-sensitive to his caress.

"Don't you want to finish this last dance?" Winter asked.

Nick grabbed her by the hand and gently pulled her towards the foyer. "I don't. We only have a few minutes before the entire crowd stampedes out into the street. I want to walk you home in the quiet darkness and enjoy the stars before everyone else comes outside."

He tipped the coat check and retrieved her wrap. His breath skittered across the skin of her neck as he draped it around her shoulders. A shiver of longing raced down her spine. Liquid heat pooled low in her abdomen. And in that instant, she knew she was going home with him and was going to take everything he offered.

His kindness and attention had changed something in her. Silently, she prayed that he had protection because she was going to take him up on his deliciously naughty offer. The only question was where they would go.

"Your place or mine?" she whispered. Stepping close to him, she brushed her lips across his ear and darted out of the community center, leaving him behind. She was well down the street when he caught up to her. Laughing he swung her into his arms.

"Winter, you're a tease and a minx. I didn't realize you had a lighter side. I'm pleasantly surprised."

Warmth glowed inside her. No longer could she ignore the connection between them. It was dynamic and growing, like a living thing, and it filled her with happiness. He was still the same teasing man she'd met before, and he still threw out those crazy puns and board game names. Only now she realized that despite all his friends, he was somewhat socially awkward, and that was how he coped. It had gone from an annoyance to mildly endearing, though she suspected there were times when it could still get on a person's nerves.

She snuggled into his side, and their arms wrapped around each other's waist. As they wandered down the street arm in arm, the distant sound of other partiers echoed behind them. She couldn't wait to get home and be with him. He was wonderfully warm against her side in the cool night air. The pleasant warmth sparked thoughts of two hot, naked bodies moving together in the dark of night. *Oh yes, she was ready for this.*

"My place, I think." She paused. "That is, if you have protection with you." She threw him a questioning glance and was relieved when he said he was prepared.

Laughing they leaned on each other and hurried up the street and into her house. They kicked off their shoes and raced down the hall into the bedroom. She eased the door shut behind her. The last thing they needed was Aunt Muriel's cat interrupting a private moment.

Chapter Twenty

It was barely after four when Nick's internal alarm clock woke him. He stayed motionless for a moment, recalling last night's erotic events and reliving every moment of passion. Winter wasn't what he expected at all. With her military background, he somehow expected her to take charge, to take control. Instead, she gave as much as she took, moving with him, loving him, and letting herself be loved by him.

Moving slowly to avoid waking her, he rolled toward her and opened his eyes. She lay on her side facing him, her hands clasped under her cheek. Even in the dim light, he could see the tangles their activity had created in her glistening black hair. His fingers itched to smooth away the knots. Instead, he contented himself with just enjoying her beauty.

His heart swelled with love. Waking beside her was something he could easily get used to. Damn, he loved this woman. He realized now that what he thought was love in his previous relationships was nothing more than serious infatuation. What he felt right now, at this moment, was pure sweet love. The kind of love that lasted forever.

He didn't want to get up, nor did he want to wake her. But it was time. Despite the long weekend, he had a business to run, bread to bake, and four dozen cookies left to ice. He debated letting her sleep and leaving without waking her, but in the end, decided that he wanted to talk to her and steal a few sweet kisses before going to work.

He stroked his index finger across her forehead, in front of her ear, and down onto her neck and shoulder. Her skin was silky soft and warm. Peace and contentment stole through him.

"Hey, beautiful," he whispered. "I know it's very early, but I have to go. I didn't want you to wake up alone and think I abandoned you. Unfortunately, I have to go to work."

She murmured low and snuggled deeper into her pillow. "This is not how I wanted to start my day." She snuggled deeper under the covers and inched closer to him. "I wanted to sleep late and snuggle before we got out of bed."

"I'm with you on that one hundred percent. But this is the life of a baker. Early mornings almost every day. Trust me, I'd much rather stay here with you. On the plus side, I'll be free by ten so we can go to the celebration together."

Unable to resist, he smoothed back her hair and leaned in for a kiss. She turned into his lips and met him eagerly. Knowing it was too early to say the words, to tell her he loved her, he poured his feelings into the soft brush of his mouth and the tender caresses of his hands. In only a moment, he was lost in her, and the sensations she wrought in his heart and his body. His last thought before losing himself in her was to hope that she felt the same way.

One kiss led to another...

·♥·♥·♥·♥·♥·

He was late for work.

He was never late for work. Ever.

Thank heaven for reliable staff. Uma managed to finish the cookies and bake the bread while the others prepped the shop for the day's sale.

Nick loaded a flat dolly with boxes of cookies. Then loaded a second dolly with boxes of cupcakes, muffins, and napkins. After locking up the shop, they hurried to his booth in the town square. Winter had gone ahead to organize the booth and prep the tables for the delicacies he was bringing.

He was still more than a block away when the first strains of the high school band warming up, and the excited chatter of children hit him. This Victoria Day fundraising event was a fabulous idea. If the sound of the crowd was any indication, they were going to raise a lot of money for the new clinic. One thing about Havenites, they loved to support local charities.

The sun was bright and warm, the days were getting longer, and excitement bloomed in his heart. He was going to spend the day with Winter. The entire day. He wasn't one to look a gift horse in the mouth, but after their incredible loving the night before, he hoped for more. A lot more.

"Morning, Nick," Grace greeted him at the edge of the green space. "You're late." She laughed lightly. "You look tired. Rough night?" Her grin was pure teasing evil.

"I'm late because somebody, and I mean you, demanded a bazillion cookies." He winked at his good friend, more than certain she could see his happiness. "Where do I get my stamp card?"

"Right here." She handed him a printed card. The top read, Happy Victoria Day. At the bottom were twenty-five numbered boxes.

Each visitor would get a card. Each box could be checked by participating vendors. Once all twenty-five boxes were checked, the cards could be dropped in a draw box. The prize was a weekend at West Edmonton Mall in one of their suites. Additionally, there was a table selling tickets for the grand prize trip to Mexico. There were, of course, many subsidiary prizes in both draws.

"Don't forget to put your name on the back, in case you drop it."

He saluted. "Yes, ma'am." He hurried away when she pretended to threaten him. "Gotta go. My staff isn't waiting around." *And Winter was waiting!*

The event wasn't slated to start until ten, but now, at only nine-thirty, the park was brimming with people chatting and holding paper cups of coffee. His covered tent was halfway down the left side of the square. He cut diagonally across the square, his eyes fixed on his destination, and the beautiful woman standing there, laughing with Uma.

Winter's raven hair shone in the morning sun. He paused to look at her. She'd filled out over the past few weeks. She'd never been tiny, but she'd lost the look of someone who'd been unwell. His gaze traveled her curves, and he suddenly realized she was wearing black denim jeans, a matching jacket, and a bright pink T-shirt with sparkles on the front, and not her usual khakis. The change stole his breath. She looked nothing like the exhausted woman who had stumbled into his bakery only weeks ago. She was thriving in Haven.

All he had to do was convince her she was destined to stay here.

She looked up and caught his eye. A slow smile spread over her face, jolting him into action. He hurried across the field and snuck into the back of their tent, stopping at her side. He leaned toward her and brushed a quick kiss across her cheek.

"Good morning."

"Morning. Again." She whispered the last word. "Did you bring me coffee? I'm dying for a cup."

"Not yet. I thought we'd set up and then find coffee for everyone." His staff was scheduled to take two-hour shifts at the table. That way, everyone had the majority of the day to celebrate and visit the other booths.

"Nick. Nick. Nick. I thought you knew me better than that. I can't function without coffee."

"Fine. You are dismissed. You can go get coffee for everyone." He looked around. "There's a free coffee booth somewhere. The fancy coffee booth is near the gate." He pointed back the way he'd come.

"Nothing fancy for me. Did you want one?"

"Absolutely. Just plain. You know how I like it?"

"I sure do. On it, boss." Her grin was saucy, and he was tempted to kiss it off despite knowing she wasn't likely to enjoy any more public displays. He'd been startled that she didn't shy away from his earlier kiss.

She scooted under the table and headed in search of coffee. Helpless to stop himself, he watched her go, fully enjoying the way her jeans cupped her derriere and the seductive sway of her hips.

"She's a lovely woman," Uma said.

"She is that."

"She's good for you. You've never been unhappy, but lately, since she arrived in town, you're fairly bursting with happiness. I'm happy for you."

"Thanks. I just hope she stays."

"I guess you'll need to give her a reason to stay." She elbowed him and went back to setting out the packages of cupcakes and muffins they were selling.

A reason to stay. The words echoed in his head, stealing some of his happiness but increasing his resolve. He'd find a way to keep her here. Somehow.

Chapter Twenty-One

Winter was astounded at the sheer volume of people in the park. Nick was at the other side of their tent, selling baked goods while she handled the free cookies. She gave a school child a maple-leaf cookie and a napkin. "Are you having fun?"

"Yes! I got a stuffed puppy." She waggled the blue dog in the air.

"Your puppy is adorable."

"Say, thank you," the child's mother advised.

"Thank you." Cookie crumbs exploded from her mouth with the words.

The mother smiled, repeated the thanks, and they stepped aside so the next person in line could take their place.

A pretty woman stepped forward. "Hi. Nick looks pretty busy. Can you give him a message for me?"

"Nick," she called over her shoulder, "this lady would like to talk to you."

"I'll just be a second."

"Oh my. I didn't want to distract him." She thrust out her hand. "I'm Belinda. I run the women's shelter ranch outside of town."

"A ranch in the mountains?"

Belinda laughed. "Yup. My husband inherited the land. We're not high up, and there's plenty of grazing for cows before the true hills start."

"And it's a women's shelter?"

Belinda stepped to the side before she answered. "It's for battered women and their children. To help them get back on their feet. After my husband passed, I wanted to do something for battered women, because a dear friend of mine was battered by her ex. After her husband died, I decided to open the shelter. It's been a lot of work, but after two years, I'm finally open."

"Amazing." Winter turned to the next person in line and handed them a cookie. "Hi. Happy Victoria Day. Don't forget to check out the other great treats we have for sale. The funds raised go toward an updated medical clinic. Enjoy your day."

"Belinda. Hi. How are you?" Nick stepped up beside Winter and greeted the woman with a big hug like he'd known her all his life. Something close to jealousy slipped down Winter's spine.

"Better than I have been. I know this isn't the time, but I'd like to talk to you about baking or cooking classes for my residents. I want to give them some life skills to carry forward when they leave us. I was thinking I could bring them to you?" She posed the idea as a question with a hope-filled voice.

"I'd love that. If you hang around a bit, we can work out some details."

"Oh, thank you. I'm back in town on Wednesday for my weekly shopping trip. Can we do it then?"

"Absolutely." He grinned. "That's probably easier than battling the crowds today." He offered his hand. "See you next week."

They shook as if they were making a deal. "Thanks so much, Nick. Nice to meet you." She smiled broadly at Winter. "Maybe I'll see you around?"

"That would be nice." There was something about Belinda that made Winter smile. Maybe it was the way Nick was completely professional with her that made the jealousy fade away in an instant.

"Well," Belinda declared, "I best find Natalie, or she'll never forgive me for being in town without saying hello." She waggled her fingers and walked away just as Uma and her husband arrived at the booth.

"Off you two go. Reuben and I have this handled. Enjoy a couple hours of freedom."

"Are you sure?" Nick smiled at Uma. "I could use a break."

"Shoo." She made a go-away motion with her hands. "Two full hours and not a second longer or less."

Winter threw her hands up in mock surrender. "Yes, ma'am. We'll go."

"Do something fun," Uma called as they walked away.

"Where to first?" Winter slipped her hand into Nick's. "How about something to eat?"

"How can you be hungry? I saw you snacking on the free cookies," he teased.

"I'm starving. Somehow," she gave him an accusatory stare, "I missed breakfast because someone kept me in bed."

"Ingrate." He laughed. "And it was you who kept *me* there. Let's hit the food trucks. I could go for a chili dog and onion rings."

"Wonderful. That sounds perfect." They walked along, shoulders brushing, dodging through the crowd. Peace washed over her. Being with Nick, doing something as simple as walking together, percolated feelings she'd never had before. Her nerves simmered like a pot about to boil...but in a good way.

The enticing aromas from the food trucks tickled her nose and the joyous calls from the festival guests were music to her ears. If the sheer number of people was any indication, they'd raise a ton of money for the new clinic. She was proud of the effort they'd made and the apparent success.

"Tell me about Belinda," she asked when they entered an area with a few less people.

"She's Natalie's friend. Nat was heading for Belinda's ranch when she was run off the road. Clint saved Nat and her son's lives. The rest, as they say, is history."

"I knew about Clint saving Nat. I was asking about Belinda."

"I know her from events at Clint and Nat's. Beyond that, all I know is that she's opened her ranch. She's running it from the insurance from her husband's passing, and inheritance from her parents. I'm not certain, but I think Nat funds it as well." His shrug was eloquent.

"I wonder if she'd want me to teach some self-defense classes?" The idea made her heart jump happily. "I mean for as long as I'm here."

Nick frowned.

Her joy vanished. "I'm sorry, Nick. I like you and what we have together, but I can't, no I won't, lie to you and say I'm staying. I don't make promises I can't keep." She gripped his arm until he looked at her.

"I'm giving you what I can. I hope that can be enough."

His brows pinched together and he pushed out a ragged breath. "Winter, I'm willing to take what I can get. No promises, no commitments." His smile was wobbly and fake. "Now, let's get you fed before you turn into a grouch."

He sprinted the last twenty yards to the food trucks. She recognized the attempt to outrun his feelings. She wished he realized this wasn't any easier for her. She raced after him, dodging people all the way.

They ate and visited every vendor, getting their event passes stamped at each one. "Are we even eligible to win?" she asked as they stood beside the local knitting group's display.

"I have no idea. You're on the committee."

"So are you!" She swatted effortlessly at his arm.

"I'll double-check with Grace. She's commander-in-chief of this *Operation*." He dropped the comment without cracking a smile.

"Oh, nice military reference. I thought you only did pop culture." She winked.

"I'll have you know...I'm a *Chess* master of puns." He draped a forest green scarf around her neck and turned to the lady manning the booth belonging to Haven's charity knitting group. They sold their products, and the funds or the items themselves went to different charitable organizations. "Matilda, I'll take this one."

"What? You can't buy me a scarf." She unwound it and set the incredibly soft item back on the table.

"Why not?"

"For one, it's not even winter."

"No, but you are."

She gaped at him for a moment and snapped her mouth shut so she wouldn't laugh at his play on words. His mind worked almost too fast to keep up with.

He draped the scarf back around her neck. "Accept it with good grace, Winter. Snow will be back, and wherever you are, I want you to think of me."

"I'll still be here in winter. It's only the end of May. I'm here until Aunt Murial gets back in March. That's nine months." *Nine months. Enough time to have Nick's baby. Her knees went weak. She was not going there. Not now. Not ever. No way.* But the image of herself holding a baby with Nick's sea-green eyes wouldn't stay away. *When had she started wanting children? This town was destroying her resolve to get her life in order. It chased away her dreams and tried to slide in new ones.*

She fingered the soft scarf. "It is a lovely scarf."

"Good. I'll get to see you use it."

"How much, Matilda?"

"For you, Nick, and for love...absolutely nothing." She pushed away the money he offered.

"Oh no. That's not right," Winter objected. "We're not in love."

"Fine then." The septuagenarian crossed her arms. "For the possibility of love."

"Isn't the money going toward the new clinic?" Nick asked, folding Matilda's fingers over the cash. Matilda nodded.

"In that case, here's a donation." Winter dropped a twenty onto the table. "Thank you both for the lovely scarf." She nodded decisively and walked away before anyone could object.

Behind her, Matilda said, "She's one good woman. You should keep her."

"I'm trying, Matilda. I'm trying. She's as elusive as the perfect crème brûlée."

A smile crept over Winter's face. There was something sweet and endearing about a man who wasn't afraid to admit publicly that he had feelings. Squeezing the scarf, she told herself she'd think of Nick every time she wore it.

She shouldn't have accepted it. It was just another way to lead him on. But how could she reject the chance to carry forward a lasting and tangible memory of today? She needed to stop seeing him. He was too much temptation, and he was laying siege to her heart.

·♥ · ♥ · ♥ · ♥ · ♥ ·

"I am baked." Nick dropped onto his sofa.

"Me too." Winter sat beside him. "I really should go home."

"No, you should stay and I'll make dinner." He shifted slightly to watch her. Ever since he'd given her the scarf, she'd been jumpy and keeping her distance.

She was quiet for so long that he wondered if she was looking for a way out of the invitation. "What do you say? Dinner and movie?" They could cuddle together, and he'd steal a few kisses. She kept saying she wasn't sticking around town, but as long as she was here, he'd keep courting her because he was one hundred percent certain she cared for him as much as he cared for her.

"I'll buy dinner."

"And stay for a movie?" He wasn't even embarrassed about the hope in his voice.

"Nick. Nick. Nick. Are you ever going to give up?"

"Winter. Winter. Winter. No."

Her abrupt laugh startled him.

"Fine. I'll stay, but I want to pick the movie. A Christmas movie."

"In May?" He'd watch anything if she stayed. "Fine. We'll watch a Christmas movie. Go ahead and order whatever you want to eat. I'm going to change."

Thirty minutes later, the food was ready, and they were sitting, side by side, eating and watching what turned out to be a rather romantic holiday movie. When they finished eating, he cleared the mess and sat back down beside her. Winter looked sleepy and as sexy as anyone he'd ever seen. He slipped his hand behind her neck and pulled her closer to his side. "Get over here," he whispered.

She sighed but cuddled up close. He kissed her cheek. She turned so their lips met, and before long, the movie was forgotten.

He'd been hoping to make love with her. He hadn't expected it, but he had hoped. Knowing she was leaving Haven...he stole the pleasure she so willingly gave and refused to think about her moving on.

Chapter Twenty-Two

The sun's heat was scorching through her long-sleeved T-shirt. She'd learned the hard way not to wear short sleeves outside all day. When she'd worked in Afghanistan, she'd been tanned nut-brown. In Alaska, she'd been nearly as white as the snow. Now, in Haven, after a long winter of rehab, she had a hint of a tan, but eight-hour days under the burning sun were too much for her still winter-pale skin. Though at this rate, she'd be tanned in no time.

"Hey, Winter," Mrs. Trench called from her front step. "Come onto the porch. Get out of that sun." She lifted a frosty glass in the air. "I've got iced tea."

Now, there was an offer she couldn't resist. After an hour of kneeling, going from bed to bed weeding Mrs. T's gardens, she rose carefully to her feet. She tucked her gloves into her pocket on her way to the deck.

"That looks divine." She climbed the steps. The shade's blessed coolness brought instant relief from the unrelenting heat. Who knew the mountains got this hot? Certainly not her.

"Young lady, I don't know why you push yourself so hard. You need to take more breaks." She passed over the sweating glass. "Sit, dear. Sit." She took a seat on the wooden rocker.

Winter sat on the adjacent porch swing. She hated to sit on it and risk getting it dirty. But every week, Mrs. T insisted that it was fine because the cushions hosed off with no damage. She chugged half the glass before her companion passed her a glass of water.

"Have some water and some cookies. I baked them this morning. Peanut butter chocolate bombs."

"Oh, I shouldn't." But how could she resist? Mrs. T used top-end milk chocolate drops in the center of each cookie. They were ooey-gooey goodness and utterly irresistible. She set her tea down and grabbed a cookie. Like the chair argument, fighting over cookies was a sure way to lose.

"You do make the best cookies, but really, you shouldn't have." Mrs. T wasn't old, probably in her mid-fifties, but she had a mothering gene as wide as the Rocky Mountains.

"Come now, spill the tea."

Hastily, Winter looked down. She hadn't spilled anything. "I'm sorry, what?"

Mrs. T laughed. "Come now. Spill the tea. Dish. What's the scuttlebutt? Catch me up on all the gossip. You must hear a lot being out and about every day. Start with you and Nick. How's that going? I see you walking together a lot."

Winter choked on a bite of cookie and sprayed crumbs over the deck. Mrs. T chortled.

"Um. Nick and I are just friends. There's no tea to spill." She stumbled over the unfamiliar expression. "Mostly, we spend time together because we're both single and all our friends are married." Not exactly a lie.

"Oh poo. That's not true. I see you together. He can't keep his eyes off you, and you're no better. You're as smitten with him as he is with you. Are you engaged yet?"

"Mrs. T, there's no engagement. There will be no wedding. We're friends." This was a new twist on their weekly conversation, and one she wasn't thrilled about. "Let's talk about you. Did I see you with Gypsy's great-grandson? He looks to be about your age, and he's quite handsome."

Mrs. T blushed. "First, call me Emily. I just bumped into him, Stetson, of all the silly names. He's just taken early retirement. He was an engineer. We had coffee, but only because there wasn't an empty table, so we had to share."

"Come now, Mrs.—Emily. You were together at ten when I grabbed a coffee, and you were still there at one when I picked up my lunch."

Her client straightened her shoulders. "He's a good conversationalist. He's a well-traveled man. He's lived all over the world." Her cheeks pinkened. "I'm too old for that sort of thing."

"Mrs. T, if there's one thing I know, you're never too old for love. My grandmother got remarried at eighty. Much to my father's disgust. He said it was 'unseemly', of all things."

Of course, her parents thought a lot of things were improper. Like the military. They fully supported the troops—as long as the troops were not their children. She shoved the negative thoughts away.

"I'm just saying, don't let fear hold you back." She bit back a snort at the hypocrisy of the comment. She was utterly terrified of embracing, or even admitting, the depth of her feelings for Nick.

Mrs. T was quiet for a while. "I might consider that. *If* you consider that what you have between you and Nick is more than friendship."

Great. Now, they were negotiating love. She nodded. "Fine." Mrs. T. smirked, and the conversation turned to the heat and Winter's other yardwork clients.

"How many yards are you doing a week?"

"Fifteen. I think I've reached my max. Unless I start working seven days a week, I can't take on any more."

"And you like it?"

"I do, but I'm not sure how I'll fill my time once winter comes. I need something more. I'm not sure I want to shovel snow all winter."

"Gracious, no! We get tons of snow here. In the 80s, we had twelve feet."

Winter rocked back in shock. She knew there was more snow high in the mountains but hadn't thought there would be that much. "Definitely not shoveling for a living." She laughed. "Thanks for the warning."

After a twenty-minute break, Winter stood. "Well, I better get this garden finished. I have plans tonight."

"Are you going to the movie with Nick?"

"I am. Tonight is *Raiders of the Lost Ark*. I haven't seen it in years." Once a month, the library held a movie night. This month, they were running an Indiana Jones festival. It was fun to join everyone for a night of food and snacks.

"Well, maybe I'll see you there. Stetson and I are going. *As friends*." She put a sly emphasis on the last two words.

"See you tonight, then. Thanks again for the rest and the treats. You don't have to feed me, but I do appreciate the time off my knees."

·❤·❤·❤·❤·❤·

She was late finishing up her mowing for the day, and by the time she arrived at the library with Nick, there were only two seats left in the far back corner.

"I told you we'd be late," Nick teased.

She jabbed him with an elbow. "Hush. It's starting. And we would have been on time if you hadn't insisted on feeding me."

"Well, I couldn't sit here all night and listen to your stomach growl, and there's no outside food in the library." They were sitting in the library's meeting room, which held up to a hundred people if you packed them in tightly enough. There were only sixty tickets available for each movie. Each ticket came with a bucket of popcorn and either a soda or water. There were also hotdogs and potato chips for sale. The events were fundraisers for more equipment and books.

"My stomach would not have growled. I ate two cookies today."

"Not enough food to survive on. That's why I fed you. Besides," he leaned in to whisper in her ear, "this way, we're almost hidden, and we can hold hands and cuddle.

She leaned into him. "Good point. Maybe you're smarter than you look."

The movie was just as fun and sappy as it had been the first time. The outrageous stunts and plot just made it more entertaining. Having Nick beside her was the cherry on top.

Twice, the librarian had to shush them for laughing too loud at Nick's outrageous comments and wordplay. Winter got in an amusing quip or two of her own. Before tonight, she hadn't thought of herself as funny. Maybe Nick's sense of humor was contagious.

For certain, she felt lighter and happier than she had in a long time. But lingering unease nibbled at the back of her mind.

Chapter Twenty-Three

In the unofficial parking area of Haven's second lake, Nick paused beside the box of his truck and studied Winter as her gaze traveled around the surrounding forest. Poplar and pines towered over them like sentinels guarding Mother Nature. It was early. The sun had barely risen, and the air was still cool. He was bundled up in his high-tech, weather-resistant hoodie. She looked lovely in her army green hoodie. He hoped she had something wind and rainproof with her. "Are you sure you want to do this?"

"I said I did, didn't I?" She stared right back at him. "I don't say things I don't mean. I said I'm good with camping for a few nights, and I am. Let's do this." She paused and raised her eyebrows like she was mocking him. "Unless you're having second thoughts."

"Definitely not. It's already late July, and I've only been camping once this year. And it sucked because Cam and Sterling had to leave early and left me to break camp alone."

"Aw. Poor little Nicky. Such a tough life."

Her laughter tickled down his spine. "Last time I did this, it took three days to get all the way around the lake. I've booked five days off work, just in case. That good for you?"

"Yes. I found a couple of teens to do my yards for me. We'll be fine." She shouldered her heavy pack and grunted. "I'm so out of shape. I used to be able to tote twice my body weight."

"I can take more."

"No." She curled up her nose in disgust. "I'll manage. It's not that bad." She waved toward the path. "Let's do this. I'm stoked. How much bigger is this lake than the one we went around this spring?"

"It's about four times as far. Give or take. Depending on fallen trees and any spring flooding, there may be slight detours. It will be cold because we're higher up. Nights can get chilly."

"I brought mitts and extra socks. I'm good to go. Why are we hanging out here and not hitting the path?"

Her tone was gruff, and he realized that over the past few months, she'd been much more cheerful. She'd even started making smart comments and dad jokes. He wondered why today was different. He studied her a moment longer, and with a mental shrug and decision to worry about it later, he waved toward the path. "Lead on."

With the sun only just rising, it was dark in the forest. Slowly, as they hiked west, the sun's light increased along with the temperature, though it was still cool in the shade. Neither said anything, instead, they stepped quietly and listened to the relative silence of the forest. There was no wind, and birds called to each other, their twittering sounds bright in the morning air. There was peace in the wordless companionship.

In the distance, an animal barked and yipped a few times before falling silent. "I wonder what that was." Winter pivoted back toward him as if asking for his opinion.

"If I had to make a guess, I'd say dog, though it might have been a coyote. Didn't sound right to be a wolf."

"Cool. Do I need to worry?" Her tone was casual.

"Probably not. But it's always good to be aware."

They followed the path for nearly two hours, the lake's water sparkling through the trees and underbrush. "I'm ready for a break," Nick said. "There's a nice spot by the water just around the next bend. It's rocky, but it will be sunny."

Winter impressed him with the way she walked along, offering occasional questions, and pointing out different things, like interesting mushrooms, pretty flowers, and once, a small deer family. She was very observant and snapped dozens of pictures with her phone.

They reached the spot he'd mentioned. A small stream ran into the edge of the lake. "You can drink the stream water. It comes from a spring twenty yards back." They had brought water and a water filter, but there were plenty of streams for cool, fresh water. "Granola bar?" he offered. They'd split their supplies into the two packs. His just happened to hold the snacks.

"Sure."

"How long are we walking today?"

"Tired already?"

"Nope. Curious."

"It's probably about eight hours, at a slow pace, with lots of breaks. I have a spot I'd like to camp. It's got a pretty meadow and lots of access to fallen trees for a fire."

"If we can have a fire, why did we bring the stove?"

He knew she was teasing, so he said, "Just so you had to carry extra weight."

She pitched a small rock at him that landed harmlessly at his feet. "Jerk."

·♥·♥·♥·♥·♥·

"It's beautiful here." Winter spun in a slow circle, taking in the details of their camping spot. There was even a ring of rocks on the gravel beach, about six inches across, for a fire pit. Someone had stacked a bunch of deadfall and sawn logs just under the edge of the trees. "Look, there's firewood."

"Yup. There usually is. A couple of guys from town like to come out and play with their chainsaws." He chuckled. "Apparently there aren't enough things to use them on in town. They camp and cut wood for fun. I usually gather a bunch myself. I like to leave a pile when I go. Just in case the next people need it."

Nick was so considerate. He was a clean hiker, even picking up the odd bit of garbage they'd seen on the path, and he provided treats for town events, helped neighbors move if they asked for help, and sometimes showed up when they didn't. Nick had been nothing but kind to her. Exactly the kind of man she'd be interested in. If she was looking.

"I'm going to try and catch a couple fish for dinner. There's nothing like pan-fried trout. Even a jackfish or pike is delicious. Want to join me?"

"I'll set up the tent and then meet you by the water." Her survival training wouldn't let her delay setting up shelter in favor of food. Especially when they had brought more than enough to get them through the short trip. Still, the thought of fresh fish had her salivating.

The tent went up in minutes, and she spread their thin foam mats and sleeping bags inside. She kneeled in the short dome and stared at the beds. Would they end up cuddling? It might be awkward in

LOVING WINTER AMAZON PRINT 189

the small space, and their bags were different so they wouldn't zip together. Still, the idea of being with Nick made her heart race.

"Woohoo." Nick's shout startled her. She jerked backward and tumbled onto her backside.

"What?"

"Got one! She's a beaut. Come look. It's big. I think we'll only need one."

They ate the trout with scalloped potatoes made from a dehydrated kit Nick had purchased from a friend who made his own travel meals. Surprisingly, the potatoes were as delicious as if she'd made them herself.

The sun was going down by the time they finished eating. She threw a few small sticks in the fire and settled down on a blanket against a log to watch the flames. She sat slightly sideways, her legs to the right of the small fire, her right shoulder against the log. Nick sat beside her, his shoulder just touching hers, his legs facing the opposite direction.

They both had a view of the flames dancing against the growing darkness. She could only see Nick if she cranked her head left. As night crept in, so did peace and contentment.

"I need more in my life," she blurted. Why did darkness bring out things you would otherwise not mention?

"Oh?"

Thankfully, he didn't turn to face her and ruin the emotional safety of the darkness.

"Do you ever wish there was more to your life?"

The fire crackled and popped into the silence that stretched between them. She'd begun to think he wasn't going to answer when he finally spoke. "No. I don't think so. I'm quite content. Sure, there are things I'd like to have that I don't have. But I'm happy and pretty content. How about you?"

She ignored his question and asked her own. "What don't you have?"

"I asked you first."

She tipped her head back until it rested on his shoulder. She stared up at the stars dotting the night sky. "Purpose." His head tipped back until it touched hers. It felt like he was asking her to say more.

"It's hard to explain." She took a moment to gather her scattered thoughts. "Doing yardwork is great exercise...but it's not enough. I spent every minute of my life, from the moment I turned eighteen until the IED blew us up, working. I lived for the service. Helping strangers. Protecting my country and my family. It was important."

"Yardwork is service, too. It's just a different kind."

"It's not enough." She sipped the hot cocoa he'd made before sitting with her. "I need more. Why can't Aunt Muriel come home early?"

"What would that change?" His tone was interested, but the words felt accusatory.

"I'd be free to go wherever I wanted."

"So, go. I'll watch her house for you. She's a dear friend of mine. I was watching it until you got here. Follow your dreams. Leave Haven." His voice had the snap of hurt and anger.

"I don't know what I want," she whispered. A tear streaked down her cheek. She wiped it away just as Nick turned to embrace her. He pivoted so his legs were beside hers and wrapped her in his arms, her back against his chest. Solid warmth washed over her and her fear and uncertainty faded.

She still didn't know what she was going to do with her life, but whatever she did, Nick would be there for her. At least until she left Haven.

Chapter Twenty-Four

A week later, after several quiet evenings with Nick, Winter finally made a decision. Now, she shifted impatiently as she waited for the realtor to unlock the door of the vacant shop just down from the bakery. *This is a mistake. You're getting yourself in too deep. You aren't staying in Haven. Don't put down roots you can't pull out.*

"Come on in. It's dusty and needs a coat of paint, but I think you'll like it." Mary-Beth Rivers held the door wide open and waved Winter in. "It's been vacant for years. I've been a realtor in Haven for five years, and it's been empty all that time."

"Is it for sale, or rent?"

The light flicked on, illuminating the small space, and her questions piling up in her head vanished like mist in the wind. There was a bar height, ornate wooden cash desk near the front, and several shelves down the sides of the fifteen-foot-wide space. Near the back, a cooler with sliding doors towered over everything and created a division between the front and back areas.

Her heart skipped a beat. It was perfect for a plant and flower shop.

"What used to be here?"

"A catering company. The back room was a small industrial kitchen, but the appliances are gone. They used the cooler for food, but it could be easily adapted for your purposes. Back to your earlier question: it is for rent or purchase. I've contacted the owner who left town years ago. You'll be responsible for half of the utilities if you rent. If you decide to buy, sixty percent of your rent will be deducted from the purchase price."

"Wow. I wasn't expecting that." She walked into the back of the shop, where the kitchen had been, to see how much work it needed. Rent to own was perfect. She wasn't committed to owning a building, but when she left town next year, she could sell her supplies, or just abandon everything.

She winced when she thought about leaving.

Winter, this isn't about the long term. This is about making some money and feeling useful. Mowing lawns and watering flowers was lovely work, but it wasn't fulfilling enough. At least not for her.

She needed more, and flowers brightened her heart. She'd been putting together arrangements with the spring flowers in her garden, just for practice. They weren't blooming well yet, it had only been a few weeks since she planted them, but with the help of videos and fake flowers she'd ordered online, she was getting the hang of it.

Aside from a battered stainless-steel work surface in the center of the room, the rear space was empty. The walls were pale blue with large unpainted gaps where the appliances must have been.

"I can work with this. It's clean enough, but it needs paint."

"And I'd recommend a fire inspection. I'll get the owner to start on that if you are interested." She checked her tablet and told Winter the price of the rent and the average utility costs. "Of course, those costs are for no electric use, and basically no heat. There are two parking spots out back. There is an apartment upstairs. It's accessed by a staircase outside and rented to the grade three teacher. Of course, unless you buy the building, having a renter doesn't affect you." She paused for a moment.

Winter walked around the back area, planning how to use the space, and returned to the front. With a coat of paint, a few tables, shelves, and a cash system, she'd be ready to go. She twisted her hands together, uncertain if she was ready to take such an enormous step. She was torn between wanting to be more productive and not setting down roots.

"What do you think?"

For a moment, fear consumed her. Her mind rolled through her life and potential futures, both in Haven and elsewhere. A sense of rightness washed over her. Opening a shop was a step, a temporary one, but it was the right one.

"I'll take it. Just renting for now, but with the option to purchase later."

"Wonderful. Let's go to the office and do the paperwork. I'll see about immediate access so you can get set up. Painting and such takes time. I've got the number of the local refrigerator repair guy. He'll check out that cooler for you."

· ♥ · ♥ · ♥ · ♥ · ♥ ·

Winter sat beside Lisa, across from Grace's tidy desk in the bookshop.

"What's up? What can I help you with?" Grace straightened the single stack of paper on her desk to align with the top left corner.

"I need advice." She swallowed hard and looked back and forth between her friends. "I just did a thing. I mean...I rented the old catering shop. I'm opening a flower shop, and frankly, I have no idea where to start running a business." She was giddy with excitement and shaking with nerves.

Grace leaped up and rounded the desk. She threw her arms around her friend. Lisa threw her arms around them both. "Oh my gosh," Grace exclaimed.

"That's so exciting. I'm glad you're staying in Haven." Lisa squeezed tighter.

"Um. I'm not."

Grace didn't hide her confusion. "You're opening a business but not staying? How does that work?" She perched on the edge of her desk. "I know you didn't plan to move here..."

"I didn't. I'm here until my aunt gets back. But I need to be productive, and this is a way to do it. The shop has nearly everything I need, except inventory. Startup won't be too costly. And maybe by the time I leave, there'll be someone around who is interested in buying it."

Lisa dropped back into her chair. "It's just weird. At least to me. No offense."

Why were the words that came with the statement 'no offense' always offensive?

"It's okay if you don't understand. I'm doing what I feel I need to do, to stay sane while I'm here. I'm accustomed to being busy. There's no downtime in the service. Haven needs a flower shop. I like flowers. It all meshes perfectly."

"Well, when you say it like that...I think I get it. Congratulations. What are you going to call it?" Grace sounded genuinely excited.

"I'm thinking. Blooming Perfect." She frowned. "It sounds silly when you say it aloud. Is that too corny?"

"You're asking the owner of The Book Nook? Of course not. Our jokester friend will love that it's a pun. Have you told Nick?"

"Not yet."

"Told me what?" Nick's voice came from behind her, and she jumped guiltily.

"Nick. Hi."

He raised a tray of coffee. "Hi. I saw you from across the street. I brought you ladies coffee and butter tarts." He set the tray down and handed them each a cup. "What didn't you tell me yet?"

Her friends looked like they wanted to crawl away and hide.

Shoot. She'd wanted more time to formulate how to tell him. She hated going into conversations, especially important ones, without adequate preparation. A good soldier was always armed with the proper procedure. Now, she found herself flat-footed.

Nick looked at her, a thousand questions in his eyes.

She didn't want to get his hopes up or crush him.

"I'm renting the old catering place. For the rest of my time in Haven, what's left of it that is, I'm going to run a flower shop. Until I leave in the spring."

"That's fabulous. Congratulations!"

"You aren't upset?"

Grace snuck between them and left the office with her coffee and a tart in hand. Lisa was hot on her heels.

"Why in the world would I be upset? You love flowers. You always have them at your place. You've given me several houseplants, and your aunt's are thriving under your care. I'm glad you've found something you want to do. This is amazing."

"I'm not staying." She had to be sure he understood.

"So, you've said. Repeatedly." His voice cracked. "I'm still happy for you." He smiled widely, but it didn't reach his eyes.

"Do you want to see it?"

"Of course! Were you finished with Grace and Lisa?"

"Oh. No. I'll meet you at the bakery if you have the time this morning. Shall we say eleven hundred hours?"

"See you in an hour." He leaned in and brushed her lips with a kiss. "Congratulations, Winter. I know you'll be amazing at this. You've got the drive and the discipline to run a successful business." He winked and walked out.

Her friends came back in as if they'd been waiting outside, giving her and Nick privacy. "He took that well."

"I think he's hiding his true feelings, but I appreciate that he's trying to be happy for me. Back to why I popped in, got any advice on getting started?"

"So much advice," Grace said. "First, set up your social media and ask Havenites what their favorite flower is. You might as well open shop knowing what they prefer."

The trio launched into a planning session. She was late getting to the bakery for Nick's tour.

·♥·♥·♥·♥·♥·

Nick trudged alongside Winter to her store. "You're going to be great at this."

"You don't sound like you mean that." She unlocked the door and went inside. The owner had given immediate access, rent-free, for the rest of the month. It was barely two weeks, but it would allow her time to get set up, if she hurried, by Canada Day.

"Honestly, Winter, I'm trying, really trying, to be happy for you. I am thrilled and excited that you are following your dream, albeit a temporary one. But knowing you still plan to leave me hurts. Give me some time to figure out what's going on in my head. And my heart."

His words floored her. *Did he care that much?* They were still sleeping together on occasion. *Did he want it to be more? Was he upset about losing his bed partner, or her, the person?* She blinked back a tear. "I can do that." She turned on the lights. "What do you think?"

He looked around. "You know, if you painted those shelves white and the walls a sunny yellow, it would be really cheerful in here. It's perfect for a flower shop. Is it going to be big enough?"

"It is. There's room in the back for storage and making arrangements. I'll put in a couple of grow lights back there for an overstock of live plants. I'll sell plants on these shelves and keep the arrangements and single stems in the cooler." She pointed to the items as she talked.

"You could do a red and white theme for Canada Day if you're open by then. When do we start painting?"

"We?" *Was he offering to help?* It sure sounded like he was.

"Of course I mean we. You can't do this all alone. We'll have to run to the city for paint." The local hardware store was small and didn't do much business in paint. He pulled out a tape measure. "Let's figure out how much you'll need."

Chapter Twenty-Five

Winter was rolling the last of the paint on the front walls when someone pounded on her window. She set her roller down, lowered the volume of the radio, and peeked past the paper covering the front window.

Nick.

She'd been painting for a week and was on the final coat. Nick had made a habit of stopping by on his way home from the bakery every day to check on her progress and to walk her home. The day had gone so fast that she didn't even realize the time. It must be after six, or he wouldn't be here.

She flipped the latch and pushed the door open. "Is it that time already?"

"It sure is. Get cleaned up. We're going out for dinner with Grace and Sterling."

"What's wrong with what I've got on?" She waved at the paper jumpsuit that covered her clothing and the plastic shower cap that covered her hair.

He stepped in and kissed her cheek. "Was that a joke? I'm shocked. But seriously, there is absolutely nothing wrong with that outfit. You look stunning. You're perfect as you are. But I'm guessing Sid's doesn't allow paper garments." His wink stole her breath.

As much as she loved being with him, she was getting in too deep, and it was beginning to hurt to think about leaving him. She couldn't stop a frown.

"I was just going to go home and chill. I'm exhausted." She wasn't but hated to beg off without a reason.

"We planned this last week. Don't you remember? It'll be fun. We won't stay long. Just dinner and then home to rest." He put a slight emphasis on rest, implying that there might be other bedroom activities.

Heat flooded her body, then her face.

"Get your mind out of the gutter...it's stepping on mine."

"I am so tired. I guess I can go, but you have to promise, no baking puns." She shook her painty finger at him.

"Hey, I can't help myself. Baking puns pop up when you *yeast* expect them."

"You did not go there." Shaking her head, she picked up the roller and headed for the industrial sink she'd added in the back room. "Let me clean up my tools first."

"Good plan. Every *Operation* needs clean tools."

She glared at him over her shoulder and turned away before he could see her smile. "Bring that can of paint, please." It took fifteen minutes to clean everything to her satisfaction. "I'm so glad to be done with this outfit." She balled up her coverall and shoved it into the garbage. "There's as much tape as paper on this thing." She'd patched a dozen rips over the past few days.

As they walked to Sid's after going home to change, Nick's hand brushed hers twice before he finally tangled their fingers together.

It felt so right, but she reminded herself that she wasn't getting attached. Not to Haven, not to the people who lived there, and especially not to Nick Blackstone. Her phone chimed, and she paused to look at the screen. She swiped the screen and put it back in her pocket.

"Not going to answer that?"

"It's not important. I can call them back." *Or not.*

He squinted at her like he thought she was odd. She ignored the guilt that followed his appraisal.

Grace and Sterling were approaching the restaurant from the other direction as they arrived. "Evening." Grace greeted Winter with a hug. Nick and Sterling shared a solid handshake.

"I reserved a table last week." Nick held the door open for everyone to enter. He always held the door for her and for everyone they were with. It wasn't a big gesture; it wasn't anything more than common courtesy. The fact that he never failed to do so made it seem like more than it was, and it never failed to make her feel special.

"Thank you." She squeezed his fingers and tugged him in behind her. When she tried to release his fingers, he clung tight until he pulled out her chair at the table. Once she was seated, he took the chair beside her and squeezed her hand one last time before turning his attention to their friends.

Losing that touch shouldn't have hurt, but it did.

"How is the painting going?" Grace asked.

"I just finished the final touch-ups, and just in time. I get my shelves and tables for the back room tomorrow morning, and the first shipment of stock arrives in the afternoon. The non-perishables. The plant pots and hangers. Plant food, and some trinkets. That sort of stuff. Wednesday, I get my plants, and I'll be ready to open Thursday before Canada Day. I'm super excited." Beyond excited, but it wasn't her way to spew her emotions in public.

"That's wonderful," Grace exclaimed. Do you need help with anything? I can spare some time tomorrow."

"Me too." Nick smiled. "My *Life* is yours. Working together, we can *Beat the Clock* and get everything done."

She chuckled at his wordplay, though she'd heard the clock pun too many times. Funny how she had slowly gotten used to his ways and started to enjoy his goofy mannerisms. She swallowed a sigh. He'd gotten under her skin. Leaving him and all the other Havenites was going to be hard; she'd make memories and enjoy her time with them while she was here. She pushed away the mood and forced herself to be cheery.

"Thanks for the offer, Grace. I'm not sure how long everything will take, but feel free to stop by anytime. If nothing else, you can keep me company while I work. What are your plans for the long weekend?"

"A sale, of course," she chuckled. "Focusing on children's books this time. I like to have a theme. Nick's making me dinosaur cookies. So, of course, all dinosaur books will be on sale. Plus, ten percent off orders over sixty dollars."

"Doesn't that cut into profits?"

"You'd think so, but people often round up just to get the discount; in the end, I come out ahead. And by more than you'd think." She shrugged eloquently. I'm getting the hang of this bookstore thing."

Sterling nudged Grace with his elbow. "Don't be modest. You're doing fabulously. I've seen the books."

Grace flushed and smiled, obviously flattered by her husband's praise.

They talked business while they ate their main courses, and then the discussion turned to family and summer plans.

"Is your family coming out to see you this summer?" Nick asked.

"Probably not." Winter winced. "We don't talk much."

"What a shame. Why is that?" Grace asked, her voice filled with concern.

Winter sighed. She knew this topic would come up eventually. She just didn't want it to be now. Or ever. "Let's call it a difference of opinion and leave it at that. Okay?"

"Is it something you can work out or that we can help with?" Nick stroked her hand, which was balled into a fist on her thigh.

"No." She pushed some thoughts around before she spoke again. "They didn't approve of my decision to join the service." Her friends made sounds of disbelief. "They support the military, but not me being in the service. They wanted me to go into the family business. I'm not cut out for that."

"Cut out for what?" Sterling asked.

She sipped her water and wondered where the waitress was. She could use a stiff shot of something right about now. "Office work. Corporate fundraisers. Parties with politicians. That stuff."

"What do they do?" Grace's voice was kind.

Here we go. Knowing who and what her family was would change everything. She didn't want to talk about it but had the feeling they'd persist until she did. "My maternal grandmother inherited a bit of money." Like, multi-billions of dollars. "She wanted to put the money to good use so she started a charity. When you have that much money, the interest alone is substantial and hard to spend."

"Wow," Nick murmured.

"Ya. Anyway, after she passed on, my parents took over the company. They'd both been working there. My brother works for them as well."

"What does your charity do?" Grace smiled like she felt bad for asking.

"Not my charity. Their charity. Don't get me wrong," she waved her hand like it would help them understand how she felt. "I fully believe in what they do. I just don't want to work there. I'm not a sit at your desk person. I'm a doer." She swallowed the anger that built in her heart every time she thought about the business. "They build housing for those who can't afford homes. There's a whole process to be approved for a unit in their developments. People live there rent-free or at reduced rates, depending on their circumstances. It allows them to save for their own places. The charity also builds and sells homes, at a discount, to the same people when they have the resources to purchase."

"That's incredible," Nick enthused. "And you don't want to work there?"

"No. I do not. I need to be active. I can't sit at a desk all day. According to my mother, 'It would be unseemly' to work on site. So, I went my own way and joined the service. Now that I'm injured, they're nagging me to come back to the business. They'll double down if they find out I'm discharged."

"You didn't tell them?" Grace frowned.

Winter shook her head. Beneath the table, Nick stroked her thigh. The touch calmed the edge of her hurt and anger. "I'd just as soon not tell them, or see them and continue the same old argument. I want to be me. The way I want to, and they don't understand that, so I keep my distance."

"That's very sad." Nick patted her leg again. "I'm not close with my family, but we're not estranged. I admire your dedication to serving our country, and to sticking to your guns about your life."

For a moment she wondered if the guns reference was yet another pun or military reference, then decided it didn't matter. She clapped her hands. "Anyway, I'm ready for dessert." The discussion was dropped, though the intermittent and slightly awkward silence as they ate tiramisu was a clear hint that their thoughts were stuck on family dynamics.

Rather than argue over the tab, Sterling paid for himself and Grace, and Winter paid for herself and Nick. He objected until she reminded him that it was her turn. They'd started taking turns paying when they went out or ordered in.

"I'll walk you home," Nick said, pulling her chair out for her.

"You literally have to pass her house on your way home." Sterling laughed. "Don't try and make it sound all magnanimous, dude." He slapped Nick on the back.

"I'd walk her home if it were two miles in the other direction. Get a *Clue*."

"So, if I lived two-point-one miles away, I'd be on my own? Nice, Nick. Very nice."

"That's not what I said!" he blustered. "Fine then," he faked hurt feelings. "Walk yourself home. I'll just walk half a block behind." Laughing, they headed out together.

Nick didn't make her walk home alone. They chatted and strolled along. Twice he tried to capture her hand, but she deftly avoided his grip. He walked her to her door, kissed her cheek, and stood there until she was inside. Her dreams were filled with things she couldn't have. Like a life in Haven, Nick, kids. She pushed the thoughts aside and climbed into bed.

Chapter Twenty-Six

As if avoiding his hand after dinner with Grace and Sterling hadn't been hard enough, Nick continued to meet her at her shop on his way home every night. They walked home together. It was growing harder and harder to avoid him. And she didn't want to. But if she was going to do her time in Haven and then move on to do something useful with her life, she couldn't risk getting any closer to him. She cared for him too much to hurt him unnecessarily.

The last Wednesday in June, she tossed and turned in bed, unable to sleep. At four-fifteen, she gave up and got in the shower. It was hours before the grand opening of Blooming Perfect, but she had too much on her mind to sleep.

She was pacing the living room, sipping her third cup of coffee when she heard whistling outside. She peeked through the blinds. Nick. He must be headed to work. On impulse, she raced to the front door and called out to him. "Hey, Nick. Wait up. I'll walk you to work."

"Morning, beautiful."

"Morning." She grabbed her keys, locked up, and hurried down the sidewalk.

"You're up early. Excited for the launch?" He draped his arm over her shoulder, tugged her close, and brushed his lips across her cheek. "You smell amazing."

She leaned into him briefly before pulling away. "Thanks. I am excited. And worried. What if nobody shows up? What if this is a bust? What if there isn't enough business for a flower shop?"

"Isn't that why you added some gift items and souvenirs?"

"Yeah..." she trailed off.

"Come on. All your friends will come to support you. Plus, Haven is crawling with tourists visiting the lake and hiking in the mountains. It's the start of our busiest season."

His calm tone smoothed the edges of her anxiety. "I can't rely on my friends to keep me in business. This was a huge mistake."

He stopped, grabbed her shoulders, and gently pivoted her to face him. "Look at me, Winter. This is not a mistake. The grocery store can't keep enough flowers in stock to meet Haven's needs. The town needs this. Add your gift items, and you'll do great."

He caught her gaze and looked into her eyes for a full minute before continuing. "I know that you don't feel you do enough. It must be very hard to replace the feeling of usefulness that serving in the military gave you. This need is genuine, and by filling that need, you are useful, just differently than you were before. My only concern here is that you don't overdo it and strain that knee. I notice how you limp slightly when you've overworked, or have stayed on it too long."

She ducked her head, touched that he'd seen her so clearly. "You're good for my ego." She grabbed his hand and tugged him forward. "Let's get you to work. I need a muffin."

It was all she could do not to squirm under his long, hard assessment.

"If you want a muffin, I'll give you one. Though it'll take at least an hour. I have some cookies that might fill the gap while you wait."

"What about a breakfast sandwich instead?" As much as she loved cookies, the pure sugar mightn't be the best idea when she was nervous.

His laugh rang out through the quiet morning, startling some chickadees into flight. "Fine. I'll make a sandwich while the oven preheats for my bread." He'd told her several times about his method of overnight proofing so the bread was perfectly risen to pop into the oven first thing every morning.

An hour later, sated by her breakfast and two cups of coffee, she sat on a tall stool in the kitchen, watching him work.

"You're very quiet. Still thinking about the opening? It's going to be a game changer for Haven."

She shrugged. Her thoughts were deeper than that. "I'm thinking about a lot of stuff." More than she'd ever admit. Like how much she loved watching him work. How much she'd miss him when she moved on. Plus, his earlier assurances that her store was a useful endeavor kept ringing in her ears because she couldn't quite believe he was right, though part of her wanted to believe. She was like a child learning there was no Santa. She wanted to believe, but deep down, she knew she couldn't. The shop was nothing more than a lark, a boondoggle, a fun way to pass the time.

Of course, it could have interfered with her yardwork clients, but they had all agreed to let the two university students she had hired do the job under her supervision. She'd gotten popular in the past month and had too much work for one person but not enough for two. Luckily, the boys were willing to work part time.

He gave her a puzzled look, then washed and dried his hands. Two quick steps had him standing in front of her. He grasped her fingers in his. "Your hands are like ice." He blew onto her fingers. The intimate act sent shivers up her spine. She was going to miss him when she moved on.

"Calm down, Winter. You're going to do well. Honestly, I think you'll do amazing. Will you be as busy as a city shop? Probably not. But Haven needs this and I can see your passion for flowers and growing things, which I expect comes from seeing so much destruction during your tours of duty." He shook his head. "Sorry, sidetracked my own thoughts." He chuckled.

He squeezed her hands lightly and looked right into her eyes. "Blooming Perfect is going to do well because you are filling a need."

The soft assurance in his gaze stabilized something inside her. Maybe she could do this. She squeezed his hands back. "Thanks, Nick. It means a lot that you support me."

"And I will support you by being your first customer. As soon as Uma gets here, I'm coming down to buy a plant for the front window. I've thought about getting one for a long time, but now that I know someone with the skills to help me keep it alive, I'm diving in with something tall and green."

She laughed at his self-mockery. "I can do that." She tugged her hands free. "I guess I should go and get set up. There isn't much to do, but I think I'll feel better if I'm ahead of the game."

Nick pulled her into his arms and placed a gentle kiss on her forehead. "You'll do great, Winter. Ironic that Winter is bringing flowers to town. I guess Mother Nature doesn't have a *Monopoly* on growing things." He smirked.

She swatted his shoulder. "Ugh. Enough wordplay and game references." She smiled.

"You love them, they make me irresistible."

He wasn't wrong, but she sure wasn't going to admit it. "Dream on, Blackstone. Dream on."

"Your lack of humor *Boggles* me. It's got me all *Scrabble*-d up."

"You are irrepressible."

"And fun too. Now, can I get you a coffee for the road?" He stepped back and helped her into her light jacket.

"No. I'm good for now. I've already had five cups, but if you wanted to bring me one later, I'd appreciate it."

"As you wish. Though I can't believe you aren't vibrating from all the caffeine."

She followed him to the front door and stepped outside. She was thirty feet away when he shouted, "You've got this, Winter. You'll be great."

She sure hoped he was right!

· ♥ · ♥ · ♥ · ♥ · ♥ ·

The sound of low voices tickled Winter's ears as she headed from the back room toward the front of the store. Ten seconds to opening. There was no reason she hadn't opened a few minutes early, except fear. The door was tinted to block the sun, and she'd pulled the window blinds closed, not wanting anyone to peek until she opened. She envisioned the opening as being like a surprise gift. No peeks until the last second.

Steeling herself with a calming breath, she flipped the deadbolt. Immediately, the door was pulled open from outside.

"About time," Grace chided with a smile that lit her entire face. We've been waiting. She threw her arms around Winter. "I'm so excited for you. Congratulations. I'd have brought you a bouquet to celebrate your opening, but the flower shop was closed." She winked. "I got you this instead." She thrust a package of the high-end chocolates she sold in her shop into Winter's hands. "Congrats."

"Um. Thank you." She smiled so broadly it hurt her cheeks as a dozen people filed in, each congratulating her on her opening. Several brought small gifts. In minutes, the shop was buzzing with conversation and people asking questions about the house plants and flowers she carried.

Surprisingly, there were unfamiliar faces among her friends. Total strangers who must be from out of town, and locals whose names she didn't yet know.

Her first sale was a pretty floral mug and a box of specialty tea. The morning flew by in a sea of congratulations and sales. Before she could catch her breath, Nick strolled in looking entirely too handsome and smug. He stepped up to the end of her cash desk and slid a takeout box and cup on the end. "I was by earlier with coffee, but I couldn't get in the door. I hit Sid's and grabbed lunch for you." He looked around. "Man, it's busy."

"This is quiet," she whispered, half afraid to say the words aloud. "I can't believe how many people came out." The tiny chime over the door rang out as another person came in. She greeted them with a smile.

"Why don't you eat and I'll help out."

Since her computerized sales system was the same as his, she agreed. Leaning back against the counter, she dove into the chicken caesar salad he'd brought. It was exactly what she wanted, and she gobbled it up quickly. Now that the stress of potentially failing on her first day was over, she was ravenous.

As she watched Nick joking and teasing with her customers, a sweet sense of peace and belonging crept over her. Clichéd though it might be, she felt like she'd found a safe haven here in Haven. She pushed aside thoughts of leaving. She had almost nine full months before her aunt returned and the future once again became something she had to deal with.

Charlie Lindburg, the new owner of Haven's online newspaper, popped in, snapped a few pictures, and asked for a video interview.

Initially, she balked. Wanting to avoid publicity was part of why she refused to join her parent's charity.

"Why not do the interview," Nick suggested. "It might gain you a few new customers. Think of it as free advertising."

From a business perspective, it made sense. From a personal one, it terrified her. Okay, Ireland, you've faced down insurgents and terrorists, and survived an IED. You can handle half a dozen questions from a small-town reporter. Mentally braced, she turned to Charles. "Where do you want to do this?"

"Away from the windows because the sun's too bright over there." She'd opened the blinds after unlocking the door, wanting her plants to get the sun's full benefit.

"How about back here, by the cooler? It's light enough, and the flowers will make a nice backdrop." She waved toward the cooler.

"Perfect." They walked over together. "My wife will video us while we talk. I'll ask a few questions. Don't worry if you need time to think. I can edit out any pauses or mistakes."

He ensured his wife was recording and began with a few simple questions which were easy to answer. Then he started getting more personal. "What brought you to Haven?"

"I'm recuperating my knee after an injury. I thought this would be a nice way to pass my time. It's good to stay active." The questions went on and on, she did her best to keep her answers pleasant and generic. She didn't want anyone to trip onto the fact that her family was stupid rich, or as her military brothers said, her family had "F-you" money.

Finally, she was done answering questions. "Look, I appreciate the interview, but I have customers, and it looks like Nick is having some trouble." He wasn't, but that was irrelevant. "Can we finish up?"

He did a quick wrap-up, thanked her, and left.

Between bouts of busyness, she fretted over whether or not doing the interview had been wise. She voiced her concerns aloud.

Nick squeezed her hands. "Maybe it'll go viral and you'll become famous and bring a ton of business to Haven. Wouldn't that be awesome?"

The words hit home like fists. Her head went light and she swayed on her feet. If this went viral, her parents might see it. Dread settled over her shoulders like a lead shroud. "Let's hope not." She turned away from his puzzled, questioning expression, unwilling to answer any questions or discuss her fears.

Chapter Twenty-Seven

When a full month had passed and her parents didn't appear, Winter began to relax. Business was booming in the shop and her yardwork clients were all happy. Her physio was going great and the only pain left in her knee came from overdoing things.

"Morning, Nick," she called out as she entered the back door of the bakery. The air was delicious with the scent of fresh baked bread and cinnamon. The kitchen's warmth was a blessing after the cool morning breeze. She couldn't wait for the full heat of summer to arrive.

"Morning, Winter. Beautiful day, isn't it?" He glanced at her over his shoulder and turned back to spooning batter into muffin papers.

"It is. A bit cool, but still very nice. The clouds are amazing. I have a question for you."

"Ask me anything. I'm an open book. I'll be done in two shakes. Why don't you grab us a couple coffees?"

By the time she shed her sweater, poured coffee, and came back to the kitchen, he was sliding the muffins into the oven. "What can I do for you?" He dropped his oven mitts onto the counter.

"I have to go to the city tomorrow, for a check on my knee. I was wondering..." she trailed off, suddenly feeling insecure about asking him to join her.

"I'd love to come. There's a new supply store I want to check out. I mean, if you have time."

Laughter bubbled out of her. "That's what I was going to ask...if you wanted to join me. My appointment is early, ten am, so we'd have to be on the road in the wee hours. I thought a second set of eyes might be nice as deer can be active then."

He clutched his chest. "And here I thought it was my wit and amazing personality that you were after. I'm heart broken."

"Keep it up, funny man and I'll leave you at home."

He dropped to his knees. "Please, ma'am. Don't leave me. I'll be good. I swear it. Plus, getting up early is kind of what I do. I'm perfect for watching the road. Or, I could drive and let you sleep. I know you're like *Sleeping Beauty* and like to snooze all day."

"We'll leave at four-thirty. Can you get someone to watch the bakery for you?"

"I'm sure Uma won't mind the extra hours. I'll let you know once she comes in today. How about Blooming Perfect? Who's minding the store?"

"Lisa will be working for me. She's free because the restaurant at the garage is closed down for kitchen renos starting tomorrow. The timing couldn't be better for me."

"That's right. I knew that. Clint put in a large bakery order to keep people looking for snacks happy while they're closed."

"You just forgot that?" she teased.

"Naw. I'm ready. It's mostly cookies anyway. They're baked and packaged for individual sale. Same with some muffins. I'm ahead of the game. I'm so far ahead that I've got time for dinner and a movie tonight. Want to join me for some takeout and television? There's a *Star Trek* marathon on cable."

"That's the one with the Wookie, right?" She tried to bank her laughter and it came out as a snort.

"Funny. Very funny. That, as you well know, is *Star Wars. Star Trek* is Kirk and company. I find your lack of knowledge of old pop culture disturbing."

"Actually, I'm more of a Captain Archer fan. Kirk gets around too much. But either way, I'm good for a quiet evening." More than good. She'd love to sit beside him and she sure wouldn't object if they ended up spending the night together. It had been too long since their last time.

·♥·♥·♥·♥·♥·

Nick rolled over in bed and stared down at the beautiful woman sleeping beside him. He'd never get enough of watching Winter sleep. She was lovely with her long lashes resting against her cheeks. Her perpetual frown was replaced by a small smile that he wanted to kiss.

In the brief time they'd known each other, they'd spent half a dozen nights together. Not nearly enough for his liking, but he didn't want to push too hard and scare her away. She seemed to be warming up to Haven, probably more than she'd ever admit, but she was still skittish when the subject turned to the future.

He'd marry Winter today, and would have a week after meeting her. There was so much about Winter to love. Her intelligence. Her cute figure, her lovely black hair, her serious demeanor, her caring personality. Her dedication to her country. Even her skittishness was attractive. The only thing that bothered him about Winter Ireland was her troubles with her family. It wasn't right. They should accept her for who she was.

Her eyes fluttered open. "You're thinking very hard." She sounded sleepy. "Want to talk about it?"

"No, I'd rather kiss you."

"Is that the *game* plan?"

"Mm." He brushed his lips over hers. They were still slightly swollen from last night's lovemaking. "Two kisses. Then a shower, and we have to go."

"What about kisses in the shower?" She rolled away from him and off the bed.

He caught up with her in the bathroom.

Half an hour later, she was pulling on her jeans. "We probably should have stuck to those two kisses."

"It's not my fault that your naked body is irresistible." He nuzzled her neck until she pulled away. He trailed his fingers over the satiny softness of her neck and down her arm as he stepped away to get dressed. He was not ready to walk away from the delights they'd just shared, but if she was going to make her appointment, they had to get going. "We'll be picking this up where we left off as soon as we get back."

She blew him a kiss but didn't comment. But then, she never did comment when he made emotional remarks, especially when they referred to the future. She was fine with physical intimacy but avoided all things emotional. He walked to the chair where he'd left his jeans last night and rubbed the sudden pain in his chest.

"Are you okay?" She stepped to his side.

"Heartburn. I should eat something." He winced at the lie. Lying didn't come easy to him. "I'll grab a banana on the way out. I'll be fine."

She squinted at him, disbelief clear on her face. "Nick? Are you having a heart attack? Chest pain?"

"No." At least not the type she meant. He slid into his jeans and a clean henley. "Get your clothes on and run home to change before I do something that will make us even later. He waggled his eyebrows suggestively. "We can take my truck. It's a bit newer than yours."

"There is nothing wrong with my truck." Her voice was muffled by the T-shirt she was pulling over her head.

"I didn't say there was. But my seats are more comfortable, and my box is covered." He grinned when she glared at him. She was very owly today. He swatted her backside. "Meet me at the truck. I'll pack snacks." Working in the bakery he liked to taste everything he baked and had grown accustomed to nibbles here and there all day. He grazed like a cow rather than having breakfast and lunch most days.

Three hours into their five-hour trip, he gave up on trying to engage her in conversation. She answered every question with a single word.

"You aren't worried about my heartburn, are you? It's really no big deal."

"No. I believe you." She turned to look out the side window where trees and hills were giving way to flatter ground.

"Want to tell me what's going on in your head? You're awfully quiet this morning."

"I'm just tired. I didn't get much sleep last night."

That was on her as much as it was on him. She certainly hadn't objected to his advances and met each of his kisses with growing ardor. Something had shifted between waking and getting into the truck.

"Why don't you sleep?" He caught her shrug out of the corner of his eye. After passing two semis, he turned to glance at her. Her head was back and her eyes closed. She wasn't asleep, her body was rigid and her fists clenched. Something must really be eating at her. He debated leaving her to her fake nap and decided against it.

"You must be worried about this appointment. I don't think you need to be. You're moving much better than when you arrived in town. I'm sure you'll do fine."

"I hope so." He thought he heard a tremor in her soft reply.

He wasn't sure why not being perfectly fit mattered so much. She was more than capable of doing everything she set her mind to. Perhaps she didn't have the degree of perfection the military required, but that career was gone now.

"You'll do great. I've seen you jogging, lifting weights, painting walls. You can do virtually anything."

"Except serve my country. I lived for the service. I was useful. I helped people. Now I'm just..." She waved her hands vaguely and shrugged.

"You do know that you're the only person who doesn't value what you do, right?" He wanted to shake some sense into her. He snuck another quick look. She was hunched forward with her arms wrapped protectively around her middle. He slowed, pulled into the end of a farm's driveway, and stopped.

With the truck out of gear and the emergency brake on, he unbuckled, turned, and grasped her hands. "Winter Ireland, you run a very successful yardwork business; your flower shop is doing great as well. It's always busy. You might not be fighting terrorists or bringing down dictators, but what you do brightens the lives of everyone you deal with. That, in itself, is valuable. I can't think of anything better than bringing joy to other people's lives." He squeezed her hands between his when she didn't look at him.

"Losing your career due to injury doesn't make you less important. I think it can give you better insight into other people's loss.

That will roll into being a better person. Which isn't to say you weren't a good person before."

He pushed out a hard breath. "I'm messing this up. I don't have a clue how to say it correctly. Game pun *not* intended...this time. You're filling a need for the people of our town, and that's more than enough."

Slowly, she raised her eyes. "Do you believe that?" There was a tear in her eye and a glimmer of hope in her voice, like she wanted to believe his words but didn't quite trust him.

"I really do." He struggled for the words. "Maybe your role on earth is in helping brighten people's days and not in fighting off evil." He smiled. "My superpower is making people smile with jokes and my baking. Your superpower is in your sweet smile and the beauty your flowers bring. Neither one of us is a police officer, a medic, or an ER doctor, but what we do is valuable in other ways. Not everyone is meant to be Gandhi or Mother Teresa. The world needs more small heroes. Everyday heroes. Like us."

For the first time since she got in the truck, she smiled a full and true smile. One that went all the way to her eyes and turned up the corners of her mouth. She was breathtaking. His heart gave a joyful thump.

"Thanks, Nick. I needed to hear that." She rolled her hands over to hold his. "It means a lot that you try to understand what I am going through...that you see me. You were the first person I met in Haven, and you've been there for me from the start. I appreciate it. Thank you."

"You are very welcome." Slowly, he lifted her hands one after the other and pressed a kiss on each palm before buckling his seatbelt. "We best hurry, or we'll be late." He smiled before putting the truck in gear. "We have to improve our time management."

She swatted him on the arm. "We'll be fine if you step on it."

"If I get a ticket, you're paying...because you forced me into the shower with you." Her light laughter brought out his, and the joyous ringing cleared the air between them. They chatted for miles.

A soft buzzing sounded. She pulled out her phone and looked at the screen.

"Are you going to answer that?" Nick glanced at her.

"Nope."

"Why not?"

"Obviously because I don't want to talk to the person on the other end. Not that it's any of your business."

He hated that she didn't want to talk about it, and he couldn't help but wonder if she was avoiding calls from her family.

The uncomfortable silence between them returned like an Arctic cold front.

Chapter Twenty-Eight.

For the first time in ages, Winter didn't stop at the bakery on her way to work. She couldn't. Her heart wouldn't let her. She unlocked the flower shop door and stepped inside. Leaving the lights off, she wandered toward the back, straightening a pot here and there.

She loved this place.

Almost as much as she loved Nick.

And that was why she had to stay away for the rest of her time in Haven. Leaving him was going to hurt as it was. There was no way she'd be able to move on if they grew any closer. Besides, he was mad at her.

After she refused to tell him who was on the phone and why she didn't answer it, they'd barely spoken for the duration of their trip. The only good thing that came out of that day was a clean bill of health on her knee. She was free to use it fully. Not that she hadn't been, anyway. In any other career, except maybe professional sports, she'd be back at her job. Too bad the military never changed their mind once a decision was made.

She worked her way through her morning prep. She checked the water level in the buckets of cut flowers, watered the plants that needed it, and counted her float. Then she sat at her computer to surf the internet.

"I should have brought a road cup," she muttered into the silence. "I need coffee." She hadn't gotten around to buying a coffee pot for the shop. She didn't care for the coffee from pods, it always tasted stale to her. She also couldn't see the sense in brewing a whole pot for one person.

"Suck it up, Ireland. Go to the bakery and get a cup."

Someone tapped on the door. Her brows knit together. Who would be here this early? Maybe it was Grace or Lisa. Both liked to pop in early in the morning, though not before she opened. Shrugging mentally, she went to unlock the door. She didn't bother to lift the privacy screen that covered the door.

"Morning." Nick gently eased past her, a large go-cup of coffee in his hand. "You didn't stop for coffee." His tone was mild, with hurt behind the words.

"Ya. No. I didn't."

"Is there a reason why not?" He walked to the cash desk and set the cup down.

She fumbled for an excuse and, after much too long, managed to say, "I didn't think we were talking. We weren't exactly on the best terms after yesterday."

He nodded seriously. "I get that. But I thought we were friends. Friends can disagree and still be friends."

Could they, really?

And friends?

Weren't they more than that, despite her insistence that friends were all they could ever be?

She swallowed a sigh.

Friends with benefits.

That's what this was.

Ya, if that's all you have between you, why are you running away from him like your pants are on fire?

"Are you going to say something? Or shall I just go?" He stuffed his hands in his front pockets and rocked back and forth on his heels. "I get it. What you do, or don't do, in terms of your phone is none of my business. I should have kept my mouth shut."

"Yes. You should have."

"In my defense. I don't like when families are uncommunicative. Grace was estranged from her family when I met her. Now, they're talking again. Her sisters are even moving to Haven to be closer to her. I think she's happier now."

"I'm not calling my family. We have nothing in common. They'll just disapprove of my life choices again. So, drop it. Okay?"

"Consider it dropped." Slowly, he moved forward and pulled her into his arms. "Now, where's my morning kiss?"

She shook her head and hid her smile. "You're a pain in my backside, Blackstone. A royal pain."

"Ya, but you love me anyway."

Unfortunately, she did.

She shut him up the only way she knew how. With a kiss. Three heart-pounding moments later, they shifted apart. "Thanks for the kiss. And the coffee," she whispered against his lips.

"Dinner tonight?"

Heaven help her, she was going to accept. How could she not? But how could she? "Sure, why not?"

"Bank that enthusiasm." He kissed the tip of her nose, and a shockwave of desire rocked him to his toes. Her arms slid around his waist, drawing him closer. "A nice intimate dinner for two and then..." He left the idea hanging and stepped back. He wanted nothing more than to kiss her senseless, but now wasn't the time or the place. He stepped in and brushed a sweet kiss over her lips. "I can't wait. I'll pick you up at seven."

·♥ · ♥ · ♥ · ♥ · ♥·

Hand in hand, they walked toward Sid's.

"Look at that." Nick pointed down the street, where an enormous white stretch limo was parked out front of Sid's. It was parked along the sidewalk taking up half a dozen or more spots. "You don't see many of those here."

Winter froze beside him. "Oh, hell no." She pivoted and headed back the way they came.

"Where are you going?" He raced after her.

"Anywhere but there. I'm out of here. I'll drop Muriel's keys on your porch. Nice knowing you, Nick." She sprinted away, her low-heeled sandals clacking against the sidewalk as she went. One flew off. She paused long enough to kick the other aside and kept going. She didn't even pick them up.

"Winter! Wait." *What the hell was wrong with her*? He grabbed the shoes as he passed.

She sprinted up her front steps and inside. The screen door banged shut. He finally caught up with her in the guest room where she was frantically tossing clothing into a duffle bag.

He grabbed her shoulders from behind and stilled her frantic actions. "What's going on, Winter? Talk to me. Please."

She shook her head and pulled against his grip.

He held tight but loose enough that she could have pulled away if she wanted to. "Talk to me. Who is it?" He dropped his hands. "Oh my, God. It's your parents, isn't it?"

She nodded. "Probably."

Slowly, he turned her into his embrace and pulled her close. As he stroked the tension from her back and shoulders, her arms slid around his waist. "We can skip dinner."

"It's only a matter of time before they're knocking on the front door. I'm surprised they even stopped somewhere else, let alone to eat." Her voice trembled, and his shirt was growing damp from her tears.

"I'm leaving. Now. Not later." She hiccupped, then sniffed. "I can't deal with them."

He took several long minutes to consider the thoughts bouncing around his head. "No judgment here, but don't you think it's time you talked to them?" She jerked out of his arms and glared at him with her arms wrapped around her middle like she was trying to hold herself together.

She couldn't leave. He couldn't stand it if she was gone.

He held up his hands in a stop or slow down gesture. "I don't know the whole story. But I do know that there's a mountain of history I know nothing about. Maybe it's time for peace talks."

"No."

"You told me you miss your brother and his kids. I'm guessing you aren't talking to him because it could get back to your parents. For the sake of your relationship with your nephews, maybe you should try to bridge the gap."

"Was that another damn game pun? *Bridge*? Seriously? Do you ever quit?"

"Unintentional, I swear. But you're avoiding life. Aren't you a soldier? Aren't you used to combat? This is just another battle that needs to be fought. If for no other reason than your peace of mind. When's the last time you saw them? When's the last time you tried to talk?"

"Talk? I stopped going home on my leave after the third year. It wasn't worth the fight. I did see my nephews until two years ago. Then my brother started telling my parents I was coming and they'd be there too."

She'd run away from the fights. That didn't seem like her. She was one of the toughest women he knew, and he wasn't thinking in terms of the military. She was a strong person, up for any challenge. Except, apparently, this one. Now, she was running like a pack of wolves were on her tail.

·❥·❥·❥·❥·❥·

Winter glared at Nick. How could he even suggest she talk to them? "You have no idea who they are or how they are!" Her voice shook, and she clenched her fists to still her shaking nerves.

"True enough," he said thoughtfully. He perched on the edge of the bed and patted the mattress beside him. "So, tell me."

She paced back and forth in the small room, unable to stay still. "Both of them are lawyers. Mom grew up rich. Stupid rich. Have you ever heard of the Ireland Foundation?"

"Yes."

"Well," she waved her hands up and toward herself, "that's me. My mother is Rosalee Ireland. My father is Kenneth Winter...hence my name. My maternal grandmother inherited some money. Stupid money. Twenty-five billion dollars. Her father was in gold somehow, and she got more from her second husband. I don't know the details. They never mattered to me. She started the Ireland Foundation which builds low-income housing all over Canada, though mostly in big cities."

She paused for a deep breath because she was practically shouting and this wasn't Nick's fault. "I never fit into the family. I was more like Aunt Muriel, Dad's sister. I hate fancy balls and stuffy dinners. I like the outdoors and doing my own thing. The first fights started when I turned sixteen and refused to go to a fundraiser. I'd been to several, and I hated every second. Fat lot of good refusing did. I might as well have been shouting into a hurricane. I went. I hated it. I hated them all. They enrolled me in university to get my business degree. The first step towards my MBA.

"That doesn't sound so bad. There's nothing wrong with a good education."

"Screw you, Blackstone. There is if it isn't what you want. They had me slated for a desk job with the goal of taking over, with my brother, when they were ready to retire. So, when I turned eighteen, I hopped the bus to the recruitment office and signed up. I was in basic training within three days. I won't lie and pretend I didn't use family money to grease some palms to make it happen that fast."

Nick nodded, though it was clear he didn't understand how she felt.

"How would you feel if you were told you could never cook or bake again? What if someone denied you your dreams and kept you from living your happiness?"

"I'd hate that." He patted the bed again.

She sat beside him, almost close enough to touch. "Since I was twelve and watched a video on how the military helps around the world, I wanted to serve my country. My parents said no. To do so would be 'unseemly'. That's their favorite word. I swear, if I hear it again, my head will explode."

Jumping up, she resumed pacing to ease the tension making her heart pound and knees shake. She'd love to go ten rounds with a punching bag. "When they heard I was injured, they were ecstatic. Now their missing daughter would come home and fall right into the rigid role they had all laid out. I won't!"

"How many years, actual years, has it been since you tried to get them to see reason, without losing your temper?"

"It's been…" she swallowed her chagrin and anger, "it's been never. We don't talk without fighting. Ever."

"Maybe this is your chance," he said softly, reaching out and snagging her hands. He clasped them between hers. "Your hands are like ice." He rubbed them until the chill melted away.

"They won't listen."

"They're all about image, right?"

"Yeah," she responded slowly, unsure where he was headed.

"So, let's go to Sid's. Catch them there, in public, and quietly tell them you're not going back. If they are that concerned about image, they won't cause a scene and you'll have the chance to put your view forward."

"I can't."

"So instead, you'll run every time they catch up to you? What kind of life is that Winter? You may not want to settle in Haven, but eventually, you'll find your path and want to settle down someplace. Don't let them take over your life. Isn't that exactly what you're fighting against?"

Fudge. He made sense. Except it wasn't that easy.

"It won't be easy." Nick smiled softly. "I'll go with you. I'll be your wingman."

"That's dating, dipshit."

"Not if you're in the Air Force." Nick grinned. "Fine then, army girl. I've got your six. Isn't that how they say I've got your back?"

"On television, yeah." Her hands trembled and her heart pounded. Fear kept her pinned to the bed beside him. She couldn't do this.

Could she?

Chapter Twenty-Nine

"I can't do this." She pulled back against Nick's arm, where he was trying to urge her into Sid's. They'd stopped six times along the way, and he'd talked her into continuing each time.

He turned her toward him. With his hands on her shoulders, he stared at her until her gaze met his. "You can do this. You've faced down terrorists, fought insurgents, and survived a freaking IED explosion. You've got more balls than anyone I've ever met. You. Can. Do. This." He gave her a little shake. "Don't let them win."

He opened his arms, and she slid into his embrace. "You're strong enough," he whispered in her ear. His lips slid down her cheek and he captured her mouth. Softly at first, then savagely, like he was daring her to fight him.

Somehow, the pressure, the force, fueled her resolve. After kissing him back until they were both breathless, she stepped away. "I'm going to regret it, but let's do this."

"Damn the torpedoes. Man the guns. Ain't no way they're going to sink our *Battleship*."

She swatted his shoulder. "You did not just call me a battleship."

"Would I do that?"

"Beam us in, Nicky. Beam us in." Somehow buoyed by his teasing and confidence in her, she made the bad *Star Trek* reference. "Okay." She pushed out a breath and squared her shoulders. "One way or the other, this ends tonight. Wish me luck."

"Nothing doing. You don't need luck. You've got this. We've got this."

She pecked his cheek, grabbed his hand like it was a lifeline, and dragged him inside. She took a moment to get her bearings and with her shoulders high and a smile plastered on her face strolled toward her family. They were all here. Her mother and father. Her brother and his wife and their boys.

"Mom. Dad. Fancy meeting you here." She pulled Nick to her side. "Welcome to Haven. I'd like you to meet my boyfriend, Nick Blackstone. Nick, these are my parents, Rosalee, and Kenneth. This is my brother, Carl, and his wife, Tracey. These two adorable munchkins are James and John."

The boys leaped up to hug her. "Auntie Winnie." Their hugs were bolstering.

"Nick and I won't bother you. We'll let you eat in peace. Why don't we meet at Aunt Muriel's in about ninety minutes? Do you have the address?" She knew they did.

Her father stood and thrust his arm toward Nick. "Nice to meet you, Mr. Blackstone."

"Nice to meet you, Mr. Ireland."

Winter bit back a smile. She knew damn well he'd used the wrong name on purpose.

Her father's face went red. "That's Kenneth Winter."

"Oh, I'm so sorry. My mistake." Nick leaned past her father and smiled at her mother. "Mrs. Ireland, it is lovely to meet you. I can see where Winter gets her good looks."

Her mother's cheeks went pink. "Mr. Blackstone, why don't you join us for dinner? I'd love to get to know the man keeping Winter away from us."

Nick looked at Winter. "What do you think, dear? Shall we join them? I'm perfectly happy to continue on our romantic date."

She had to stifle a laugh at his outrageous mannerisms and the stunned expression on her mother's face. Nobody refused Rosalee Ireland. She leaned toward him and pecked him on the cheek. "Why don't we join them? Just this once. We can pick up the romance after dinner." *Romance. Ha. Friends with benefits.*

She paused. No, that wasn't true. Nick was very romantic. Letting her choose their meals, bringing her coffee, treats, and pretty rocks, and anticipating and looking after her needs. He was romantic, just not showy about it. The realization shocked her.

"Well, as much as I'd love to be alone with you, I think we can join them. It might be fun." That last part was for her benefit. It was his way of saying he had her back.

Sid bustled up to them. "Winter. Nick. Can I help you find a table?"

"Sid. Hi. Can we pull one up here? This is my family. I didn't realize they were here until just now, and we'd love to catch up."

A table was pulled up and everyone shuffled around. Winter ended up beside Nick and across from her parents. Her brother's family took the outside of the booth of the new table.

There was no conversation until they ordered. Just as Sid went to put the order in, Nick said, "Put that on my account, please."

Sid looked startled. "Absolutely, Mr. Blackstone." She hid a smirk as she strolled away.

"So, Nick. Tell us what you do?"

"I'm a baker."

Her mother's eyes narrowed, and she practically sneered.

"Oh, he's being modest. He's a famous chef from New York City. He sold his restaurant, Tamier, and owns the bakery here."

Her mother straightened up and smiled. One thing Rosalee Ireland knew was the best restaurants. "Fascinating."

"You must come for dinner," Nick proclaimed. "I'll make you some of my signature dishes."

He has signature dishes. Who knew? She bit back a grin. He was very subtly putting them in their place.

"You are going to love Winter's flower shop. She's got the greatest plants, and you cannot believe how busy she is. People from all over the province come for her merchandise. She's going to make a splash in the flower industry."

Why the hell had he brought that up?

"What about your military career? Oh, my goodness, you aren't AWOL? Are you?"

"Absent without leave? Relax, Mom. I am not AWOL. I've been honorably discharged."

Her parent's mouths gaped like fish and her brother hid a chuckle.

"Aren't you coming back to The Ireland Foundation?" Her dad barked.

"Honestly, I'm quite happy in Haven. I love my store. I have dozens of friends."

"I know," Nick blurted. "We must have a party and introduce your family to all our friends."

"Oh, that's not necessary. We're only here for a couple of nights."

"I insist." Nick clapped his hands. "We'll have it catered."

The server came and began placing meals. For a few moments, silence reigned. Finally, Mrs. Ireland spoke. "But what about the foundation?"

"Mom, Dad. I know the foundation does good work. Fabulous work. But honestly, the dinners, the meetings, the publicity, it all crushes my soul. All I want is to find my way. Maybe that's here, with my flower shop. Maybe it's someplace else. All I do know is that I'll never be happy with the foundation."

"But we need you," her father blustered.

"Do you? Really? What use do you have for a discharged GI with no education?"

"We work for families, with families. It's important to show our family is strong."

"Can't it be strong without stifling your daughter's happiness?" Nick quirked his left eyebrow.

Her parents reared back in unison, and her brother laughed aloud. It seemed her brother was considering Winter's side of the argument.

Her mother blinked, and for a moment, Winter thought she saw a tear. But that couldn't be right. Her mother was calm and rational. Occasionally, she lost her temper, but Rosalee Ireland did not cry.

"Is it that bad?" her mom whispered.

"It is. I believe in what you do, but to be stuck at a desk or in fancy dress functions kills me."

"I had no idea." Her mom twisted her hands together and stared back and forth between her husband and Winter. "Can you give us one dinner a year? Maybe the spring gala?"

Winter was about to say no when Nick squeezed her knee. "One gala a year. No more," she relented. Her parents' smiles were ecstatic.

After their awkward compromise, they got through dinner with only a few awkward moments.

"I guess we should find a hotel." Her father looked at Nick like he'd have a recommendation.

"Not in Haven this time of year. We have two B&Bs, and they're likely full. Why don't you stay at Muriel's? I'm just down the street.

Winter can sleep in my spare room so there's enough room for all of you."

Winter kicked him under the table. He kicked back lightly.

Rosalee and Kenneth looked at each other, and Winter would swear silent communication passed between them. "That will be fine." Kenneth's smile was weak, as if staying in his sister's house was beneath him.

·♥ · ♥ · ♥ · ♥ · ♥·

Alone in his house, Nick high-fived Winter. "You were awesome."

"Did you see Mom's face when you said you were a baker? I nearly died trying not to laugh. Dad nearly choked when you told Sid to put dinner on your tab like you were some kind of bigshot. I'll pay you back for that."

"No, you will not. It's the least I can do for my *girlfriend's* family," he teased.

"Yeah, sorry about that."

Her wince went straight to his heart. "Why? Isn't that what I am? Your boyfriend?" Anger and frustration rocked him back on his heels. The rejection so close to their success cut deep.

"We've never...never defined what we are." Her face went red.

"I didn't realize it needed defining. We're friends. We're lovers. We're exclusive. I thought that meant we were in a relationship. Boyfriend and girlfriend, and all that goes with being a couple. The two of us, maybe working toward something long-term. You embraced it when it suited you and now you wince? Why is that? What am I to you, Winter? Where do I fit?"

It was all he could do not to shout. He was tired of her playing hot and cold. He thought she had finally come around and was getting serious. "I'm going to bed."

He trudged up the stairs. She followed without speaking. *Why didn't she fight back?* He tossed her duffle into the master bedroom. "You sleep here. I'll sleep in the spare room."

Chapter Thirty

A t four-thirty-two, the door eased shut behind Nick. Winter leaped to her feet to go after him. What would she say? She didn't even know what the hell had happened last night. She'd been riding the high of finally getting her parents to listen. Granted, it had only happened because Nick insisted. Somehow, after they got back to his place, things had SNAFU-ed.

She flopped back onto the bed and covered her face with the pillow. She would not cry. There was nothing to cry over. They were friends. Nothing more.

So, why did it hurt so badly that he was upset?

She screamed into the pillow.

What was wrong with her?

She was a tough, strong soldier.

"Only you aren't anymore, are you?" Up on her knees, she pounded her frustrations on the mattress. "He'll never talk to you again." She buried her face and screamed again. "I don't need this crap. I should be sleeping."

She'd been up most of the night. She'd managed to keep from pacing, only because she didn't want Nick to hear and know his desertion had slashed her heart. She'd lain in bed and argued with herself. Over and over.

Finally, she got up, showered, and went to the shop. At least there she'd be busy. Maybe she could distract herself enough to stop fixating on Nick because she had the feeling that this could be the end of their friendship.

"Stop thinking about it." She forced herself to walk calmly to Blooming Perfect and snorted at the thought that her life was anything but perfect. Living in Haven wasn't supposed to hurt. It was where she was going to find herself...before she moved on. So much for that!

Inside the shop, with the door securely locked, she crumpled to the floor, sobbing. She wasn't supposed to fall in love with him. He'd never leave Haven, and she couldn't stay. This was nothing more than a little R&R, Rest and Recuperation.

Blooming Perfect was a lark. A way to make some money and pass the time. Lord knows she couldn't spend her time doing nothing. As much as her knee was healed, she knew that mowing lawns full time was going to be too much for it in the long run.

Arms wrapped around her knees; she wept until she had no tears. She sat there shivering, more from hurt than the cold floor. She stayed there until someone knocked on her door just as the phone began ringing.

She didn't want to talk to whoever was outside, so she struggled to her feet and trudged to the phone.

"Blooming Perfect, how can I help you?"

"Winter? Thank God! I've been trying to find you."

"Grace?"

"Yes. I stopped by the bakery and Nick's a wreck. What the hell happened between you two? He won't talk about it."

Me neither.

"It's fine. Nothing to worry about," the lie tumbled off her lips without thought.

"Don't give me that bullshit. Let me in." The door rattled.

"It's too early to open."

"It's after eleven. Let me in or I'll call Mac and have him bust in. I'll tell him I'm afraid you've hurt yourself. He'll do a wellness check."

Crap.

She hung up and trudged toward the door.

How had it gotten so late?

Grace pounded on the door. "Let me in. I swear I'll call Mac."

She flipped the lock and walked away. She didn't have the strength for this discussion. Not now. Probably not ever.

The bell chimed as Grace entered, and then the lock snapped shut.

"Get over here," Grace demanded. "Let's talk about it."

"There's nothing to say. We're over." She whirled round, dashing away fresh tears. "We were only friends, now we're not."

"Of for f--- Pete's sake. You were more than friends. You were a couple. I know it. Nick knows it. Everybody knows it. Except you. Why can't you admit it?"

Wasn't that the ten-thousand-dollar question?

"Because it isn't true. We're friends. He knew that going in. I'm not staying here. I'm leaving as soon as Muriel comes home. This is just a spot of R&R."

"Oh, bull cookies. If this is temporary, why did you open a business? Why are you on three special event committees? Why are you giving self-defense classes at Belinda's ranch? Why did you date him at all?" She huffed out a breath and drew Winter into her arms. "Oh, honey, don't be afraid to love or to fight for your guy. Maybe you didn't plan to stay in Haven, but who says plans don't change."

She gave Winter a little shake. "This isn't the service, things can change. I never planned to end up in Haven. I was on the run from my family and stopped here. I was shooting for a life someplace else, and here I am. Happily married with two kids. My grandmother used to say, "Your goals are like distant stars, aim for the heavens, but don't be afraid to alter your aim for a new destination or goal." I used to think it was a stupid thing to say. Now I know better."

The words resonated within Winter, though she didn't want to admit it. "He's just so...so jokey."

"He is at that. But so what? Does it matter? He might be laughing his way through life, but it brings joy to those around him, and he never makes light of serious things. I hated his joking when we met, but it kind of grew on me. It'll grow on you too."

It already had, but that was her secret.

"I don't know..."

"Just think about it. Don't cut down the trees looking for the forest. Recognize what you have and go for it. Shoot for the moon, girl. Shoot for the moon. Now, I have to run and grab Travis from Sterling. I'll be back in a flash with coffee and breakfast. And, by the way, your mother is looking for you. You didn't answer when she pounded on the door."

"Shit. I totally forgot about them."

"She seems nice, by the way. Last time I saw her, she was screaming at Nick to get his shit together and find you. For someone who dresses like a million bucks, she sure cusses like a sailor."

"My mother does not cuss. She's too uptight for that."

"Your mother's language would put a rig worker to shame. She's great. I'll bring you food and I'll tell her you'll be home shortly. Okay?"

Not even close to okay.

"Fine. Bring me a breakfast sandwich and a cinnamon bun."

"Eating your feelings isn't going to help."

"It won't hurt either." She stuck out her tongue at Grace's back as she left the shop. This had been the suckiest twenty-four hours of her life. The only worse day was the day she'd blown herself up. And while Grace had made her feel marginally better, she still had no idea what she wanted to do.

"I'll burn that bridge when I get there. I guess."

Two days later, she was standing beside the limo, bidding her family goodbye. "I'll fly home this summer. I promise. But only if you promise me no dinners, no press, no functions."

"One dinner party, close friends only."

"Mo-om. No. Your idea of an intimate dinner is sixty people. No. Just plain no. I'll go to the spring ball next year. That has to be enough."

"And you'll make up with Nick? He seems like a nice boy. He didn't even lose his cool when I lost mine." She shook her head. "He just gave me a coffee and a maple pecan tart and listened to me rant. Why the boy even locked the store so we weren't interrupted. You know that he loves you, right? He'd make a fine son-in-law."

"Don't even start. I told you that I haven't made any decisions. I'm not rushing into anything. I think I'm still running away from the trauma of my injury. I'll double up my counseling sessions and reconnect with my injured platoon mates. I'm taking my time and doing what's right for me. With, or without Nick has yet to be determined. I will keep you updated."

"See that you do." Rosalee leaned in and kissed Winter on the cheek. "I may not understand you, but I do love you. Don't disappear on me again, okay?"

The pain in her mother's voice brought heat to her face. Hiding hadn't solved anything. It had only hurt her family. "I won't, Mom. I swear."

She hugged everyone goodbye, watched as the limo rolled down the street, and breathed a sigh that was half relief, and half regret for the pain she'd caused.

·♥·♥·♥·♥·♥·

"I don't know what to do. She won't talk to me." Nick flopped into the extra chair in Grace's office. "Winter's totally shut down. We used to see each other almost every day. Since her family was here, she won't even talk to me. What the hell do I do?"

"She needs time to think, and, honestly, I think you do too."

"What?" Her words scratched against his conscience.

"Judging by what you both told me...you were pushing her for something she wasn't ready for. You were so hung up on your needs that you ignored hers. You fixated on what you wanted without caring that she was scared."

Had he done that?

"Did I?"

"Come on, Nick. You aren't an idiot," Sterling chimed in from behind him.

"Hey, Sterl."

"At least you're not stupid most of the time," Sterling added. "She ran away from her family because they were controlling, and she ended up in the service, where her every move was dictated. Weirdly, she loved the army. But when she was discharged, she had no idea what she wanted or needed. She's never had the chance to make decisions for herself. Then along comes this nice guy, but he's pushy."

"And I pushed too hard."

"Too hard and too fast." Grace shoved a box of chocolates toward him.

He didn't want one, but he picked a nut cluster and chewed it while he gathered his thoughts. "And I promised we could just be friends." He cracked his knuckles. "I didn't count on falling so hard. I got excited."

"Dude, please." Sterling held up his hands in mock horror at the unintended double entendre.

"What do I do? How do I get her back?"

"That's exactly your problem, Nick." Grace shook her finger at him. "You're still making it about you. Back off. Give her time to miss you."

"Time? It's been two weeks."

"It could be months. Or maybe never," she said.

He rolled off a mental grocery list of cuss words. "Fine. I'll back off. But it won't be easy."

"Nothing worth having ever is. I waited years to find Grace." Sterling rounded the desk and kissed his wife. "Look at us now. Happily married and raising a family."

He was happy for them and at the same time extremely jealous of their obvious bliss. Speechless, he nodded.

"Go back to work, my friend. Leave me alone with my wife. Give Winter some time. Maybe she's like the season and will come around again."

"God, I hope so." Waiting was going to kill him. Especially if he kept seeing her all the time.

Chapter Thirty-One

Winter closed up Blooming Perfect for the day. Lisa, Grace, Natalie, and Belinda waited on the sidewalk out front so they could go for dinner at Sid's. Every Thursday for the last three weeks, since her breakup with Nick, the ladies went for dinner while the men played poker. Of course, her friends never mentioned the men unless they had to. Especially Nick.

"Boy, Travis was fussy today. I spent the whole day walking the store with him in his carrier," Grace grumbled.

"It must be the moon," Lisa added. "Amy was like a feral cat on steroids. I didn't think she'd let me leave the house."

"Funny," Natalie said, "I didn't have any trouble getting away."

"And here we are!" Belinda declared. "Five hot women going out for dinner." She sighed. "I really need a man."

"Nobody needs a man," Winter grumbled. "Men are nothing but trouble."

"Of course they are," Grace laughed. "Wonderful, sexy, cuddly trouble. Speaking of which, mind if we pop into the bakery for a sec? Sterl asked me to get Nick to bring sausage rolls and cookies."

Winter stumbled. She hadn't been in the bakery since the big fight. She'd lost ten pounds without her daily diet of Nick's goodies. Well, she didn't have to talk to him, which was good because she had no idea what she'd say.

She missed him like crazy, but not enough to reenter a relationship with him. At least not as things stood between them. She might have to forgive him, though. She was staying in Haven whether he liked it or not. This was her home; her friends were here, her store, Aunt Muriel. It wasn't the one she was looking for, but it was exactly what she needed. Nick, or no Nick.

Liar. You'll be heartbroken if you don't get back together. You love him. You just want him to come crawling back to you. Ya, and he's probably waiting for you to crawl back to him. Then he'd make a stupid joke about winning the game. Well, Nick Blackstone, this isn't a game! And you aren't going to win!

They stepped into the bakery. "Where's Nick?" Grace asked Uma, who was polishing the display counter.

"In the back doing the milk order. He's in the cooler."

"Oh, Winter, can you go ask him to bring what Sterl wants? I have to pee." She raced toward the bathroom like she wouldn't make it on time.

"Can't one of you guys go?" She looked back and forth between her friends.

"We have to talk to Uma about the party next week," Lisa said, her cheeks pink. Uma looked surprised but agreed.

Dirty little liars! They just wanted to force her and Nick together. Well, she'd show them. She'd talk to him, and that would be the end of it.

"Fine. I'll do it." She stormed into the back room and stuck her head in the open door of the walk-in cooler. "Nick."

He whirled round, an uncertain look on his face. "Winter. What are you doing here?" He set his tablet on the shelf. "I mean, how can I help you?"

She stepped forward without meaning to. It was agony to be this close and not touch him. *God, she missed him.* "Grace asked me to tell you that Sterling wants—"

Bam!

The cooler door slammed shut.

"What the hell?" She spun around and grabbed the handle. It didn't move. "Didn't you get this fixed yet?"

"No! The parts didn't come in. They're back-ordered."

She pounded on the door. "Let me out of here!"

"Did you plan this?" Nick glared.

"No." She crossed her arms over her chest and glared at him. "Jeez, it's freezing in here."

"It's called a cooler for a reason."

"Ha. Ha. You've got a joke for everything, don't you?"

He opened his mouth and slammed it shut. "It's a coping mechanism." He emptied a milk crate, flipped it over, and slid it toward her. "Have a seat."

"Coping mechanism for what? I thought your life was picture perfect." She pounded on the door again.

"They won't come. I expect this is Grace's way to get us talking."

"I have nothing to say."

"Maybe not." He paused for a full minute, then slipped out of his zip-front hoodie and draped it over her shoulders. "But I have a few things to say. Some stuff I'd like to clear up...since we have time and no place to go."

Pushing her crate back until she could lean against the door, she closed her eyes. She didn't want to hear this, she just wanted out of here. "Let me out," she screamed one last time.

"Not until you guys talk. I'll be back later."

"Oo, she's such a witch."

"She means well." Nick stuffed his hands into his jeans' pockets. "I like you, Winter."

As if she didn't know that already.

·♥·♥·♥·♥·♥·

Sweet heaven, she was so beautiful. She'd lost some weight, and she looked tired. Still, she was the loveliest woman he'd ever seen. And man, did he love. More than he realized.

He had to admire Grace's spunk in shoving them together. He'd have to thank her later. For now, while he had a captive audience, he had some things to say.

"I do joke a lot." He ignored her eye-roll. "It started when I was thirteen. That's the year my dad and grandfather died in a car crash." He bit back the hurt the memories brought.

"I'm so sorry."

He shrugged. "Thanks. We were devastated. My sister and I took it hard. But not as hard as Mom. She gave up on life." He blinked away tears. "She didn't die or anything. She just took to her bed for months. I didn't know what to do. I just looked after Tabby and Mom. Tabby's a year younger than me."

"I'm sorry for your loss." Her eyes were filled with sympathy. Nice, but not what he was aiming for.

"Dad loved jokes. The worse the pun, the better. He had a million private puns for Mom. When she wouldn't leave her bed and would barely eat, I skipped school to be with her. I was afraid she'd suicide. I studied online and stayed within earshot. Just in case...." He scraped his fingers through his hair and jammed them back into his pockets.

"About the fourth day, I accidentally cracked an egg joke, and Mom smiled." He grinned at the memory. "It was incredible. I can't tell you how happy and relieved it made me. I started telling jokes all the time. Just to see her smile, and she did. Not big smiles, and not for long."

"That's wonderful."

"I think it was a turning point of sorts. Eventually, she got out of bed. She was an artist. She's never picked up a paintbrush since. But at least she joined us in the land of the living." He swallowed a lump of emotion that threatened to choke him. "But she told me…she told me…never to tell her another joke. She couldn't take it."

"But the stupid irony is that jokes had become so ingrained they were second nature to me. I couldn't, can't stop. Sometimes, I think it's my way of keeping Dad alive."

Winter stared up at him and blinked several times. It was so wrong, but he wished she was blinking back tears because maybe she understood him better now.

"I talked to a shrink about it. It's kind of my scar from the trauma of their deaths and from having to step up and be a parent at thirteen. She told me to embrace the jokes. They weren't hurting anything." He snorted. "At least they weren't until I met you."

"That's an awful story. I'm sorry you went through all that. But it wasn't the jokes, Nick." She twisted her hands together. "They were part of it, maybe the straw that broke the camel's back."

"I know. It was me. I pushed too hard. You told me that we'd never be anything more than friends and occasional lovers. It wasn't enough. I thought I could handle it, but I wanted more. I needed more. And I pushed for what I wanted without any consideration for what you needed. I am truly sorry, Winter. More sorry than I can ever express, and I apologize."

"Thank you. I forgive you." She bit her lip. "It wasn't just you. It was me, too. I got so hooked on my plan to leave to find a better life that I didn't realize how wonderful my life is here, in Haven, with you."

"You mean that?" He stared wide-eyed at her.

·♥·♥·♥·♥·♥·

"I do. I've made a decision." She'd only made it while listening to him bare his soul. "I'm happy here. I love my shop and my new friends. But mostly, I love you, Nick Blackstone. And if you'll forgive me, I'd like you back in my life."

He leaped up, grabbed her, and swung her around. "Hell yes." He rained kisses on her face and wiped her cheeks. "You're crying."

"Well," she snort-laughed, "You don't have a *Monopoly* on hurt feelings."

He leaned back and grinned at her. "You did not just say that!"

"Unfortunately, I did. Now, take me home so we can make love."

"Nope."

Her heart dropped to her toes. He was refusing her? What the hell?

"I'm taking you out to dinner and then home to make love. Book someone to work for you tomorrow because we're not getting out of bed until Monday. I must be a *beaver* because, *dam* I missed you!"

She snorted inelegantly and broke into laughter. "Get me out of here."

He pulled out his phone and swiped the screen. After a moment, he spoke, "Grace, get us the hell out of here. I need to feed my woman and make love to her." He put the phone away and pulled her into his arms. "If it's okay with you, I'm going to kiss you."

"Yes, please." Her words were breathless and low.

"Hot damn." He swept his lips over hers. Once. Twice. And again. This time, he lingered. She opened to him, and their tongues danced. Gentle and frantic. An apology, a greeting, and a whole lot of love passed between them without words.

Bliss.

The door popped open, and they jerked apart, breathless.

"That didn't take long," Grace smirked. "I knew you two would see eye to eye."

"Thanks, Grace," Winter said. "Now get out of our way."

Laughing, they brushed past her.

"You're welcome," she called as they left the store.

Chapter Thirty-Two

T he sun blazed in the September sky. Already the leaves were turning and mornings were cool. Fortunately, there was no inclement weather forecast for today. Her wedding day.

How had five months passed so quickly? It seemed like she'd just arrived in Haven without a plan or a future. Now, she was giddy with the anticipation of tying the knot with Nick.

Sweet Nick.

She'd been blessed when the universe thrust him into her path. The road had been rocky to start with, but slowly they were paving the way to the future. Together.

"Are you ready?" Aunt Muriel called through the bedroom door.

"Almost. Come in."

Muriel burst into the room like a tornado. "Sweet heaven. You're still in your underwear." She slammed the door behind her. "What if your father or brother had been in the hallway?"

"They're at Nick's getting ready, aren't they?"

"Yes, but still. And why are there cookies on your underwear? Shouldn't you be wearing white lace?"

"You're such a traditionalist. The dress is the traditional white. That'll have to do. And Nick will love the cookies." She hugged her aunt, pouring all her love and gratitude into the embrace. "I cannot believe you ended your vacation to come home for this."

"Not ended, just a break. I'm heading back out next week. I've met a wonderful man. We're driving to the Grand Canyon together."

"No way. Is that safe? How well do you even know him?"

Muriel patted her cheek. "Relax, honey. He's my friend's brother. She vouched for him. And I had a PI investigate him. He's got no criminal history, no hidden wives, and lots of money. He's very charming and sexy too."

"Oo, I do not want to hear that!" She unzipped her gown bag. "Help me into this monstrosity." The dress wasn't a monstrosity, it was quite simple and unique. The fabric had been hard to find, but it suited her perfectly. She couldn't wait to see the look on Nick's face when she walked down the pathway to the gazebo in the park.

Someone rapped on the door, and her bridesmaids bustled in. Grace, Lisa, Natalie, and Belinda looked incredible in their simple green dresses. Each dress was designed to fit its wearer's shape. She'd become quite close with Belinda while teaching self-defense classes to the battered women housed on Belinda's ranch. It was part of their healing process, taking back their lives and power.

"Let's do this thing." She pulled the dress over her head, her friends rushing to assist her.

$\cdot \heartsuit \cdot \heartsuit \cdot \heartsuit \cdot \heartsuit \cdot \heartsuit \cdot$

"What if she changes her mind?" Nick paced back and forth in the front of the gazebo.

"She's not going to," Cam said. "Calm down. Nat told me Winter is calm and ready to marry you. Though I don't know why anyone would marry your ugly mug."

"Ha ha."

"Sh," Mac hissed. The men stood in a line across the front of the gazebo in the park. Nick just right of center. Then came Cam, Sterling, Clint, and finally, in his red serge dress RCMP uniform, Mac. Nick was blessed to have so many good friends. Haven had been good to him. He clasped his hands behind his back to keep himself steady and in place. *Where was she?*

Low music began to swell, and Amy, Lisa's daughter, walked out from behind the screen hiding the female half of the wedding. She walked up the sidewalk in her pink floral dress, with a basket of rose petals in her hand. She tossed flowers as she walked quickly up the aisle. Natalie's son Mathew, in a black suit, followed, carrying the rings securely tied to a satin pillow.

Grace came first, her eyes on Sterling. Then Lisa who focused on Cam. Natalie only had eyes for Clint. Even from the other end of the line, Nick heard Mac suck in a breath when Belinda stepped forward. Interesting.

Then, Winter stepped from behind the screen, and his knees went weak. Sweet God in heaven. She was beautiful. Her hair was piled on her head in a sexy, messy hairdo. Her dress was simple. No fancy lace, no beads. Just a floor-length gown with no sleeves and a high neckline.

She met his eye and smirked.

She was laughing?

She came closer, and he did a double-take.

What was she wearing?

Camo? White camo?

He laughed aloud. There was no way to keep his amusement in. She was wearing winter camo. *And were those white combat boots? She did love her boots.* Her laughter joined his, and the entire crowd laughed with them.

"Nice dress," he whispered when she stood beside him.

"I thought you'd like it. I was worried it wouldn't be finished for today, but the seamstress finished it...in...the Nick of time." They laughed until they were breathless, and he swept her into his arms for a long steamy kiss.

Someone cleared their throat. "Ahem. It's customary for the kissing to take part *after* the vows," the minister said, doing his best to be serious.

"Gosh, reverend. Sometimes a guy just can't wait."

About Katie O'Connor

Best-selling author Katie O'Connor lives in Calgary, Alberta, Canada. She married her high school sweetheart and is living her happily ever after. She is the mother of two grown daughters and is extremely proud of her five grandchildren.

She is the founder of The Write Chicks, a private romance writers' group set up with the sole purpose of supporting each other's writing careers. Currently, she is past president of the Calgary Association of the Romance Writers of America. In the past, she's been their secretary and has also served on the organizing committee for When Words Collide, a reader and writer conference in Calgary, Alberta. In 2025, she will be a Story Coach for the Alexandra Writer's Center Society in Calgary.

Katie's career path has been long and twisted, with most of her life devoted to her family. She's been a waitress, chambermaid, cashier, store manager, as well as a lab and X-ray technician. She's been a small business owner and is an avid quilter and crafter.

She's dabbled in writing since high school because something drives her to create stories. She swears it's impossible for her NOT to write. Unsatisfied with one genre, Katie writes contemporary romance, erotic romance, fantasy/paranormal romance, romantic suspense, and erotica.

She believes in all things magical, including dragons, fairies, UFOs, ghosts, and house pixies. But most of all, she believes in love, romance, and hope.

Where to Find Katie

Website: katieohwrites.com

Email: katie@katieohwrites.com

Mailchimp Signup: http://eepurl.com/Q2nRr

Website: https://katieohwrites.com

Facebook: http://www.facebook.com/katieohwrites

Bookbub: https://www.bookbub.com/profile/katie-o-connor

Books by Katie O'Connor

Their Christmas Love
Their Perfect Christmas
A Silver Fox Christmas Box Set
Heart's Haven:
Running Home
Building Trust
Saving Grace
Heart's Haven Box Set
Three Moon Falls:
Fire Magic
Water Magic
Earth Magic
Stand Alone Books:
Carly's Heart
Matchmaker Christmas
Cupid's Charm
Gingerbread Dreams
Christmas in Silver Creek
Fake Dating at Half Moon Bay
Sleigh Bells Inn
Hearts in the Spotlight
To a Tea
Bulletproof Heart
Protecting Josie
Rekindled Fire
Winning her Love
Ticket to Her Heart
Coming Soon:
Air Magic
Midnight Magic

Lemon Sugar Cookies

INGREDIENTS

Lemon Sugar:
- ⅓ C (71 g) granulated sugar

- 2-3 tsp fresh lemon zest (from one large lemon)

Cookies:
- 1 C (227 g) butter, softened to room temperature (not too soft!)

- 1½ C (318 g) granulated sugar

- 1 tbsp fresh lemon zest (from one large lemon)

- 1 large egg

- ¼ C fresh lemon juice

- ½ tsp vanilla extract

- 2¾ C + 2 tbsp (409 g) all-purpose flour (see note)

- ½ tsp baking soda

- ½ tsp baking powder

- ½ tsp salt

INSTRUCTIONS

- For the lemon sugar, combine the sugar and zest in a bowl and rub the lemon zest into the sugar with your fingers until super fragrant and the zest and sugar are evenly and well combined. Set aside.

- Preheat the oven to 350ºF. Line two large, rimmed baking sheets with parchment paper and lightly grease with cooking spray.

- In the bowl of an electric stand mixer fitted with the paddle attachment or in a large bowl with a handheld electric mixer, cream together the butter, granulated sugar, and lemon zest until light and fluffy, 3-4 minutes. Scrape down the sides of the bowl as needed.

- Add the egg, lemon juice, and vanilla and mix again for 1-2 minutes until the batter lightens in color. Scrape the sides of the bowl as needed. It will look a bit curdled; that's totally fine.

- Add the flour, baking soda, baking powder, and salt and mix until combined. Don't overmix – just mix until no dry streaks remain.

- Scoop the cookie dough into rounded balls

- Stir or crumble the lemon sugar to break up any clumps. Roll cookie dough balls in lemon sugar and place on the prepared baking sheets about two inches apart (about 12 cookies per baking sheet).

- Bake for 9-11 minutes until slightly crackly on top (don't overbake).

- Let the cookies cool for a few minutes on the baking sheet before removing to a cooling rack to cool completely.

www.ingramcontent.com/pod-product-compliance
Lightning Source LLC
Chambersburg PA
CBHW020820260626
47169CB00003B/762